Praise for the I

"A fast-paced thrill of a ride from start to finish."

Library Journal on *Target Acquired*

"Lynette has another hit on her hands. *Target Acquired* grabs hold with nonstop action."

Dani Pettrey, bestselling author of *One Wrong Move*, on *Target Acquired*

"Eason skillfully metes out details of the families' backstories, adding depth to a zippy plot."

Publishers Weekly on *Target Acquired*

"Lynette Eason at her best. Smart plotting, action-packed suspense, well-developed characters, and sweet romance. . . . I devoured it in one sitting."

Reading Is My Superpower on *Double Take*

"Eason's first book in her Lake City Heroes series grabs you and doesn't let you go."

Booklist on *Double Take*

"I thoroughly enjoyed the characters, the banter, and the suspense."

Jaime Jo Wright, ECPA bestselling author of *Night Falls on Predicament Avenue*, on *Double Take*

"*Double Take* is phenomenal and had my heart racing from the moment I started reading. Brilliant plot. Incredible story."

Kimberley Woodhouse, bestselling and award-winning author of *The Secrets Beneath*, on *Double Take*

SERIAL
BURN

BOOKS BY LYNETTE EASON

SERIAL BURN

LYNETTE EASON

Revell
a division of Baker Publishing Group
Grand Rapids, Michigan

© 2025 by Lynette Eason

Published by Revell
a division of Baker Publishing Group
Grand Rapids, Michigan
RevellBooks.com

Printed in the United States of America

Library of Congress Cataloging-in-Publication Data
Names: Eason, Lynette, author.
Title: Serial burn / Lynette Eason.
Description: Grand Rapids, Michigan : Revell, a division of Baker Publishing
    Group, 2025. | Series: Lake City heroes ; 3
Identifiers: LCCN 2024024571 | ISBN 9780800741211 (paperback) | ISBN
    9780800746728 (casebound) | ISBN 9781493448623 (ebook)
Subjects: LCGFT: Detective and mystery fiction. | Thrillers (Fiction) | Christian
    fiction. | Novels.
Classification: LCC PS3605.A79 S47 2025 | DDC 813/.6—dc23/eng/20240213
LC record available at https://lccn.loc.gov/2024024571

Cover design by Ervin Serrano

Baker Publishing Group publications use paper produced from sustainable forestry practices and postconsumer waste whenever possible.

25 26 27 28 29 30 31   7 6 5 4 3 2 1

Dedicated to Jesus,
who is faithful even in the hard times.

For my thoughts are not your thoughts,
neither are your ways my ways, declares the Lord.

Isaiah 55:8

PROLOGUE

Someone had to stop her. She was going to ruin everything if left to do what she had planned. He clenched the steering wheel and narrowed his eyes. He'd have to be subtle. He couldn't let her find out he was involved. He couldn't let *anyone* find out. The price was too high.

And he was already paying a very high price—one he couldn't afford to pay anymore. Refused to pay it. He could run. At the thought, he kept one hand on the wheel and reached out with the other to touch the bag on the passenger seat. He had enough money to leave, but a life of always looking over his shoulder wasn't for him. And she'd never stop looking for him. No, it was better this way. Get rid of her once and for all.

His gut tightened, nerves thrumming as he followed her. If he was truthful, he was afraid of her. Of what she would do if she caught him . . .

But no. His plan was solid. She'd never know it was him. And at this point, he had no choice. He had to risk it. She *had* to be stopped. He fingered the bag once more and thought of all the years of pain and abuse. Of what the bag's contents meant.

It was his means to the end. Period.

Without putting himself at risk.

He took a deep breath and went to implement the first step in the plan.

ONE

Deputy State Fire Marshal Jesslyn McCormick surveyed the charred remains of the building that used to house a thriving church community—*her* church community. It had burned last night, and firefighters had worked tirelessly to put the blaze out.

This afternoon, she'd been able to do her walk-through with the structural engineer and established a safe path from one end of the scene to the other while she examined and collected what she could. It had been enough.

Now she stood in silence, helmet on the ground beside her, gloves tucked into her protective coat pockets, working hard to contain her anguish. And even harder to suppress her tears at the thought of sweet Mr. Christie, a member of the cleaning service, lying in the hospital with second-degree burns and smoke inhalation that might very well kill him.

FBI Special Agent Nathan Carlisle stepped up beside her. "Are you all right?" His compassionate blue eyes nearly destroyed what was left of her composure. She wasn't supposed to cry on the job.

"No." Maybe she couldn't cry, but she could be honest. Nathan

11

and his partner, Andrew Ross, had been called in because burning a church was considered a hate crime. She wouldn't be able to prove that intent until the suspect was caught, but best to bring in the FBI right from the start. ATF was also involved, along with the Lake City Police Department.

He placed a hand on her shoulder. "I'm sorry. I mean it, Jesslyn." His kind eyes said he really did. "Thanks."

"Do you need to sit this one out?" he asked, his voice low. "I'm sure another marshal wouldn't mind taking this one off your hands."

She shook her head. "No way. This one's personal." Which meant she probably *should* sit it out, but . . . nope. Not unless she was forced to.

"I don't blame you. I'd feel the same way."

She'd met Nathan a few months ago. He and Detective James Cross had become good friends during a law enforcement training event two years ago. When James needed a temporary partner at the Lake City Police Department, he put in for it while waiting for a position with the FBI. He was fortunate to get assigned to the Asheville, North Carolina, resident agency not long ago. There was some drama with his family, that much she knew, but no details were shared. Which was fine because the more she knew about him, the more she liked him. If she was honest with herself, she'd admit she'd grown fond of Nathan in record time. Too fond? Probably, but she wasn't going there. Not today.

But she *was* honored she got to work with him—with all of them.

And go to church with most of them.

Until now.

"A building isn't the church," he said.

She slanted him a glance. "You're a mind reader now?"

"Not exactly, but I read facial expressions pretty well."

"I'll save you the effort. The person who did it either didn't know Mr. Christie was there working, despite the vehicle parked right beside the back entrance, or he—or she—didn't care. Either way, a good man is in the hospital, and while I'm upset about the damage

LYNETTE EASON

to the church, I'm more upset about Mr. Christie." She wanted to talk to him when he woke up. If he woke up. It was possible he saw the arsonist. But she'd have to get in line. Nathan and Andrew would be the ones doing the questioning.

"Of course." Nathan paused. "Can I ask what you saw that makes you say it was arson?"

"Let me do this one time." She waved over Fire Chief Kurt Laramie.

"What do you have, Jesslyn?"

"I was just explaining a few things to Nathan and wanted you to hear as well."

Chief Laramie nodded. "Go on."

She turned toward Nathan. "Fires usually burn upward and outward. They create a V-shaped pattern." She pointed to the smoldering, blackened structure. "There are multiple V-shaped patterns inside. So what would you deduce from that?"

"Multiple starting points," Nathan said.

"Give the man an A." She sighed. "And the detection dog alerted to an accelerant. Which could mean nothing more than someone stored cleaning products together, but you don't store those in the pulpit, Pastor Graham's office, the kitchen, and the nursery."

He winced. "Someone deliberately burned the nursery?"

"They did."

"That's a special kind of evil," he muttered.

"Part of me wants to take it as a message of some sort. Another part, the rational part, knows it was just a good place to make sure the fire spread hot and fast since the nursery was next to the kitchen—in which all of the gas burners had been turned on." She shrugged. "And in the nursery, you have things like baby oil, wipes, plastic or vinyl mattress covers, and more. Stuff that burns fast and hot. Whoever did this was determined this building was going to burn to the ground. But, here's the kicker. What's interesting is the purple stains."

"Why is that interesting?" Nathan asked.

13

"It indicates a specific kind of accelerant. One that's homemade and easy to make, relatively safe to handle, but I'll know more once I talk to Marissa at the lab."

"You think this is a one and done?" the chief asked.

"If it's a hate crime and they simply wanted to burn the church down to make a point, then . . . maybe. Or maybe they'll hit another church. No way to tell right now." She turned to Nathan. "You get to investigate and figure that part out."

Chief Laramie patted her shoulder. "I'm glad to have you working this one, Jesslyn. Your dad would be proud of you."

"Thanks, Chief." He and her dad had been good friends, and the chief had welcomed her into the role of fire marshal with open arms. He walked off and she chewed on her lip.

She guessed her dad would be proud. She could only take the chief's word for it.

"How do you do it?" Nathan asked, breaking into her thoughts.

"Do what?"

"Your job. James told me about your house burning down when you were a child and losing your family. I can't imagine. And then you have to face fire every day?" He shuddered. "I hate fire. Don't even like bonfires."

She was surprised he brought it up. Her past wasn't a secret, but it did seem to be a taboo topic for almost everyone around her. "I'll admit, it's not easy," she said, "but I wasn't there when it happened."

"Sometimes imagination is worse than the actual thing."

"True." She cut him a glance. "And mine is an educated imagination. I've studied the case notes. I know exactly what happened. I know how they died, what they might have suffered. I just don't know who did it." She nodded to the church. "But this? It's my job, my passion. One I chose as an attempt to honor my family. An arsonist killed them and was never caught. I can't describe what that feels like. I never want another child or family member to go through that." She blew out a low breath. "Each fire reminds me of why I do what I do."

"Makes sense." He went silent for a moment, and Jesslyn waited for him to get around to asking whatever he was thinking about. "I caught the interview you did a couple of days ago. The plea for someone to come forward with new information that would lead to the capture of the arsonist before the twentieth anniversary of the fire."

"You saw that, huh?"

"You did a great job. Your love for them and your passion for justice came through loud and clear—especially your intent to keep looking until you found the person who killed them."

"Oh. Yes. I probably should have toned that down a bit."

It had been the first time she'd publicly spoken out about her family's deaths, and the surge of anger and grief that had swept over her caused her to lose a fraction of control over her emotions. She'd jabbed her finger at the camera. "If you're alive, I just want you to know that I'm still searching. You killed my family twenty years ago. They didn't deserve that and neither did I. I hope you can't forget that night. I hope it lives with you and torments you each and every hour of each and every day. You may think you've gotten away with it and that people have forgotten, but I'm here to say you haven't and people haven't. In fact, I have a plan to make sure everyone remembers that night. Remembers my parents for all the good they did before their premature deaths. Remind the world that my sisters never got to grow up. My dad was one of the most prolific builders in this area, and he and my mom had a dream. I bought a building that will help fulfill that dream. They wanted to create a youth center where any and all are welcome to have a place to go after school. In doing that, my parents will be remembered for their dream of changing lives for the better, while you will be caught and punished for what you did. Because I will catch you and that's a promise I intend to keep."

Replaying her words made her frown. Had she overdone it? Come across too strong? She swallowed against the sudden surge of emotion and looked Nathan in the eye.

He offered her a gentle smile. "No, I don't think you needed to

15

tone it down. It was raw and honest, and people will admire you for what you're doing."

"Thank you," she whispered, then cleared her throat. "I just don't want my family forgotten. They deserve more."

"Absolutely."

"I meant what I said. I plan to find him. As long as he's still alive, I'll find him."

His eyes lingered on her, studying her. Dissecting her?

She snagged his gaze. "What?"

"The more I talk to you, the more you intrigue me."

Okay, that was bold. "Hm."

"Too blunt?"

"No." Too perceptive maybe. She'd have to remember that if she wanted to hide her feelings from him. But right now, her interest in getting to know him a bit better overruled her caution. "You know my story. What's yours?"

He raised a brow. "I have a feeling I'm missing a few details."

"Not many." Okay, maybe a few.

"Jess?"

She turned to see Pastor Chuck Graham walking toward her, sorrow in his blue eyes. She looked at Nathan. "Excuse me a minute?"

"Of course."

She hugged the older man, who looked like he'd aged another few years overnight. "I'm sorry, Chuck."

He pressed fingers to his lips. "Just . . . why?"

"I don't know. Only God and the arsonist know the answer to that. So, until one of them talks . . ."

Chuck blinked back tears and nodded. "Well, this won't stop us. We'll just rebuild and find a place to meet in the interim."

Jesslyn nodded. "Absolutely." Other church members had started to gather outside the perimeter of the crime scene tape, and Chuck walked over to them, his shoulders held straight, chin lifted high. When he reached the group, they hugged one another, shoulder to shoulder, then started to pray. Jesslyn ground her molars and swept her gaze around the onlookers. Sometimes arsonists liked to watch the fallout of their work, but no one in particular stood out to her.

Then again, whoever was responsible wouldn't be wearing a sign labeled "I did it."

"You think he's here?" Nathan asked, his voice low.

She spun to face him. "You really need to stop doing that. It's unnerving."

His lips twisted into an amused smile that sent her heart racing in ways it hadn't done since . . . ever.

All righty then.

"You're an investigator," he said. "It's not hard for another cop to tell what you're thinking." His gaze slid from hers and scanned the crowd just as she'd done. "We'll get some video footage and pictures, but I don't think he's here. At least not in view."

"Well, he doesn't have to be." She pointed to the TV crew camped out to the side, cameras rolling. A helicopter buzzed overhead with more cameras. "He can sit at home and watch the whole thing from the comfort of his recliner."

THIS WAS THE FIRST TIME Nathan had gotten to work with Jesslyn, and he had to admit, watching her in action was downright impressive. He'd heard there wasn't anything she didn't know about fires and accelerants, but hearing her talk about purple stains and what they meant was fascinating.

Hanging out with her at a friend's lake house was very different from sharing a crime scene with her. While reserved by nature, at the lake house she was relaxed and witty when she decided to speak. Here, she was intense, focused, and dead serious.

Impressive.

Admirable.

Attractive.

Okay, maybe that last one wasn't exactly wise, but the truth was, he'd been interested in Jesslyn long before now. The moment he'd met her, he decided he wanted to get to know her better. Which was why he'd kept his distance. Mostly. He had issues. Burdens he'd never share. He'd keep his attraction tucked away—which meant he needed to find his filter and keep his mouth shut. What in the world was he thinking telling Jesslyn she intrigued him? She did, but that didn't mean he needed to announce it. No one knew he and Jesslyn had a whole lot in common when it came to their growing-up years. That they'd both lost people they loved to a fire. But while Jesslyn seemed to race toward a blaze, he avoided it at all costs. Fire terrified him. To find himself investigating it was fine. Just don't ask him to get close to it.

Andrew Ross, his partner of a few months, had no idea of any of that. They were still building that bond of trust most partners grew into. And while Nathan would die for the man if it came down to it, he wasn't ready to share his deepest, darkest secrets. That kind of trust took time and he was in no hurry to move it along. Thankfully, Andrew tended to mind his own business.

Nathan transferred his thoughts to the woman beside him and gave her a sidelong glance. She had her auburn hair pulled up into her standard ponytail, her naturally pale skin a shade lighter than usual. She continued to stand silent and still, her emerald gaze on the scene giving no indication she was aware of his presence.

Another reason to keep his interest in her six feet under. She might not appreciate it and they had to work together.

"How's the Airbnb? Comfortable?"

"Yes. It's fine. Roomy, which is nice." They were talking about nothing, but that was fine. It kept things on a low simmer, a distraction from the charred church.

"But you like living in Asheville?"

He studied her. "These days I like Lake City better."

Her eyes widened a fraction and a blush pinkened her cheeks. She looked away and the color faded. Andrew headed toward them and Nathan cleared his throat. "I'll call you if I have any questions," he told her.

"Of course." She turned to him and offered a slight smile. "It was good to see you despite the circumstances."

He really needed his heart not to do that thing it did every time she barely smiled at him. Andrew stopped to talk to one of the other firefighters, giving Nathan a few more precious seconds alone with Jesslyn. "You too. I'll be in touch."

She nodded and her smile slid away. Then she took a deep breath and picked up her helmet. "I've got a report to write. I'll see you later."

"Later."

She walked away, straightening her shoulders and lifting her chin, like she was preparing herself for battle. Because that's what the investigation was going to be. A battle to find the arsonist before he struck again. They both knew the odds were that he would. They'd have to alert every church in the vicinity.

On that cheerful thought, he turned to his smirking partner, who'd snuck up on him. "What?"

"Why don't you just ask her out already?"

So much for Andrew minding his own business. But Nathan heard the friendliness behind the mild teasing. "Why would I do that?"

"Because you want to?"

He really did, but . . . "I can't."

"Can't or won't?"

"Both."

Andrew's smirk turned into a frown, but Nathan ignored him and headed for his Bucar—a Dodge Charger. While he liked the vehicle, he much preferred his Rhino XT—despite the ribbing he got from fellow officers for having such an expensive ride. But his brother-in-law, Kip Hart, was a personal injury lawyer and had presented the vehicle to him as his Christmas present. Nate tried to refuse, but the pleading look on his sister Carly's face had him caving—with the caveat that when his twelve-year-old nephew was old enough to drive, Nathan could gift it back.

"We'll cross that bridge when we come to it," Carly said.

And now, Nathan had two more years of driving the cool SUV before he had to figure something out. In the meantime, he had an arsonist to find and a woman to put out of his head.

As soon as he climbed into the driver's seat, his phone rang, and he answered it with a quick swipe of the screen before he registered the name. *Rats.* "Hey."

"Wait, is this a recording?" Eli, Nathan's eldest brother and all-around know-it-all, said.

"Stuff it, bro. I've got reports to write. What's up?"

"Ah, you didn't check your caller ID before answering, huh?"

"Eli . . ."

"I know you avoid me until you just can't anymore."

"Only because you annoy me." Saying the words without heat didn't make them any less true. Lately, his brother's calls were about to send him over the edge. Changing his number was starting to look like a good option.

"Why do you think that is, Natty?"

His brother the psychiatrist. Always trying to psychoanalyze him. Did Eli truly not understand how obnoxious he was? For a guy who spent his days counseling people and helping them navigate their relationships, Eli refused to let go of the one topic Nathan didn't want to talk about. And that one topic was driving them further apart than they'd already been.

"It's Nathan." Natty was in the past when life was fun and innocent. But Eli would call him whatever name Eli wanted to call him because he was Eli. And Eli only cared about himself. Always had, always would. "Tell me what you want or I'm hanging up."

"Fine," Eli said, "but one day you're going to need to stop taking your anger at yourself out on others. Come to counseling with me, Nathan. Please? We can go together. It's way past time you forgave yourself for—"

Nathan hung up.

Ten seconds later, his phone buzzed again and he let it go to voicemail. Through the driver's window, he could see Jesslyn standing beside her car three spaces down, on the phone. He watched her, wishing once more things could be different. That he could be different. That his past was different. She lifted her head and caught his eye before he could look away, freezing him on the spot. He lifted his hand in what he hoped was a casual wave and drove out of the parking lot.

TWO

Jesslyn had planned to leave the scene and go grab some rest before writing her report. Instead, she stayed put, reluctant to leave. She wanted answers and she didn't have them. Not that staying here was going to make them magically appear, but still . . . she stayed.

The crime scene photographer was gone, the evidence was collected and on its way to the lab, and she was the only one left—not counting the two firefighters taking first shift on watching for any residual sparks that might reignite the blaze. A chill swept through her that had nothing to do with the dropping temperatures, as her uniform kept her nice and toasty.

No, the shiver had more to do with a feeling. She swept her gaze over the area, the gold-and-orange sky tinted with pink capturing her notice only for a brief second before her attention landed on a car on the other side of the parking lot. A lone figure outlined by the streetlight right behind him sat in the driver's seat watching the activity.

Or the lack thereof at this point. She couldn't make out his features, thanks to the backlighting, but she could feel him watching her.

So who was he?

A reporter?

A looky-loo?

The arsonist?

While she stood there debating the wisdom of approaching, the engine rumbled to life and idled. All right then. "Let's see what you're doing here and what you want." Jesslyn walked toward him. Deputy fire marshals in North Carolina didn't generally carry weapons, but she did most of the time. Thanks to her background in law enforcement, she was authorized.

The vehicle lurched forward and headed out of the parking lot. Jesslyn pulled her phone from her pocket and aimed the camera at the disappearing vehicle. An older model Chevy Malibu. Dark blue or black. Maybe even a dark green. She snapped a few more pictures before the taillights blinked out of sight.

With nothing more to do at the scene, Jesslyn headed back to her Jeep, climbed in, and sped toward home. Her stomach growled, reminding her it had been a while since she'd eaten anything. Using voice commands, she texted Lainie Jackson.

> Hey there, I'm starving. I know you're working the late shift, but have you had dinner yet?

Three seconds later, she got a response.

> Nope, wanna grab something in the cafeteria with me?

> Sure. I need to change, though. I'll hit the restroom and see you in about 20.

> I'll be in line.

The hospital was just one exit up the highway and on the way to Jesslyn's home. Thankfully, the cafeteria food was downright awesome and people often came just to eat there whether they had someone in the hospital to visit or not. Which meant the line could get long. But at this time of night, the wait shouldn't be too bad.

Bright headlights fell in behind her and she flipped the mirror to soften the glare. When she made it onto the interstate, she kept watch on the tailgating offender and was glad when the car finally zipped past her.

Sometimes she wished she carried a police badge. But only in instances like this.

As soon as she drove onto the off-ramp, she put the reckless driver out of her mind and made it to the hospital with ten minutes to spare. Plenty of time to get inside, change, and meet Lainie in the line. She parked near the entrance closest to the cafeteria and texted her friend.

> On the way inside.

> Want me to order for you?

> My usual. Thx. I have cash.

She climbed out, the cold wind whipping her messy ponytail around her eyes and sending shivers down her spine despite the protection of her gear.

Her phone pinged with a text and she glanced at the screen. Her aunt Carol.

> I'll have breakfast ready if you can still make it in the morning.

Jesslyn sent her a thumbs-up just as another chill sent goose bumps pebbling beneath her heavy coat, and just like that, the sensation of being watched returned full force. The parking lot was well lit with cameras and security monitoring 24/7, but she'd feel much better inside the building.

She grabbed her bag from the back seat of the car, slung it over her shoulder, and headed for the door. She walked fast, keeping her eyes on her surroundings, but didn't see anything that might have set her internal alarm ringing.

Shoving off the feeling, she directed herself toward the cafeteria, the delicious smells growing stronger the closer she got. She zipped inside the nearest single bathroom, changed clothes, washed her face, and brushed her hair into a fresh ponytail.

When she walked into the cafeteria, Lainie was fourth from the end. Jesslyn stepped up beside her. "Thanks for holding me a spot."

"Sure thing." No one minded her breaking in line.

Once they had their food, they found a table at the back. "Pot roast," Jesslyn said. "My favorite."

"I know. I figured that's why you wanted to come eat."

She laughed. "I actually forgot it was on the menu tonight." They said grace and Jesslyn took a bite, savoring the rich, hearty flavors. The tender meat rich with herbs and seasonings exploded on her tongue. She swallowed. "Okay, I'm never cooking again."

"What do you mean *again*?" Lainie said. "Has there been a first time?"

Jesslyn waved her full fork at her friend. "I should throw this bite at you for that, but I don't want to waste it."

"I knew I was safe." A full minute of silence passed before Lainie looked up. "So, are you okay?"

"I am. Or I will be. It's Mr. Christie I'm worried about."

"I was here when they brought him in. Nathan and Andrew are upstairs hoping he'll wake up so they can talk to him."

At the mention of Nathan's name, heat flooded Jesslyn's neck and into her cheeks. She ducked her head to focus on her food and hope the pink faded before Lainie saw it. But she was fooling herself. With her fair skin, she probably resembled a lobster.

After another bite and swallow, she glanced up and saw Lainie's speculative look. Yep. Lobster.

"He's a nice guy," Lainie said after a few seconds of silence.

"Who?"

Lainie laughed. "The guy who shall remain nameless so you don't turn red again."

The heat flared once more. "Ugh. It doesn't matter. Why do I do that? He's just a guy."

"A handsome, kind, compassionate, fiercely loyal, very protective guy. And rather mysterious." She nodded. "Can't leave out mysterious."

"Accurate."

"So, what's the problem?"

"Who said there was a problem?"

Lainie dropped her forehead into her palm with a groan, and Jesslyn bit her lip on a smile.

"Fine. He's great. I like him a lot."

"But?"

"But . . ." She shrugged. "It's not a good time to pursue something."

"Will it ever be a good time?"

Lainie's compassionate gaze made Jesslyn want to squirm. "I don't know. I'm so committed to the job there's nothing left for anything—or anyone—else."

"Because your job may one day lead you to whoever it was that started the fire that killed your family."

"Exactly."

"Or it might not. I saw your interview."

"Is there anyone who hasn't seen it?"

"Not that I can think of."

Jesslyn nodded. "They keep playing it and asking for anyone with any information about that night to come forward. I should be thankful. The more people who see it, the more awareness there is about who we're looking for and why." She took another bite, searching for how to express what she was feeling. She finally found the words. "I remember being seven years old and understanding that someone killed my parents and sisters with fire. On purpose. And I remember thinking someone should have stopped him. I didn't understand why no one had. When I realized there were jobs that people did to catch murderers like that, I wanted to do that job." She paused. "I don't know if I know how to do anything else."

Lainie studied her with a frown and Jesslyn returned it.

"What?" she asked.

"I've wanted to ask you something for a long time now, but haven't because I'm afraid it might make you mad."

Okay. "Since when did that stop you?"

"That's valid." She put her fork down and took a sip of her water. "I guess I just wonder what your family would think of you dedicating your life to finding the arsonist. To the point that you have no life of your own. In other words, sacrificing your life for their justice."

"What? I have a life. One that I'm very happy with."

Liar.

She shut that little voice down fast.

Lainie raised a brow. "Are you? Really? You don't long for more?"

Okay, she did. She sure did. But admitting it out loud would break something inside her. If she put words to her thoughts, she might lose the will to keep going after the killer, and if she did that, she had no idea who she'd be. And that terrified her more than just about anything.

"I plead the fifth," she muttered and stuffed another bite of pot roast into her mouth.

NATHAN AND ANDREW STOOD OUTSIDE Bud Christie's room with the man's doctor, who'd finally joined them in the hallway. It was late and Nathan was exhausted, but the best time to solve a crime was in the early hours of the investigation.

Mr. Christie's burns were bad, but the smoke inhalation was the medical team's biggest concern. "So, what you're saying is," Nathan said to the doctor, "he's not waking up anytime soon."

"He's in a medically induced coma. We'll bring him out of it when we feel he's healed enough to do so."

"But he'll live?"

"I'm afraid I can't tell you that. I've seen people recover from worse and I've seen people die from wounds not as severe. Only God knows for sure."

"Right." Andrew rubbed a hand down his cheek. "Will you let us know when you're ready to bring him out of the coma?"

"Of course." The man shook his head. "I've known Bud all my life. I'm friends with his daughter, Vanessa. She and I went to medical school together." He glanced toward the waiting room. "She's on her way home as we speak. Should be here in another hour or so."

"Good." Nathan tucked his thumbs into the front pockets of his pants. "His wife's going to need the support."

"She'll get it. They have a lot of friends." The doctor glanced at his phone. "I've got to take this. I have your card and will be in touch if anything changes."

"Thank you."

The man left, phone pressed to his ear, and Nathan turned to Andrew, who was looking at his phone. "Any progress on security footage around the church?"

"Nothing so far. If there's anything, we probably won't have it until the morning. But frankly, it's in such a rural area, I'm not holding out much hope. Not everyone has cameras on their front doors."

"Maybe not everyone, but they're checking convenience stores, liquor stores, and gas stations in addition to the home cameras on all the routes to and from the church. Just need one."

"True, but we haven't found it yet."

"And no one driving by saw anything." He shook his head. "I refuse to believe we're at a dead end. What are we missing?"

Andrew pursed his lips. "I haven't got a clue. I'm afraid we're going to have to wait for the evidence to be analyzed before we're able to go much further."

"Let's go talk to the pastor again. He gave his statement but needs to be formally interviewed. Then we'll just start visiting the members of the congregation one by one until we find something."

"Sounds like a lot of work. We'd better get busy."

"Busy with what?" Jesslyn asked, walking up to them.

"Talking about visiting members of the congregation," Nathan said. "See if anyone knows anything that might help us figure out a motive for burning the church down. What brings you here?"

"Food. And Lainie. I was getting ready to head home to grab some sleep but wanted to check on Mr. Christie first."

Nathan filled her in on what the doctor said, then told her his and Andrew's rough investigative plan. "What do you think about that?"

"I think that's a logical next step." She glanced at her phone. "Chuck's probably sound asleep, but he won't mind you waking him if you need to."

Nathan glanced at Andrew. "What do you think?"

"It can wait until morning. He'll be at the church first thing, right?"

Nathan attended as much as he could but didn't keep up with the man's schedule other than to know he was usually there in the mornings.

Jesslyn nodded. "He'll be there by eight o'clock unless there's an emergency or something." She nodded to Mr. Christie's room. "Like visiting Bud's family." She hesitated. "You have his number, just text him and let him know you're going to stop by. He'll be there if you do that."

"Good idea. I think I need some sleep so my brain will start working again." Fatigue gripped Nathan. He needed rest if he was going to be of any use to anyone. He looked at Andrew. "Meet you there around seven forty-five?"

"Meet you there." The man yawned. "I'm going home to grab a bite to eat and some sleep. Or maybe just sleep. See you in the morning."

When he left, Nathan turned to Jesslyn. "You think you can use your influence to put a rush on the evidence analysis?"

"I've already put in the request."

He smiled. "Thanks. Any more thoughts on the fire?"

"No. Sorry. I'm like you. I need the evidence processed." She nodded to Mr. Christie's room. "He didn't deserve that. No one deserves that, but he's just the kindest soul you'll ever come across."

"I've never met him, but I'm really sorry." Nathan was there on Sundays. Mr. Christie was there during the week.

"Me too." She sighed. "On a positive note, though, did the doc tell you his face was protected? Most of his burns are on his back below his shoulders. The firefighters got to him before the flames reached his face, so that's a huge blessing."

"For sure."

"We'll just have to pray for him. But for now, I guess it's time to call it a day." She patted his arm. "Go home, Nathan. I'll let you know when I hear something."

"That seems to be the theme tonight. All right. Walk you out?"

"Sure. That'd be nice."

He led the way to the elevator, very aware of the woman beside him. He could still feel that innocent pat and almost put his hand over the spot like a lovesick teenager.

Good grief. He was losing it. He definitely needed some sleep.

She led the way outside and paused for a moment, scanning the parking lot. The night was quiet, but for the distant hum of cars on the nearby highway. The hospital's exterior lights cast long shadows between the parked cars, creating a scene that was both serene and eerie.

She shivered and Nathan placed a hand on her back. "What is it?"

"That car," Jesslyn said, squinting toward a dark sedan parked a little distance away. "I believe that's the same car that was at the church fire scene tonight. I can't say that I'm a hundred percent sure, but it looks awfully similar."

"Car at the church fire scene?"

"Oh, I didn't mention it." While she told him about the car that had been there and driven away as she approached, his gaze followed hers.

A dark car, engine running, with a solitary figure in the driver's seat. "Is he watching us?" he asked.

"I can't tell. He's positioned himself so he's backlit. The guy at the church did the same thing. Like I said, when I started walking toward him, he drove away."

"Let's see what he does this time." Hand on his weapon, Nathan started toward the car and Jesslyn followed.

As they approached, the car's headlights blinked to life, momentarily blinding them. Nathan shielded his eyes and quickened his pace, but before he could reach the car or see the driver, the vehicle backed up, then sped away, tires screeching against the asphalt.

Nathan stopped and Jesslyn caught up with him. "I'd kind of like to know who that was," he said.

Jesslyn nodded. "I didn't get the license plate. You?"

Nathan's former fatigue returned tenfold. "No."

She pulled out her phone, tapped the screen, and turned it around so he could see it. "This was the car from the church. I was hoping to get the plate. Unfortunately, it's too blurry, but do you think that could be the same car?"

He squinted. "Sure looks like it could be. Same make and model, same dark color. Same suspicious activity . . ."

"Okay." She tucked her phone away. "Is it just me or do you find that weird?"

"Definitely weird." He rubbed a hand down his face while fatigue dragged at him. "We'll figure it out. Tomorrow is going to be another long day."

They stood in silence for a few more seconds, the echoes of the car's departure still hanging in the air, before reluctantly making their way to their respective vehicles.

"I'll see you in the morning," He glanced in the direction the car had disappeared. "Be careful, okay? Watch your back?"

"Of course. You do the same."

THREE

The sound of the alarm sent Jesslyn burying her head under her pillow for five seconds before she couldn't take the sound anymore. The night had been a long one, her mind full of images featuring the faceless, backlit stranger in the dark-colored car.

No matter how tightly she closed her eyes, the figure stayed etched on the inside of her eyelids, a constant source of the unease that had settled in her bones—and the reminder of the man she used to dream about on a nightly basis. Those dreams had faded in frequency, but she had a feeling they were about to return full force.

She swung her legs off the bed, her feet contacting the cool hardwood floor. One day, she'd pull out her mother's slippers that she had tucked away in her closet. They'd been left at Aunt Carol's house from a sleepover, so they'd survived the fire.

But if she wore them, something might happen to them.

Suppressing a shiver, she walked into the kitchen to fix a strong pot of coffee, the rich aroma a balm to her senses. The weird events of last night continued to crowd her memory, and she mentally mapped out her day while cradling the warm mug. First the coffee, then a quick visit to her aunt's home, then the lab, a church inspection, a talk at the high school . . . Thinking about that sent her mind skidding to the dark car once more.

It had shown up in two places where she'd been. Maybe. It sure looked like the same car, and the driver had behaved exactly the same in both situations, so . . . for now she'd assume it was the same person. He'd been at the church and the hospital. Like he'd been following her. Or waiting on her? If she'd been alone, would the driver have approached her? She wanted to doubt it, but the fact that he'd run both times lent a rather sinister feeling to the two events.

If there was a third . . .

Jesslyn peered out the window, her eyes scanning for any signs of movement. Or the dark sedan. But the world outside was still—the only movements the leaves rustling in the gentle wind and the bird on the ground looking for his worm. "Go farther south, little dude. You're running late."

The peaceful scene did nothing to ease the tightness in her chest or the heaviness in her steps as she wound her way back to her room to get ready for the day. Someone had burned her church down. Mr. Christie had a long recovery ahead of him. If he lived to make it. He had great doctors and protection on his room to give him the best chance possible. That was all they could do.

She shook herself. She needed to throw off the emotional lethargy weighing her down. She had work to do.

Her phone buzzed just as she stepped into the bathroom. Lainie.

Jesslyn put her on speakerphone while she readied her toothbrush. "What's up?"

"How's the investigation going?"

"It's in the infant stages at the moment. I'm heading to the lab this morning, hoping to take a look at the evidence and see if that sheds some light on things. How's Mr. Christie?" She started brushing.

"Hanging in there. I checked on him about twenty minutes ago and I think there's some minor improvement. Minor enough not to get our hopes up, though." A pause. "Are you brushing your teeth?"

Jesslyn spit. "I am."

"Oh. Okay. Glad to know you still do that."

"Haha. You called just as I was getting ready so . . ."

Lainie gave a chuckle that ended on a sigh. "Let me know how the investigation goes. I'm praying that you get the guy fast before . . . well, before."

Before he hit another place and hurt someone else. Or worse. "Yeah. Me too. Thanks for the update on Mr. Christie. I'll talk to you later."

She hung up and finished getting ready, checked the time, and bolted to her car.

Thankfully, the trip to her aunt's home was uneventful, and she pulled into the drive of the familiar ranch-style house in a middle-class neighborhood a little after eight. When Jesslyn had gotten the fire marshal job, her aunt decided to stay in Lake City. Right smack in the middle of the other two girls—one in Canada and one in Florida. And now, once a week her aunt liked to do breakfast. She cooked a whole smorgasbord for the two of them and they caught up on life. This morning would have to be quicker than their usual more leisurely meal.

Jesslyn opened the front door and stepped inside to the yummy scent of pancakes, bacon, and more. "Aunt Carol? I'm here."

Her aunt had done a big remodel not long ago. To the left was the dining room, to the right was the kitchen, and straight ahead was the living area. Off that was a new sunroom and screened porch with a well-manicured lawn and more plants than Jesslyn could name.

"Carol?"

The sunroom door opened and her aunt walked in, shrugging out of her coat. "Hey there, hon. Good morning."

"Hey." She kissed her aunt's cheek and marveled that the woman could pass as her sister even though she was in her midfifties. Her jeans hugged trim hips and her sweatshirt hung baggy but comfortable on her upper body. She'd pulled her dark curly hair into a ponytail and topped off her outfit with her signature baseball cap.

"Come on in and let's eat. I'm starved."

Once the two of them had their food, they said grace and dug in.

"Okay," Jesslyn said, "I have something to run by you."

"Go for it."

"I've been thinking about this for a while now. You've told me lots of stories over the years about my parents and their desire to make a difference in their community."

"Yes. True."

"And you told me that before they died, they were talking about building a youth center."

Carol's eyes narrowed. "Yes."

"I know I've mentioned it in passing, but this time I'm serious. I want to build that center."

Her aunt set her fork down and leaned back. "I know. I saw the interview. I've been waiting for you to tell me more."

"Right. I've been thinking about this for about two years and now, in honor of the twentieth anniversary of their deaths, I want to do it. I bought the old gym at the corner of Main and Hendricks and plan to have it renovated."

"Okay . . ." Her aunt's eyes widened as she listened.

"I set up a nonprofit and bought it about six months ago with this idea in mind, and now I want to go through with it. I need your help, though. You're an event planner and you know people with money. Could you help me put together a list of potential donors? People who would be willing to invest in the building's renovation and who will believe in the project."

"And you want to put your family's name on it."

"Well, my father's anyway. He worked on a lot of buildings in this city, but you said this one was his dream, so I want to make it come true."

Her aunt swallowed and looked away for a moment. "Oh, Jess . . . I don't know what to say . . ."

Jesslyn raised a brow. "That you'll help me?"

Carol gaped for a moment, then cleared her throat and smiled. "Yes. Of course I'll help you. I just—"

"Oh good—because there's more." She used her most winsome

smile and added, "I would love it if you would be in charge. I'll need you to contact the donors and ask them if they'll do it. Basically, I need you to put it all together and make it happen. I'll pay you just like any other client."

Her aunt smiled, shaking her head, but Jesslyn thought she caught a flicker of something in her eyes. Something . . .

Jesslyn frowned. "What is it?"

"Nothing. Nothing. Yes, of course. I can do that for you."

"Wonderful." But what had that look in her eye been all about? "Are you sure you're not too busy?"

"I'm always busy with something, but I also can pick and choose my busyness. The question is, do *you* have time for this?"

"No. That's why I need you." She reached across the table and squeezed her aunt's hand. "I don't know what I would have done if you'd said no!"

"Let's work out the details then."

An hour later, Jesslyn walked out to her car. She'd stayed longer than she planned, but the lightness in her heart was worth being a shade later to the lab than she'd originally wanted. After a quick trip through the drive-through, she made it to the lab and was happy to see no dark car in her rearview mirror. At least not one that sent her alarm bells jangling.

When she walked inside with two coffees in the disposable cup holder, the lab was already humming with activity. She found Marissa Fields, the evidence technician, hunched over a microscope, her face set in concentration. The engagement ring on her left hand winked under the fluorescent light, and Jesslyn smiled, glad the woman had found her happily ever after.

"Morning, Jess," Marissa greeted without looking up. She probably recognized Jesslyn's footsteps. "I was about to call you. Found something odd in the debris." Marissa was meticulous, digging into the minutiae and coaxing stories from the ashes, residue, and forgotten fragments left behind at crime scenes. Silent witnesses, she called them. Also without looking up, she held out a hand, and Jesslyn slid the cup of the still steaming brew into it, then parked herself onto the empty stool beside Marissa.

"What've you got?" Jesslyn asked.

Finally, the woman lifted her head and took a sip of coffee. "Take a look at this."

She set her coffee aside and handed Jesslyn a clear evidence bag. Inside was a brooch the size of her palm that had somehow survived the fire's greediness.

Jesslyn turned the bag over and squinted. "What's that?" On the back of the piece was the letter *M* with a horizontal slash through it.

"Maybe a signature or the logo of the store it was purchased from?"

"Maybe," Jesslyn murmured. "Is it just me or does this look too clean? Too . . . something."

Marissa sipped her coffee, then set it back on the counter. "Like it wasn't in the fire, but dropped there after the fact?"

Jesslyn met her gaze. "Exactly."

"It's not just you. I noticed that too."

"Not only that, but the mark looks familiar," Jesslyn said, frowning.

"How so?" Marissa asked.

She blinked, trying to force the memory to the surface. "I'm not sure. How hard would it be to find out where this piece came from?"

"I can have it run through the database of jewelers and their logos and see if we get a match. If so, then really easy. If not, then at least you know not to check with those."

"In other words, this might take some old-fashioned legwork."

"Yup."

"Fabulous. In the meantime, I'll send the pictures to Pastor Chuck and see if he recognizes it as belonging to someone in the congregation." She snapped several pictures of it and texted them to Chuck, asking him to check around.

"Good thought. Do you have any suspicions as to who's behind the fire?"

Jesslyn placed the brooch back on the table. "Nothing concrete. We're just in the beginning stages of the investigation. A whole team's on this, but Nathan and Andrew are teaming up with the detectives, interviewing the pastor and the congregation, and doing background checks to see if there are any ties to an arsonist with an agenda, but honestly, I'm not sure that'll pan out." She didn't know why she felt that way, but she did.

Marissa nodded. "I'll keep digging," she said. "Maybe this brooch will speak a little louder than the rest of the evidence."

Her phone pinged with a response from Chuck. He'd put the photos on the churchwide text loop to see if anyone recognized the jewelry.

Jesslyn's eyes lingered on the small inscription, the familiar mark nagging at her. She had seen it before, she was sure of it. But where? The answer flickered at the edge of her consciousness, elusive and teasing. But . . . nothing. A sigh slipped out. It would come to her.

She stood. "Anything else?"

"Yeah, one thing. The accelerant. It's not gasoline or propane or any of the usual stuff. This is—"

"Potassium permanganate?"

Marissa's eyes widened, then she laughed. "Yes. That chemistry degree is serving you well once again."

Jesslyn smiled. She didn't tell everyone about her educational background simply because it didn't come up often, but Marissa and a few others knew she'd double majored in criminal justice and chemistry before heading off to the police academy to get the law enforcement training that would help her work her way up the fire-fighter ladder and catch arsonists. "The purple stains kind of gave it away." Residues of the accelerant had been visible as the dark purple staining around the initial burn areas—a clear indication of potassium permanganate. "Antifreeze or glycerin?"

"Antifreeze."

"Easy to get ahold of." Mixing the potassium permanganate with antifreeze would give the arsonist time to get away from the structure before the combination of the chemicals ignited and flamed hot.

"And relatively safe to use—at least until you get them all mixed together."

Anyone could buy it in hardware stores, pool supply stores, and even online. "That will take forever to track down, so we need to get started ASAP." She pulled her phone from her pocket. "I'll pass this on to Nathan and Andrew."

"Well, if you hang around a few minutes," Marissa said with a wave of her phone, "you can do that in person. They're on the way in."

"Great." Jesslyn shoved her phone back into her pocket, then picked up the jewelry once more to study the signature, but mostly because she needed something to do with her hands. Nathan was coming and she refused to fidget, because his presence always unnerved her.

"You okay?" Marissa asked.

"I'm fine, just thinking about the mark on this thing." She stared at the piece and could only hope she didn't look like she was thinking about Nathan and her weird reaction whenever he was around.

"Might help to turn it over if you want to look at that mark."

Jesslyn flushed and flipped it over, ignoring Marissa's chuckle. Did everyone on the planet know Nathan's presence had the power to wig her out?

She looked up and Marissa winked at her.

Apparently they did.

NATHAN AND ANDREW HAD FINISHED TALKING to Pastor Chuck and now found themselves in the parking lot of the lab and heading toward the double glass doors. Andrew walked beside him. Nathan had to admit he appreciated the man's silent fortitude. Most of the time.

As they entered the lab, the sight of Jesslyn, her attention fixed on a piece of evidence, caused an all-too-familiar pull in his chest. Seriously? He really needed to stop that. Hoping his expression was neutral yet friendly, he walked over to her. "Marissa said you were here. Got something interesting?" he asked.

Jesslyn looked up, her brow pulled into a mix of determination and frustration, but she lifted her lips in a small smile. "Good morning to you too."

He coughed to cover his amusement. "Right. Sorry. Good morning. Get some sleep?"

"A few hours. You?"

"The same."

"Good. Yes, something interesting. We know this brooch survived the fire—if it was even in it. It's got a mark that could be a logo or a signature. Marissa's got someone running it through the database to see if we get a hit and Pastor Chuck is checking with the congregation."

Andrew leaned over for a quick glimpse. "Definitely looks like a signature. I'd go with that."

Nathan kept his gaze on Jesslyn. "I agree. On a positive note, we grabbed security footage from the hospital parking lot. The plate from the car we saw last night was covered in mud."

She scowled. "Then it's highly likely it's the same one I saw at the church. Maybe that's why I couldn't get a good shot of the plate. Dark-colored car, hidden plate . . ."

"Sounds about right," he said. "More than a coincidence. Even if the driver's not responsible for the fire, I want to know why he appears to be following and watching you. We've got a BOLO out on him so hopefully someone will spot him soon."

"Good to hear." She frowned. "Did you talk to Pastor Chuck this morning?"

Andrew nodded. "He gave us a statement and some names to run but said he really didn't believe anyone from the church could be responsible for the fire."

"Well, he wouldn't want to believe that." She shrugged. "I don't want to believe it either, but I know it's possible."

"We'll see what comes back," Nathan said.

"All right, people," Marissa said, "out of my lab. I've got evidence to process."

They said their goodbyes and walked toward the exit, pausing at the glass doors that would lead them out into the chilly morning air.

"The arsonist has done their research," Jesslyn said. "The general population probably hasn't ever heard of potassium permanganate, much less knows that if you mix it with antifreeze you can start a fire but still have time to get away before it combusts."

Nathan nodded. "I'll pass that on to the officers interviewing church members."

"Unfortunately," Andrew said, "we don't have any security footage from near the church. Maybe Lindsay can get me a list of retailers who sell the stuff and I can start looking into that."

"That works," Nathan said. Lindsay Franks, one of the analysts at the bureau who would have the information in their inbox shortly. "She's already working on it."

"You think our guy was dumb enough to buy both ingredients at the same place?" Jesslyn asked.

"One can always hope," Nathan said. "But why use that instead of something like gasoline, acetone, paint thinner, or whatever? Something more common? Not that it'll be easy to track down where he got it, but still . . . it's an odd thing to use if you ask me. And I doubt the average person knows that by combining those chemicals, you can do what he did."

"I tried a simple internet search without the word 'permanganate' and nothing showed up. Then I used an AI software and got a hit. Then again, if this person has access to it and some chemistry knowledge . . . he wouldn't need to bother with a search. We need to be sure to question the employees at these places in addition to asking about the customers."

"Exactly," Andrew said. "We'll figure out where he got it. Eventually. Anyone mind if we grab food? I skipped breakfast."

"I'm in," Nathan said. He looked at Jesslyn. "You hungry?"

"I've eaten, but coffee sounds good."

"Cornerstone Café?"

She smiled. "Of course. I'll meet you there." Her phone buzzed and she glanced at the screen. "It's Lainie. See you in a few." She swiped the screen and walked away. "Hey."

Nathan tried not to watch her leave, but his eyes had a mind of their own. And so did his feet since he found himself following her. Andrew didn't say a word, he just stayed with him. Nathan shot him a glance. "I just want to make sure she gets in her car safely. You know. Because of that vehicle that seems to be following her."

"Right. Of course."

"Shut up, man."

The banter came easy and Nathan almost smiled. Andrew reminded him a lot of James in the way he was laid-back and chill for the most part, but could be intense and driven when he needed to be.

It felt good, building the rapport that hopefully would develop into not just a lasting partnership but a friendship as well.

Time would tell.

FOUR

Jesslyn made it to the Cornerstone Café seconds ahead of Nathan and Andrew. Honestly, she needed to get it together or she was going to lose all semblance of professionalism and come across like a love-sick girl with her first crush. Which would not be totally inaccurate.

Ugh and double ugh.

The restaurant held just a scattering of patrons, so she grabbed a booth in the back corner with a view of the front door. Nathan and Andrew stepped inside, followed by Lainie and James. Jesslyn met Lainie's gaze and grinned. Her friend hurried over and slid into the booth beside her. "Hey, when you said y'all were headed here, I talked James into picking me up so we could meet you."

"I can't think of a better surprise. How's the wedding planning going?"

"The planning is basically done. Now it's just making sure I keep all of the plates spinning in an orderly manner until the big day."

James walked over. "We're going to need a bigger table. Cole and Kenzie and Steph and Tate are coming." At her raised brow, he lifted his hands. "It's a slow d—"

Lainie shot out of her seat and clapped a hand over his mouth. "Don't you dare."

He smiled beneath her palm, kissed it, and said, "I know you're not superstitious."

"Well, no sense in tempting . . . whatever."

"Fine." His phone buzzed. "Hm. Kristine is coming too."

"Kristine?" Andrew asked. "The mysterious air marshal I keep hearing about but never see?"

Jesslyn laughed. "She flies a lot and she's been distracted with family stuff but managed to slip away for a bit."

"Oh fabulous," Lainie said. "It'll be great to catch up with her."

Twenty minutes later, the group surrounded a large table in the private back room. Andrew and Kristine had been introduced and were seated next to each other. They fell into easy conversation.

With their drinks in front of them and their orders placed with Tamryn, who served them almost every time they walked into the café, all that was left to do was catch up.

Steph cleared her throat. "So, Jesslyn, any progress on the fire?"

Jesslyn stifled a sigh. She'd known the topic would be addressed at some point. And she truly didn't mind, but Steph's query brought back the hollow feeling in her gut. Then again, it was their church too. "No, not at the moment."

Andrew waved his phone. "We do have a BOLO going out on the car Jesslyn saw at the scene and we've released it to the news outlets, just requesting the guy contact us."

"You think he will?" Kristine asked, skepticism in her eyes.

Andrew snorted. "No, but with it on the news, maybe the public will also be on the lookout and will report any sightings."

Tamryn set the food on the table and James blessed it, ending the prayer with, "And thank you for letting this group be in town at the same time and available for this gathering. We appreciate it. In your name, amen."

Murmured amens floated from the group and then silence descended for a few moments while everyone dug in. "So," Lainie said, "the wedding is fast approaching—if you consider a year from now fast approaching—and I want to make sure you've all got that date on your calendar."

Steph gaped while Jesslyn raised a brow. "You really have to ask?" Jesslyn asked.

Lainie flushed. "Well, not usually, but since I scheduled something on that very day because I didn't have it actually written on the calendar at home, I figured I'd better double-check. If it could happen to me . . ."

Kristine went into a coughing fit. Jesslyn, who was sitting next to her, pounded on her back until the woman gained control. Kristine cleared her throat. "I'm sorry, but you had to say that just as I was swallowing?"

Lainie giggled. "I can't believe it either. In my defense, it was after a particularly brutal night in the ED and I hadn't had much sleep."

"You work too hard," James said, his voice low, eyes concerned and caring.

A twinge grabbed Jesslyn in the vicinity of her heart, and she had to admit, she wouldn't mind someone looking at her like that. Her gaze slid to Nathan. A certain someone. His eyes met hers and she focused back on her coffee while she worked to keep the heat climbing into her neck from reaching her face.

Rats.

"Anyway," Lainie said, "it didn't take me long to realize what I'd done—and why I had the nagging feeling that I was missing something. It's all fixed now and in big bold red letters on my refrigerator and my phone calendars. Crisis averted. Just trying to be helpful and make sure no one else has any similar issues."

Kenzie shook her head, using her hand to cover the smirk Jesslyn had already seen. "I'm not laughing at you," Kenzie said, "really."

"And when are you two setting the date?" James asked Cole.

Cole spread his hands. "Hey, I'm ready when she is."

Which Jesslyn found shocking, but Cole had certainly done a one-eighty from his carefree bachelor days. He'd reconnected with Kenzie and been a goner. Which was really sweet, but all these couples were beginning to give her longings for things she'd always convinced herself she didn't want.

Or could never have.

At least not until her family's murderer was found.

The thought grounded her.

Only she chose that moment to look up and find Nathan's gaze on her again, so *that* ground shifted with the force of an earthquake. She grabbed her drink.

What in the world?

Kenzie laughed. "I'm getting there. Dad wants to walk me down the aisle, so I'm trying to give him some time to practice with his walker." Kenzie's father had been injured in a car accident years ago but had recently put a lot of effort into his physical therapy. He'd just advanced to a walker for short distances.

Again, Jesslyn's gaze connected with Nathan's, and she could no more look away than fly to the moon. Then he blinked, and whatever she thought was there was gone.

She wondered if she was seeing things.

Whew. He could be a complete distraction. Something she definitely did not need. She hardened her resolve. She had to find her family's killer. Then she could think about the future.

"... right, Jess?" Kristine asked.

Jesslyn jerked and took a sip of her water. "Um . . . what? Sorry, I was just thinking about . . . um, someone . . . er . . . something." She rubbed her forehead and wanted to crawl under the table.

Lainie grinned, but at least she had the grace to duck her head and snag another bite of her food.

Kristine simply repeated herself. "Andrew was saying after y'all ate, you were going to visit the businesses to ask about the chemicals used in the fire."

"He told you what was used?" She raised a brow at the man. He really shouldn't have done that. Talking about an ongoing investigation was a no-go. Which he knew.

He raised a brow right back at her. "Nope, just that we were going looking."

"Oh. Right. Yes. Sorry." She needed to shut up and get herself

46

together, so why was she on the verge of tears? "Excuse me a minute, please?" She tossed the napkin onto the table and shoved her chair back, ignoring the suddenly concerned looks coming her way. "I'll be back."

She wound her way from the back room to the other side of the restaurant and made it to the bathroom with no time to spare before the tears tracked down her cheeks. Knowing she only had a few seconds before someone came to check on her, she stepped into the nearest stall and grabbed a wad of toilet paper to mop up her face.

The door creaked open. Right on time. She supposed it could be one of the other few diners in the restaurant, but she doubted it.

"Jess?"

Lainie's voice reached her. Bingo.

"I'm okay," Jesslyn said. "Be out there in a sec."

"I'll wait."

Jesslyn shut her eyes. "Can I just have a few minutes? Please?"

A pause. Jesslyn could picture Lainie's concerned frown. "Sure." The door opened and shut once more, and Jesslyn opened her eyes and exited the stall. While she ran cold water over her face and dried it, she decided not wearing makeup most days was definitely a perk.

The door opened again and Jesslyn wondered who it was this time. Kristine? Steph? Kenzie? She reached for the paper towels stacked at the back of the sink and pressed one to her face.

Something hard dug into her left kidney and she froze.

"Don't talk," the person said. "Don't scream. Just do what I say." The voice was low. Menacing.

Her breath hitched in her lungs and she lowered her hands from her face, curling the towel into a fist. She met the man's sunglass-covered gaze in the mirror. The beanie on his head did an excellent job of covering any hair color. He looked . . . generic. Average. Completely nondescript. She couldn't even see his eyebrows. "Who are you and what do you want?"

"Walk out of the restaurant and I'll tell you. If you cause any problems or try to signal for help, I'll start shooting." He paused. "And I'll start with the mom and child in the corner just outside this bathroom."

Jesslyn walked, mind spinning, fear churning. There was no way she was getting into a vehicle with this guy, but she wasn't going to risk him following through on his threat.

The clatter of dishes and the murmur of conversation faded into a distant hum as Jesslyn followed the silent directions of the gun pressed into her back.

"Hey, Jesslyn, are you okay?" Tamryn asked, balancing a huge tray of food.

Jesslyn stilled at the question. The weapon pressed harder into her kidney. "Yes, fine. I'm not feeling well and my friend here is just helping me out."

Tamryn's brow arched like she wondered if that was true or not, but she nodded. "Okay. Feel better."

"Thank you."

Jesslyn continued the trek toward the main door, heart pounding. *Stay calm, think.* Her self-defense training was limited, but it might be enough. Especially with the element of surprise.

Outside, the cool air hit her. The parking lot was mostly empty. Just a few scattered cars including hers and those of her friends. Her eyes fell on the closest one and a plan formed. She just prayed it didn't get her shot.

She pretended to trip.

Her attacker shouted, but his grip loosened. She fell against the vehicle, slamming her hand hard on the window. The blare of the car alarm tore through the quiet mountain air, and she spun to see the weapon rising, aiming for her face. She brought one arm up in a roundhouse block while stepping closer and aiming her fist at his nose at the same time. He ducked and her punch scraped along his forehead, but it was enough.

He stumbled backward with a harsh cry, and she followed, grabbing his wrist with both hands. She spun, putting her back to him, shoved his arm up, and dug her fingernails into his wrist while jamming her right foot on his.

Another yell rattled her eardrum, but he let go of the weapon and it clattered to the ground. A surprise punch from his left hand against her head stunned her and blackness swam in front of her for a moment. At her sudden stillness, he shoved her away and she fell to the asphalt on top of the gun.

Curses trailing behind him, he ran.

She started to get up and after the first attempt decided to give herself a minute to catch her breath and get her spinning head under control. But she did notice he got into a dark blue sedan with mud-covered plates.

NATHAN GLANCED IN THE DIRECTION of the bathroom for the third time in as many minutes. Finally, after another five minutes, he set his fork down. He caught Lainie's eye, hoping his questioning look was clear.

She shrugged.

He tilted his head and raised his brows. She frowned and shook her head.

Not acceptable.

He cleared his throat and put his napkin on the table. "Excuse me."

Ignoring the questioning looks from those around him and Lainie's laser-eyed *what-do-you-think-you're-doing* gaze, he made his way back to the bathroom, hoping to run into Jesslyn coming out. No such luck. After a few seconds of hesitation, he knocked and waited.

"Nathan?"

He turned.

Lainie stood there, hands on her hips. "What do you think you're doing?"

He bit off a laugh, wondering if she realized how easy she was to read. "Checking on a friend."

"Well, she was my friend before she was yours and she asked for a few minutes to herself." Her tone was soft, friendly. And had a thread of steel running through it. "She'll come out when she's ready."

"I really think we should—"

"Excuse me." Tamryn stood there, drinks on a tray and unable to get by. They were blocking the kitchen.

He moved aside. "Sorry."

"It's okay. You're talking about Jesslyn?"

"Yes."

"She came out just a few minutes ago with a guy."

Lainie frowned. "What?"

"Yeah, it was a little weird. She looked like she'd been crying and he looked a little sketchy. I asked her if she was all right and she said she was feeling a little sick and her friend was helping her out."

Lainie gaped. "B-but—"

Nathan shot toward the front door and shoved outside into the cold air with Lainie on his heels. And there next to a truck, Jesslyn was pulling herself to her feet.

"Jesslyn!" Nathan ran to her side and grabbed her bicep to help her the rest of the way up. "What happened?"

A gun lay on the asphalt. She'd been on top of it. He started to reach for it, and she stopped him.

"Don't." She dragged in a ragged breath. "That's evidence. Need a bag."

The light went on. She'd been attacked. He glanced at one of the bystanders. "Someone find the owner of that vehicle and get the alarm off." He shot a glance at a wide-eyed Lainie who'd moved closer, her eyes on the seeping welt on the side of Jesslyn's face.

"Let me get a look at that," Lainie said.

"It's okay. He just stunned me." She touched the wound and frowned when she looked at the blood on her fingers. "And cut me. But it's not deep."

"Lainie," Nathan said, "after you check her out, can you let the others know what's going on and ask one of the guys to bring an evidence bag?"

"Of course." She examined the wound and stepped back. "It's not too bad. Needs cleaning and a bandage, but other than a headache, you should be all right."

"Thanks."

The car alarm abruptly—and blessedly—shut off.

"Now I'll go get the others." With one last glance at Jesslyn's head, she hurried back inside the restaurant.

Nathan studied her. "What were you doing out here?"

"I was in the bathroom and he came up behind me while I was rinsing my face."

"We'll get any security footage available, but you didn't happen to see his face, did you?"

"No. He had sunglasses and one of those beanie hats on." She paused. "He was clean-shaven, and his breath smelled like onions. And"—she looked at Nathan—"he got into a dark blue sedan, with mud on the plates."

Nathan nodded, his face grim. "Good observations."

The others came streaming out of the building, faces concerned. Nathan filled them in on what happened, and James gave her the once-over. "Glad you're okay."

"Thanks. Me too."

"I'll get that bag Lainie said you needed."

She nodded and winced. Then glanced at the door. Staff and patrons rubbernecked trying to get a glimpse of whatever was causing such a commotion. "Talk to Tamryn. She saw the guy, I think."

"She did," Lainie said. "She's the one who saw you leave with Beanie Man and alerted us to the fact that not all was well."

"Beanie Man?"

Lainie quirked a tight smile at her. "It's nicer than some of the names I could call him."

Jesslyn huffed a soft laugh. "Yeah. I'll have to thank Tamryn."

"We all will," Nathan said.

Kenzie was pacing the parking lot, phone pressed to her ear. She finally hung up and stopped in front of Cole, who leaned in to listen. Nathan would love to know what they were talking about. Probably requesting the security footage ASAP.

The ambulance arrived. "Who called them?" Jesslyn asked.

"I did," Tamryn said, stepping over to her. "My manager told me to."

"Oh, thanks, but I'm all right."

"They can at least put a bandage on that. Please," she said, "it would make me feel better. I can't believe I didn't act faster . . . I'm sorry. It just didn't occur to me that you were in trouble."

"It's not your fault, Tamryn."

"Come on, Jess," Lainie said, taking her arm. "Might as well, now that they're here. It'll save me from having to follow you home to do it."

Steph took the other arm. "And me to make sure she does it right."

Jesslyn quirked a smile at the three ladies, but Nathan caught her desire to run in her eyes before she blinked it away. "Sure. Fine."

Kristine walked over to him while the paramedics worked on Jesslyn. "She's a good one."

"I think so."

"I know you do. She's also got baggage, so unless you're prepared to deal with that, leave her alone, okay?"

He cut her a sideways look. Her tone wasn't mean, just matter-of-fact. He could appreciate that. "Jesslyn would probably rake you over the coals for saying that. Not because you said it—she wouldn't care about that—but because of the whole protective thing. You might be stepping just a little too close to the boundary she doesn't allow many people to cross."

She snorted, then laughed. "I see you know her better than I thought you did. Interesting."

The calculating look in her eyes made him chuckle. "Don't go there. We're just friends. And I'm not sure I *do* know her that well. But I *am* observant."

"Because you want to be more than friends."

"I see you're observant as well." He turned serious. "She's not ready for anything more than friendship. I'm okay with that for now."

She nodded. "All right then. I'll get back in my lane."

Nathan left her and walked to the ambulance. Jesslyn raked a hand over her hair and tightened her ponytail with a wince. Nathan grimaced for her. She was going to have to change that habit until she healed up.

Once they finished up all the legal necessities, Nathan nudged her gently with his shoulder. "Take inventory and decide if you feel like driving or need someone to chauffeur you."

She paused, touching her bandaged head. "I think I'm all right. I'm not dizzy or anything."

"Okay. I think someone should follow you, though. Just to make sure you get there and get settled."

"I'm not going home. I've got a job to do."

"Come on, Jesslyn," he said. "You were just a victim of an attempted kidnapping and got a conk on the head. You should probably rest."

"I . . . No. I need to analyze whatever evidence is ready and"—she waved a hand—"I need to work. Besides, it wasn't a conk. It was barely a graze." She glanced at the watch on her wrist. "I'm supposed to be at a church to inspect a new wing for code compliance. Then I'm supposed to talk to high school students about what it's like to be a fire marshal and—"

He held up his hand. "Okay, got it. But I still think you should take precautions."

Lainie walked up just in time to hear his last sentence. She frowned at Jesslyn. "You think you were targeted?"

Jesslyn lifted a shoulder. "It's possible." She waved Cole and James over. "While you're waiting on the security footage, can you guys check the database and see if there are any other crimes that match someone grabbing women in the bathroom and walking them right out the front door?"

"'And no one ever hears from them again' kind of crime?" Tate asked.

She grimaced. "Yes. Exactly."

"Sure, we'll check."

"Let's circle back to you thinking you were targeted," Lainie said.

"Well, with three sightings of the dark car and now this . . . I'm starting to wonder if I've picked up a stalker."

FIVE

Jesslyn shuddered. A deep fear that she'd carried with her since losing her family started to make its presence known in a way she hadn't felt in years. Oh, it was always there, but right now, it snaked through her like a living thing, rearing its ugly head as if to strike.

He's back.

The words were a hiss in her ears, a slithering in her veins. And his face—

"Jess?"

She jerked at Nathan's quiet voice. She met his gaze, then looked away. No need to let him know how shaken and weak she really was now that the adrenaline was starting to fade. "I'm okay."

She pulled in a ragged breath. He was *not* back. *This* arsonist had nothing to do with the one in her past. Just because paranoia *wanted* to invade her mind didn't mean she had to *let* it.

Unless she wasn't being paranoid.

What if he'd seen the news like everyone else and took her promise to catch him to heart? What if it *was* him?

"So," she said, gathering her scattered wits and glancing at her watch for the time, "it's just a little past noon. I'm going to head over to the church and do the inspection. From there, I'll head to Lake City High School. I speak for the last forty-five minutes of the day.

When the bell rings, I'll be done. After that, I'll go home and crash while I wait on Marissa to get back to me about any updates on the evidence. You guys are going to check the security footage and get that gun to the lab. Does that cover everything?"

Nathan blinked at her. "Yeah, I think that's it."

"All right. I've got to go." And pray the headache throbbing through her skull would settle down. It really had been just a graze, not a full-on hit, but it still hurt.

She pulled out her phone. She had just enough time to get to the appointment at the community church on Main Street. She texted Mr. McClure that she would be there shortly.

Nathan's hand closed gently around her bicep. "Hey," he said. "I really think someone should follow you there and stay with you."

"I really think that's not necessary. I'm a big girl. I can take care of myself."

"I know you can, but Jess, if someone's stalking you—"

"We don't know that for sure. I just said it makes one wonder. But I've got to go so I'm not late. I'll stay in touch and let you know that I'm okay if that will help."

"It'll help."

Jesslyn said goodbye to the guys and settled behind the wheel of her charcoal-gray Jeep Grand Cherokee. She'd traded in her Chevy Traverse to get it a while back. The Jeep was an older model, but she didn't care. She loved the vehicle and its dependability. The eighteen-inch aluminum wheels had never gotten stuck on a muddy back road, and that was pretty much all she required in her choice of transportation. That, and the spacious back area that held a mix of her professional and personal equipment.

Her phone buzzed with an incoming call and she activated the Bluetooth. "Hello?"

A throat cleared. "Ah, Jesslyn, how are you?"

"I'm doing all right, Dr. Stover, how are you?" He was the principal of the high school and the one who'd lined up her appearance this afternoon. An afternoon she'd packed too tight. "Everything okay?"

He'd been the assistant principal the year she graduated, and she'd always liked the man.

"Well, no. Not really. I've had a few parents express concern about your appearance at the school today."

Oh. "I see. Because of my publicly televised rant?"

He hesitated a fraction of a second. "Yes. I'm so sorry."

"It's okay. I understand. Would it be better if we rescheduled?" she asked, taking pity on the man.

"I think it might." The relief in his voice tweaked her heart. Only because he obviously didn't want to hurt her feelings.

"No problem. You just give me a call when you're ready." She paused. "Or I can recommend another fire marshal to do the program."

"No, no. I want you to do it. I just think it will be better to do it at another time." He paused. "Thank you for being so understanding and kind about it."

"It's okay, Dr. Stover. Have a good afternoon."

"You too. I'll be in touch."

Jesslyn hung up, a sense of relief pounding through her. Disappointment flickered at the reason for the cancellation, but she wasn't upset about heading home when she finished the inspection.

Ten minutes later, she pulled into the church's parking lot and paused before opening the door. Using the mirrors and twisting her body, she examined every inch of the surrounding area before she convinced herself it was safe to climb out. She texted the group that she'd arrived safe.

Maybe she should have taken Nathan up on the offer to follow her, but it just galled her to let anyone else get sucked into her troubles. She'd handle this on her own.

She grabbed her iPad that held her checklist and hurried through the side door, down the short hallway to arrive at the room labeled the office. She walked through the open door. "Mr. McClure? It's Jesslyn. I'm here."

He stepped out from the side room with a smile on his face. "Jesslyn, glad you made it. Good to see you." He shook her hand.

"Sure thing."

"I was so sorry to hear about Chuck's church—your church. What an awful thing. Do you know what happened?"

"We know what happened, just not why. We're still in the midst of investigating."

"Which means you can't really talk about it." She smiled and he patted her arm. "Well, do you need anything from me or are you just ready to get started?"

"I'll get started. It'll take me about two hours."

"Then I'll get out of your way. I have to leave in about ten minutes, but let me know if you need anything before then."

"Will do. Will there be anyone else in the building?"

"No. Just us. I didn't want anyone else in your way."

"Got it. I'll text when I'm done."

She left him, pulled out her iPad and the checklist. She started with the smoke detectors, then moved to the sprinkler systems. The fire extinguishers were accessible and properly mounted. She checked service dates and found nothing wrong. Her phone buzzed and she stopped to check the text.

Nathan.

Security footage showed the guy coming into the restaurant and sitting near the back room. He was watching us the whole time. When you got up and went to the bathroom, he followed. Kept his back to the cameras as much as possible. Beanie and sunglasses covered most of his features. Marissa promised to get to the weapon ASAP.

Shocking.

I know. Sorry I don't have better news.

It's fine. Kind of what I expected. Any other unsolved cases that are similar?

None. And it's a pretty bold move to attack
someone in a public bathroom. Anyone could
have walked in.

Agreed.

Are you free for dinner?

She hesitated. Was she? Technically. She switched to voice texting.

I am. After I finish here.

Would you be interested in getting some Mexican?
You didn't eat much lunch. If you're tired, I
understand. I can pick it up and bring it to your
place.

This conversation would have been much easier over the phone. Her head hurt and she was definitely tired. Would be even more tired later.

But . . .

Can you be at my place around five?

Was it encouraging him when she didn't want to—okay, *couldn't*— take things any further than friendship? Was she making a mistake? Or seriously overthinking the whole situation?

Sure can. See you then. Text me what you like.

Jesslyn did so, then shifted her attention to the emergency exits, counting them and checking the signage as well as making sure the routes were free of obstructions. Her phone buzzed and she ignored it. If she spent any more time on her phone, she'd never get done. She moved to the next part of the new wing, hurrying down the long hallway.

A footfall from behind her sent her pulse skittering and she spun. Nothing. "Mr. McClure?"

No answer. So, it wasn't him.

But she'd definitely heard a footstep.

Hadn't she?

Her breath caught and goose bumps pebbled her arms and scalp. She'd never been afraid of being alone in a building she was inspecting. Until now.

She slipped into a room off the hallway and listened. Nothing. Realizing she was near the nursery, she continued through to the connecting room and found herself in the hallway parallel to the one she just left. Keeping one ear tuned to the area behind her, she continued her inspection with her weapon freed from the restraint and ready for her to grab at a moment's notice.

In the nursery, she found an area of wiring that needed some fine tuning, but other than that, the building was in really great shape. She finished her report and emailed it to Mr. McClure. Her phone continued to buzz. She glanced at the screen. Twelve texts. A quick scan said there was no emergency, just her friends checking on her. Sweet, but they could wait.

She then checked the parking lot. When she didn't see anyone or anything other than a sky darkened and heavy with thick gray clouds, she set the alarm and stepped outside. The first drop landed on her cheek. She climbed behind the wheel, locked the doors, then checked her phone again.

Fourteen texts.

She sent a text to the group loop everyone was on.

> I'm fine, guys. Thank you. I'll let you know if I need anything. See you all later.

The sky chose that moment to open up, and the rain came down in sheets.

She turned the key and the engine clicked, then went silent. She tried again with the same result.

Jesslyn sat there for a moment, thinking. Hers was the only car in the parking lot. The pastor was gone.

But someone had been in there with her. If it wasn't the pastor, who had it been? And where were they now? Her hand went to her weapon on her side, taking comfort in its presence.

She had a choice. Get out and try to see what was wrong with her vehicle in the downpour—she glanced in the back seat . . . no umbrella—or call someone to come get her.

Thankfully, the church was on a main road at the edge of town. Cars swept past, wipers working. And it was midafternoon, so not exactly dark although the clouds made it seem like darkness was going to descend within the next thirty seconds.

She pulled her phone from her pocket and tapped Lainie's name. Voicemail.

She called Steph.

Voicemail.

Fine.

She dialed Nathan's number. Just when she thought it was going to voicemail, he answered. "Hello?"

"Thank you for answering. I'm at the church and my car's dead. I need a ride. Are you available?"

"Grabbing my keys and on the way. Where are you?"

She blinked at the rapid-fire response. "Wow—thanks."

"What are friends for?"

Right. Friends. Friends were good. Perfect. Because she didn't want anything more.

She was such a liar.

Movement to her right at the edge of the building caught her attention. The person dressed in jeans and a flannel shirt wore sunglasses and a beanie cap. Like her attacker from the restaurant. But he'd added a raincoat with the hood covering his head.

He lifted his hands, clutching a gun between them, and aimed it at her. She threw herself down across the seats and heard the crack of the shot.

The passenger window shattered a split second before the driver's side did. Glass rained down on her. She heard Nathan shouting on the other end of the line. Another bullet followed the same path as the first.

With no time to be terrified, she stayed low and pulled her gun from the holster. Then she opened the driver's side door and slid out onto the drenched asphalt. Wet soaked into her clothes, instantly chilling her. She'd left her coat in the car, not needing it in the church, and now she didn't have time to grab it. She looked underneath the Jeep and saw black boots walking her way. She aimed, but the rain blurred her vision. And the slow traffic on the busy road behind him made her hesitate. If she missed, she could hit—

The gun fired again.

He was closing in. Nathan was on his way but wouldn't arrive in time.

And closer still the shooter came.

It was now or never. *Please let him be a bad shot.*

She bolted for the opposite side of the building, shoulders hunched, bent at the waist to make herself as small a target as possible.

The gun cracked again. Jesslyn rounded the brick corner and aimed herself for the back road, patting her pocket. Rats. She'd left her phone in the car. The rain sluiced down her hair and face, blinding her, but she continued down the road looking for a place to hide. Another glance behind her and she could see him looking for her. She ran through the My Pie restaurant parking lot, tucked her gun out of sight, and ducked into the building.

As soon as she stepped inside, everything went quiet while the three patrons and two waitresses stared at her.

One of the waitresses stepped from behind the counter. "Goodness, girl, what happened to you?"

"Can I use your phone? It's an emergency."

The woman dipped her hand into her pocket and pulled out her cell phone, tapped the screen, and handed it to Jesslyn. Jesslyn stared at it. She had no idea of anyone's number. She could hear the sirens in the distance and knew Nathan was on his way to the church.

She dialed 911 and gave an abbreviated report of her situation and location. "Contact Detective James Cross with the LCPD while I hold, please."

She waited. All eyes in the restaurant were on her and a few jaws were swinging.

Note to self. Memorize at least one friend's number in case of an emergency.

A loud crack sounded behind her. A bullet had gone through the glass door. People screamed and ducked under booths.

"Get down! Stay down!" She set the phone on the counter, pulled her weapon once more, and looked around. She had to get out of there or she was going to get people killed.

She ran through the kitchen and out the back.

NATHAN PULLED INTO THE CHURCH parking lot and slammed the car into park next to Jesslyn's Jeep. The Jeep's shattered glass glinted like spilled diamonds and the driver's door was open. He'd heard the shots, and when Jesslyn hadn't answered his frantic shouts, he could only assume the worst. James, Kenzie, and Cole arrived. Cole was out of the vehicle before it stopped rolling and was immediately soaked. "Where is she? Greene and Otis are on the way, but they're coming from another situation." Sampson Greene was the handler for the K-9, Otis, who could find Jesslyn even in the rain.

"I just got here," Nathan said. Jesslyn had called his personal phone and he was still connected to her line. He'd used his work phone to call the others.

Two more vehicles rolled in. Scott Butler climbed from one and Buzz Crenshaw from the other. The SWAT team had descended. Not because this was an official call, but because they were all friends with Jesslyn. He honestly wouldn't be surprised to see Lainie and Steph show up once they learned of the situation.

The rain continued to pelt them all while red and blue lights bounced off the church window and rain-slicked bodies. Nathan leaned in to get a look at the front seat. Her cell phone, but . . .

"No blood," he said. Relief flowed for a brief second before he straightened and looked at the others. "That doesn't mean she's not still in trouble. Her phone is on the passenger seat." He leaned back in, grabbed it, and opened the glove compartment. No weapon. "She has her gun most likely."

Or the person who took her had it. Unless she'd run. His heart pounded. He turned, searching the area behind him, the direction she would have run if she'd been able. The torrential downpour seemed to mock his frantic efforts, blurring his vision and soaking him to the bone. He shivered and fear for Jesslyn pounded him.

"Put your comms in and spread out!" he yelled over the roar of the storm. "Look for any sign of her!" Thunder boomed and lightning split the sky. Where had this weather come from? It was January. Thunderstorms didn't normally happen in January.

James and Kenzie were nodding, their rain-plastered expressions grim as they shoved in the earpieces. A drenched Cole moved like a shadow, determination on his hard features.

Nathan's anxiety eased a fraction. If anyone would find her, it would be those who cared most about her. His gaze swept the area, every sense heightened. The rain muffled sounds, but he searched for anything that might tell him which way Jesslyn went—or was taken.

His sodden feet carried him to the edge of the parking lot to the area behind the church. He glanced back at her car and its open door. If she had run, she would have come this way. Away from the shooter.

"Hey," James said, his voice coming through the comms. "She called 911. She was at the restaurant but ran when the shooter put a bullet through the front door. Keep looking! She's around here somewhere."

The woods loomed across the street, a dark, foreboding barrier. If he was a kidnapper, that's where he'd go. Assuming he didn't have a vehicle waiting.

"We need footage," he muttered.

"Already called it in," Cole said.

"Great." Nathan glanced down the road. Lights shone through the rain and he changed course. She'd gone for people. A phone. At the nearest restaurant. Now where?

A flash of something—or someone—wavered at the edge of the thick foliage. Ignoring the lights, Nathan sprinted toward the trees, adrenaline firing his pulse. "Jesslyn!" The woods and the sound of the rain swallowed her name.

The muddy undergrowth beneath his feet made each step a battle. Branches whipped at his face, leaving stinging marks, but he pushed forward. Then, a sound—not the storm, but something else. A branch cracking.

He froze, listening. Straining to hear over the downpour. There. To his right. He turned, squinting through the rain, and that's when he saw it. The shadow darting between the trees at a quick sprint. Then it paused and turned.

Nathan reached for his weapon, but before he could draw, a sharp crack echoed through the woods, a sound unmistakably different from the thunder. A gunshot.

He ducked behind the nearest tree, scanning the area. "FBI!" he shouted. "Put your weapon down!" He gave his location to the others, who hurried his way. Tate and two other officers indicated they were close by, but Nathan stopped, scoping the area. The person was gone. Nathan turned his footsteps in the direction he'd last seen him, using the trees for cover.

The rain continued to pour, a relentless cascade. Nathan steadied his breathing and scanned for the shooter.

"We've got her!" Kenzie's voice in his ear spun him around.

"Where?"

"Back at the church. She found us."

Nathan slowed. The shooter could have gone in any direction by now. "I've lost him." With one last look around, he scrambled back through the woods while the others continued to search for the man.

When he rounded the corner of the building, he found himself back in the parking lot. An ambulance had arrived during his absence, and Jesslyn now sat in the back of it, wrapped in a blanket, with Kenzie and James at her side. He hurried over to join them. "Jesslyn?"

She met his gaze. "I'm okay. Once again. But I'll tell you this. Whoever's after me wants me out of the picture for some reason." She lifted her chin and narrowed her eyes. "Well, that's a mistake, because I'm not going anywhere." She bit her lip, then sighed. "And I'm going to let you guys help me because I know you'll insist."

Nathan nodded. She was right about that.

SIX

The words sounded brave and tough, but in reality, while she meant them, they also covered the trembling deep in her soul.

One of her biggest nightmares was coming to life. One that she may have triggered with her very public, passionate promise to make sure her father's name and legacy lived on. Her recklessness both terrified her and made her glad in a strange way. Maybe she would finally find the man who killed her family.

She shoved the blanket off her shoulders and a shiver swept through her. At the moment, all she wanted was to go home, grab a hot shower, and curl up on the couch to regroup and plan. "Can one of you guys give me a lift home after I give my statement?"

"I'll be happy to," Nathan said as he held out her phone.

"Thank you." She slid the phone in her pocket, then rubbed her forehead. "I'll have to get my stuff out of the Jeep and arrange for a rental."

"You can call on the way."

She frowned. "I love that Jeep."

"It can be fixed or you can get another one."

"Don't want another one," she muttered, then shook her head. "Let me give my statement, then I'll be ready to go."

He waited, then she followed him to his Rhino-XT and couldn't help the smile that started to curve her lips.

"Don't," he said, his tone mild but the warning clear. "I was already in it when your call came." Normally he'd be in a Bucar, but he hadn't known he'd be arriving at a shootout.

"What?" She raised her brows, going for the most innocent expression she could muster. It was so much more fun to tease him than think about what could have happened. Kidnapped. Getting shot. Dying. She shuddered.

"You know what. It's just a loaner."

"Sure."

"It is."

"So you've said."

He rolled his eyes and Jesslyn couldn't help being amazed that she could feel amused after the past couple of hours. The ride to her house—with the blessed heat blasting on high—was short and uneventful, for which she sent up prayers of gratitude. "This is going to sound weird because it's been twenty years, but I have some of my dad's sweats in a drawer in the guest room," she said once they were inside with the doors locked. "The pants might be a little short on you, but they'll do for now. Second drawer from the bottom in the tall dresser."

"It's not weird. You don't mind me wearing them?"

She smiled. "No. He'd be glad to help you."

"Then thanks."

She pointed him in the direction of her guest room and bath, then went to take care of her own soaking self.

Twenty minutes later, she padded into the kitchen, her feet clad in thick wool socks. Finally, she was starting to warm up, but a cup of coffee was still mandatory for both of them.

Her phone buzzed. She walked into the den, a cup of coffee in each hand. She set the drinks on the coffee table, curled up on the sofa, and aimed the remote at the television. Leaving it on mute, she grabbed her phone and swiped to answer the call.

"Hi, Carol."

"Hey, sweetie. I wanted to run something by you."

"What's up?"

Nathan appeared in her doorway and her pulse did that little skippy thing. She cleared her throat and waved him toward a cup. With a clearly grateful look, he snagged it and settled on the other end of the couch. He filled out her father's sweats very nicely.

"Jess? Are you listening to me?"

"Um, yes, of course." She blinked. "What?"

"Is this a bad time?"

"No, not at all."

"You have company, don't you?"

"Well—"

"Is it a man?"

The gleeful tone in her aunt's voice sent her brows into her hairline. "Aunt Carol . . ."

"Okay, okay. I have a brilliant idea."

"Uh-oh."

"Oh stop. We need to have an event. I already have it all planned and want to go over your part."

"My part?"

"We'll have a dinner and you get up and give a speech. Talk about your family and why you're doing this to honor them."

"A dinner? I thought you were just going to be calling a few of Dad's friends and coworkers."

"I was. I mean, I am. Along with anyone in the community who wants to attend. They'll have to RSVP, of course, but I think a lovely dinner would be a nice touch. If we're going to ask people for money, we should at least feed them."

"Right. Okay. Sure, that's a good idea. So, what you're saying is we'll do a full-blown thing. I'll talk about Dad and Mom's dream to give back."

"Exactly. Because think about it. While the initial investment will go to renovating the space, you're going to need regular donors to keep it going. And if we have people in the community giving money, then they'll be invested in making sure it succeeds."

That was true enough. "And that's why I hired you," she said. "You're right. It's brilliant. Just send me the schedule and I'll be there to do whatever you need me to do."

"Perfect. Thank you, darling. I've decided that I'll match donations up to a certain amount. I haven't come up with that amount yet, but I will. Now, I'm off. Tell your young man I said hello."

"Aunt Carol . . ."

But her chuckling aunt had already disconnected.

She rolled her eyes and shook her head.

"What was that all about?"

"My aunt and the benefit that's now turned into a dinner."

"You sound really excited about that."

"Just thrilled." A low groan slipped from her. "I also sound really ungrateful. I'm not, I promise. And I can't say this wasn't my idea. It was totally my idea. I will say it took some convincing on my part that she would be the best one to organize this, but she agreed. She also just decided to donate a lot of the money for the project."

"A youth center in downtown Lake City. Nice."

"The McCormick Youth Project. My dad was in commercial real estate, but volunteered with a local program that tries to help troubled kids. He was very vocal about his opinion that if they had a place to go after school and during holidays, they wouldn't get in nearly as much trouble." She shrugged. "At least the ones who don't work. He was mostly talking about those who come from violent and broken homes, those who are angry and just looking for an outlet, but anyone, from any walk of life, was welcome. He was passionate about that, from what my aunt has told me."

"You don't mind public speaking. That's awesome."

"You don't like it?"

He grimaced. "Nope. I hate it and avoid it if at all possible."

"Ha. Well, you're not the first one to say that." She shook her head. "I should have known putting my aunt in charge would help make this into something I didn't envision." She sucked in a breath and let it out slowly. "And it's fine. Truly. Or it will be once I get used to the idea."

"You're going to need security in light of recent events."

"Yes. I know. I'll start looking into that."

He tilted his head and Jesslyn gulped at how handsome he was. Seriously, he was going to be a distraction.

"Tell me about your family," he said.

She pushed away these romantic leanings. "I don't talk about them much. Not because I don't want to, but sometimes when I do, I go down the 'what if' road. And the 'I wish' highway. I don't like going there. You would think after all these years, the sting of the grief would have lessened." She paused and frowned. "I mean, I suppose it has. But the anger hasn't. It's still as raw as it was when I finally understood someone had set the fire on purpose and killed them."

He nodded, his gaze compassionate, hurting for her. She shifted, not sure what to do with that. She was used to pity, but this was different. There was no pity, just . . . empathy. "I don't remember much about my sisters. I have flashes here and there when something triggers a memory, but I do remember Maria liked dolls. She was all about the dolls. The more the merrier. Gabby was the tomboy. She wanted to play baseball and carried around a little pink ball glove. She loved watching sports with my dad. Even at that young age." She smiled. "They were cute, but I do remember they drove me crazy some days."

"Siblings can do that."

"Speaking of siblings, you never did tell me your story."

He stiffened and pulled back. "What story?"

She quirked a brow at him. "The one you don't like to talk about."

If she'd sucker punched him, the look on his face would have been about the same. "What makes you say that?"

"A feeling."

His phone buzzed and he glanced at the screen with a sigh. "Do you mind if I take this? It's my brother."

"Don't mind at all. Enjoy the reprieve."

"Not exactly sure that's what I'd call it," he muttered, "but thanks."

NATHAN STEPPED INTO THE KITCHEN and answered the call. Only because in some weird way, talking to Eli seemed safer than talking about his past. "What can I do for you, Eli?" His gaze roamed her kitchen that boasted cream-colored cabinets and white-speckled granite countertops. The window over the sink was framed with gray curtains that had a subtle pattern of circles on them.

"Mom is doing Saturday brunch. Can you be there?"

"Saturday?"

"Yes."

"Maybe." Nathan raised his eyes to the ceiling, noting the smooth white surface. "What time?"

"Nine thirty."

"Who else is going to be there?"

"All of us. If you'll come."

So far the man hadn't said anything about Nathan's need for therapy. "What's the catch?"

"No catch, Natty. Mom's just making a meal. Her usual. Eggs, bacon, pancakes, and hash browns."

Eli had used his childhood nickname once again. He shuddered and ignored that. "She hates to cook."

"But she's good at it, she loves us, and she knows we'll come if she does it."

That was true. She'd cooked two meals a day, sometimes three, when he and his siblings were growing up. When their baby sister finally went away to college, she said she was done cooking on a regular basis. She'd only do it once in a while and when she chose to.

Apparently, Saturday was the day. "I think I can make it."

"Think?"

"Yes, Eli. *Think.* I'll let Mom know one way or the other." Why hadn't she called or texted him herself?

Eli had probably volunteered because he had more to talk about.

"One more question," his brother said.

And here it came. "Yes?"

"Um . . . I know you're not interested in talking to me about the past, but there's a new doctor with our practice who has a lot of experience dealing with childhood trauma. I would like us to go together if you'd be—"

"Bye, Eli."

He hung up and resisted the urge to smash his phone against the wall. What in the *world* had gotten ahold of his brother. They'd gone years without talking about the worst day of his life—had in fact gone out of their way to *avoid* talking about it, burying it deep, pretending it didn't happen—and now, all of a sudden, in the last three months, they couldn't have a conversation without Eli dredging up that day and refusing to leave it alone even after Nathan insisted. Which was typical. If Eli wanted something, he didn't let much stand in his way of getting it. Except Nathan no longer played by his big brother's rules.

"Everything all right?" Jesslyn asked from behind him.

He turned. "Yes. Fine."

"Hm."

She didn't believe him. He didn't either. "It's my brother," he said. "He's driving me batty about something that happened years ago. I keep telling him to drop it and he keeps pushing."

"I'm sorry."

He waved a hand. "Forget it. He's been a selfish handful all his life. It's a boring topic. We can move on to a different one."

"All right. I called to check on Mr. Christie and he's still being kept in a coma."

"And probably will be for a while from what I understand. It's why we're not there at the hospital waiting for him to wake up." He sighed. "Jesslyn, we need to think about who is after you. Any thoughts?"

"No, not really. I mean, someone who's mad I didn't approve their building because it wasn't up to code? Or an arsonist I put in prison with my testimony who's now out? Or an arsonist's family member who decided it was a good time to get revenge for putting away their loved one? It could be any number of people."

"And we'll check on all of that." He nodded to the den. "Wanna sit back down?"

She yawned. "Well, there you go. All of a sudden I'm struggling to stay awake. I need some more caffeine." She walked to the Keurig and fired it up.

"It's the adrenaline rush and crash," he said. "Not to mention the knock on the head. How's that feeling anyway?"

"Ibuprofen is my friend." When her coffee was ready, he followed her back into the den, and they took their respective spots on the couch. "What's next?" she asked.

"You get some rest?"

"No, I can rest later. I need to figure this out." She pulled her phone from the end table and tapped the screen. "I keep coming back to this jewelry. I've seen that mark before, I just can't remember where or when or . . ." She shrugged. "I think it was as a child, but I'm not sure why I think that." She shivered and grabbed the blanket from the back of the couch to pull it over her. "You know, after my family was killed, I went to live with my aunt Carol."

"Right. I knew that."

"About two weeks after I was starting a new life in a new town with a new school, trying to navigate the grief and just . . . not crumble, I woke one night to a man in my room."

He grunted. "What? Who?"

"I don't know. I remember being terrified of him, then wondering if it was a dream. Then totally convinced he was real. But now . . . I'm not sure."

"What happened?"

"Nothing. He just looked at me and then turned and walked out, shutting the door behind him." She paused. "Sometimes, I think he said something, but . . ." She frowned. "I don't know. Dreams change, right?"

"Maybe. And you don't know who it could have been if he'd actually been a real person?"

"Not a clue."

"What brings this to mind now?"

She gave a little laugh. "I keep saying 'I don't know,' but it's the answer that fits. Whenever I think about my family and the fire and the night they died—were murdered—I think about the man in my room." She groaned and rubbed her cheek. "You probably think I need therapy."

"I think each person has to decide that for themselves."

"Well, I *had* therapy. Years and years of it. And every time I told the story about the man in my room, no one believed he was real."

"But you did—do?"

Another heavy sigh. "At the risk of sounding like a broken record . . . I don't know, Nathan. I *really* don't know. In the beginning I did, but then everyone kind of convinced me that it was all in my head. But if he *was* real, then who was he? And why show up in my aunt's house in the middle of the night to watch me sleep unless . . ."

Nathan studied her for a few seconds. "Unless?"

"I mean . . ."

"You think it was him, don't you?" he asked, his voice low. "The arsonist?"

She bit her lip but didn't look away. "Yeah," she finally whispered. "I do. And I've been afraid of him coming back to finish the job ever since." She paused. "And hopeful too. Because then I would finally have someone to fight. I would finally have the opportunity to get justice for my family. And me."

SEVEN

Wednesday morning, Jesslyn woke, then lay in her bed and suppressed a groan. What had compelled her to spill all that to Nathan last night? The desire for someone to believe her about the man in her room? Why? She wasn't sure *she* even believed he was real. But if he was . . . did that mean she'd seen the face of her family's killer?

It wouldn't matter. He'd been just a shadow. She had no features to describe. Not even his height. From her child's point of view, he'd been a giant. In reality? Who knew?

She shifted and groaned.

Man, she was hot. She kicked the covers off and sat up, pressing a hand to her head. It ached and her nose was stuffed up. "No. No, no, no. I don't have time to be sick."

She hurried to the bathroom, filled her cup with water, and carried it back to bed.

The knock on the bedroom door echoed through her aching head. She wasn't even surprised she knew exactly who was on the other side of that door. She groaned. "I'm coming." Nathan. She had no doubt he'd stayed the night to keep an eye on her.

She padded to the door and pulled it open. Yep. Nathan. He stood there, still in her father's sweats, yet somehow looking like he stepped off the pages of a magazine.

While she—

Don't go there. "You stayed the night."

"I hope you don't mind. You kind of passed out last night and I was . . . worried. Didn't want to leave you alone in case you needed anything."

"Or someone decided to come finish what they started at the church?"

"Yeah."

"No, I don't mind." Jesslyn shoved her hair up into a ponytail, then planted her hands on her hips. Then coughed and sniffed. "Ugh."

His eyes narrowed. "You're sick."

"You think?" She stomped to the bathroom to grab a roll of toilet paper, pulled off a wad, and blew her nose. "I really don't have time for this."

When she stopped back in front of him, he pressed a hand to her forehead. "Maybe not, but you've got a fever."

"I know that, thank you very much."

"You're going to be a cranky patient, aren't you?"

"No."

"You're not?"

"No, because I'm not going to *be* a patient. I've got a to-do list a mile long and—"

"So, you're going to go spread your germs to everyone in your path?"

She stopped. And groaned. Whirled back to her bed and dropped onto it. And coughed. "No."

"I'll call Lainie and she'll bring you whatever you need to get you feeling better ASAP."

"Fine. Thank you. Then you'd better stay away. This is probably the last thing you need."

"Call whoever you need to call and let them know you're down for the count for the next few days. At least until that fever breaks."

"Right."

"Okay then. I'm going to find you some Motrin."

"I have some in my bathroom. I'll get it."

"Then I'll go fix you some soup or something."

"You'll have to have it delivered. I have nothing in the fridge." Her face was red, no doubt. Hopefully he'd chalk it up to the fever, not her mortification that he'd taken it upon himself to take care of her and nothing she could say was going to sway his decision.

A pause and then he cleared his throat. "I'll take care of it."

He slipped out of her room, and she shut her eyes, doing her best to ignore the fact that she felt like death. At least her stomach wasn't upset. It was probably just a cold, but then again, the fever indicated infection somewhere. She sniffed. Sinuses.

"God, this was not on my list for today," she muttered. She forced herself to get the Motrin, then crawled back into bed and pulled the covers over her head.

She must have dozed because when she woke, Lainie was there holding a syringe and a bag from the local pharmacy. She set both on the end table, then settled on the bed next to Jesslyn.

"I don't wanna be sick. I don't have time to be sick. Why is this happening to me? Haven't I been through enough? Now we have to throw feeling awful into the mix? It's not fair." Jesslyn couldn't help the whine in her words.

Lainie smiled, her gaze sympathetic. "I know, but it is what it is. Let's get some meds in you." She pulled her stethoscope to her ears and proceeded to give Jesslyn a full examination. Finally, she sat back. "Well, you're definitely sick."

"And people actually pay for that kind of genius diagnosis? I'm in the wrong business."

Lainie laughed. "I know. I'm sorry. Your lungs sound a little tight. Let's do a steroid shot and an antibiotic, some cough medicine, and all the fluids you can stand. I brought you an inhaler to use as well. You'll be good to go in a few days."

"I don't have time for this, Lainie."

"So you said. But the good thing is you can work from here. I'm sure you have paperwork to catch up on."

"Well, yes. That's true."

Lainie patted her shoulder. "You might want to find some nose spray too."

"I have some in the bathroom."

Lainie administered the meds, gave her a tight hug, then swept out of the room.

Jesslyn coughed, blew her nose, then fell into a restless sleep.

And dreamed of him. The man in her room. *"I'll be watching you, Jesslyn,"* he whispered.

Jesslyn yanked herself out of the dream and sat up panting, sweating, and shaking. She hurtled out of the bed and into the bathroom where she lost what little she had in her stomach. From the dream or the virus? She didn't know, but it was the first time she'd ever dreamed the man spoke to her.

She slid to the floor and lay on the cool tile while she processed everything. Had he spoken those words? That he would be watching her?

For some reason, she didn't think her brain had made that up. And maybe that was the reason a part of her was always looking over her shoulder, expecting the arsonist from her past to show up and . . . what? Kill her?

Yes. Exactly that.

She hefted herself off the floor and took some more Motrin, still thinking. Was the act of burning her church some kind of message from him? Maybe her promise to come after him had sparked his rage, and now he was setting fires to get back at her?

It was possible. Likely even. She'd awakened the sleeping beast unintentionally.

Or had she subconsciously been hoping for that very thing?

Feeling too awful to explore that possibility, she scrubbed a hand down her face and sniffed.

The smell of coffee sent her nerve endings tingling. How did she smell anything with her stopped-up nose? Maybe it was just sheer desperation for the brew. But who was fixing it? Nathan would be gone, so it was probably Lainie. She had a key and knew the code to her alarm. *Thank you, Lord, for good friends.*

Jesslyn brushed her hair and her teeth, pulled on a fleece shacket, shoved some tissues into one of the pockets, and walked into the kitchen to find Nathan sitting at her kitchen table. He was dressed in jeans and a long-sleeved black T-shirt. He looked freshly scrubbed and quite adorable. And incredibly healthy. She wanted to hate him for that, but found herself kind of melting.

No. Wait. She didn't *melt. Stop it.* Melting was for movies, not real life. "What are you still doing here?" He blinked and she winced. "Sorry. I didn't mean that as harsh as it came out. I was just expecting Lainie." And if she'd known it was Nathan, she would have taken a shower.

Oh well. At least she'd brushed her teeth. And her hair. She reached up and patted it. Hadn't she?

"How do you feel?" he asked.

"A little better maybe." She beelined for the coffee. "And just to be clear, I'm not upset you're here. You fixed coffee."

"It's pretty easy with the Keurig."

"But I don't have to wait sixty seconds for it."

"Chicken noodle soup is in the container."

"Oh, how nice. Thanks."

"It's just takeout from the Cornerstone Café."

"My morning just got a lot better thanks to you, so I appreciate it." She sipped her coffee, then looked at Nathan. And tried not to melt again. She really needed to get over whatever was making her do that. It had to be related to being sick, right? "Don't you have to work? And where did you get those clothes, by the way? They're not my dad's."

"Yes, I have to work and Andrew ran by my place to grab me a few things." He frowned. "I couldn't bring myself to leave you alone. Not with what happened at the church." His eyes narrowed. "That was really scary, Jesslyn."

"Yes. Yes, it was." She pulled a tissue from her shacket pocket and blew her nose.

He held out a hand. "Want me to throw that away for you?"

"Ew. Gross. No." She did so and washed her hands. Then returned to her coffee.

"So," he said, "what's your plan for the day, because I don't see you doing more than taking the occasional nap in between working."

"You know what else is scary? The fact that you know I'm going to work regardless of how I feel."

He laughed. "Well, we've known each other for a good bit. Maybe not like you know Lainie and some of the others, but while you're mysterious in some ways, you're an open book in others."

"I'm not sure I want to ask what you mean by that."

He offered her a soft smile. "Nothing earth-shattering. You're very guarded when it comes to relationships outside of your circle. And even with those inside it, you don't share much even though you welcome their confidences. You're driven and focused and don't like to be distracted from whatever goal you've set for yourself."

And now she needed him to leave.

HE'D STRUCK A NERVE. Or sliced an artery. He wasn't sure which, but her frozen stillness conveyed more than words ever could.

She finally gave a slow nod. "Okay, that's a fair observation. I guess you don't have to leave."

"Leave?"

She waved a hand. "It's not important."

He scrubbed his chin, regret burning a path from his brain to his heart. "I'm sorry. I shouldn't have said all that. I've always had a problem saying what I think. I've gotten better, but still . . ."

She kept her gaze locked on his. "And what about you? I feel like the pot is calling the kettle black, as my grandma used to say. So far, you've managed to avoid talking about yourself, and if you don't want to, just say so and I won't ask again."

For a moment, he almost took advantage of her willingness to let it go, then sighed. "When I was eleven, my best friend at the time was Danny Pringle. He lived next door to me, so we were always at each other's houses. We were inseparable, as were our parents. One summer evening, our parents went out to dinner like they did often. He came over and we were playing and got trapped in the old storage building in my parents' backyard."

"Oh no. How scary."

"It was, but that's not the worst of it. We were . . . playing with fire. Literally. Anyway, the short version is, a fire broke out, he died, and I escaped." He shook his head. "I've been terrified of fire ever since. It's all I can do to visit the scene of a building that's already burning. Does that make me weak?"

"Absolutely not."

His heart hummed at the compassion lacing those two words. And her eyes . . .

He had to stop thinking about her eyes. He blinked and looked away. "Well, some days it's all I can think about. And wonder why I'm here and Danny's not."

Jesslyn made a choking sound and he looked up to see tears swimming in her eyes. "Oh, Nathan . . . I . . . I don't even know what to say except that I understand," she whispered.

He fought the emotion her response elicited and offered her a small smile. "Yeah. If anyone understands, it's you."

"Thank you for sharing with me."

He'd shared, but not everything. He just couldn't.

He cleared his throat. "Anyway, I was really depressed after that, as you can imagine. My parents didn't know what to do with me. They sent me to counseling, but despite everyone's support, I decided I hated God because if he was as loving and powerful as I'd been taught—and believed—then he could have saved Danny. But he didn't, so I stopped believing in him."

"Did you ever start believing in him again?"

"I did. Sometimes, when things go bad, I can fall into old patterns, revert to believing the old lies. Like if he really was a God of love, he'd prove it and fix this world. He'd keep children safe and take out the bad guys roaming this earth, but he doesn't."

"I know that feeling. I just have to keep telling myself that nothing's going to be perfect until he comes back," she said. "Until then . . ."

"I know. He's a good God. I know that. He's proven it. I just have to stand firm on that knowledge when everything else seems to say differently."

"I sometimes feel guilty for being alive while the rest of my family is dead. Like if I'd been there, I could have miraculously saved them somehow." She gave a low snort. "Stupid. Mentally, I know that it's not possible, and in all likelihood I'd be dead too, but I can't help thinking that. Sometimes."

He reached out and gave her hand a quick squeeze. "Yeah."

She breathed in, then coughed so hard he thought she might lose a lung. When she finally caught her breath, she shook her head. "You get out of here and go see what you can find on this arsonist. I'm going back to bed." She took another sip of her coffee. "After I finish this."

"I'm worried about you being here alone."

"Yes, you've made that clear." She smiled. "And I appreciate it. Truly. But I've got my alarm system and my Glock. I'll be fine."

"You're also sick and not on your A game."

"I'm aware, thanks."

"Which is why I've called in reinforcements."

She frowned. "Reinforcements?"

"Kenzie and Cole will be here shortly."

"Nathan! They have jobs too. People who live alone get sick and don't have babysitters."

"True. But not everyone who is sick has a psycho shooter after them. So . . . since you said you'd be willing to let your friends help, I think it's better safe than sorry."

She opened her mouth as though to object, then snapped her lips shut. "You might have a point," she finally said. "And I did say that, didn't I?" He raised a brow and she groaned. "Okay. Fine. I don't have the strength to argue."

"I'll take that as a win." She glanced up at him through tired, slightly glazed eyes, and he took in her red nose, chapped lips, and wild ponytail. And still found the woman attractive. "Go to bed, Jess, I'll check on you later."

She sniffed and nodded but narrowed her eyes. "Find the arsonist. If you don't, when I wake up, I'll be joining the hunt."

"Yes, ma'am, that's the goal."

"Okay then."

"Okay."

She left and he literally had to run his hand over his lips to wipe his smile off. He liked her. Too much to kid himself that he could just be friends with her.

But unfortunately, he couldn't be anything more. Not if he wanted to keep his pain and his secrets buried. A relationship with someone—a *real* relationship—would require him to relive things he'd rather not.

When Kenzie and Cole showed up seconds later, he let them in. Along with Andrew, Tate, and James. "Brought the whole team, I see?"

"A lot of it anyway. Lainie had to go to work," James said, "and Kristine is in Paris, I think, or they'd be here too. If Jesslyn's in trouble, we're here to help."

"And since this is officially our case," Andrew said, "we can work it from here. Make sure she's safe."

"We'll do what the team did with me," Kenzie said.

Cole nodded. "Rally around her and have her back."

Last year, someone had wanted Kenzie off the SWAT team and had done everything in their power to make that happen—including attempts on her life. The team had "circled the wagons" so to speak, with Kenzie in the middle. And now Jesslyn's friends were doing the same for her. Because they loved her.

"Y'all are going to make me cry," she said from the entrance to the hallway, her voice hoarse with emotion—and the illness.

"Never on purpose," Kenzie said, "but if you need to, it's okay."

"No. I refuse. My nose is stuffed up enough, thanks." She sniffed and the others laughed. "Heard y'all come in and had to say thanks before I crashed." She waved and disappeared into her bedroom.

"Thanks for calling us," Cole said to Nathan. "We wouldn't want to be anywhere else."

Nathan smiled. "I figured that."

If Jesslyn would let them help protect her, Nathan might be able to sleep at night.

EIGHT

Jesslyn woke Friday morning finally feeling almost normal except for the stupid lingering cough, but she hoped that would fade over the next few days. And prayed the next time a killer came after her, it wasn't raining or freezing cold.

She shuddered. She definitely did not want a killer to come after her ever again.

But she had a feeling whoever had shot at her in the church parking lot wasn't gone. He'd be back.

And she was going to have to be ready.

She walked into the kitchen to find Kenzie reading a book and eating a plate of eggs and bacon between page turns. Jesslyn's stomach rumbled. "Got any extra?"

"Yep. On the stove. Let me fix you a plate."

Kenzie started to stand and Jesslyn waved a hand. "I've got it, thanks." She fixed a plate, poured coffee, and sat across from Kenzie. "You guys have been great, but you don't have to do this any longer."

"You're tired of me already?"

Jesslyn laughed. "No, I've slept away too many hours. I didn't have a chance to get tired of you. You're probably sick of hanging around here."

"Never. How's your head?"

Jesslyn touched the wound. "It's fine. Healing up nicely." She paused. "Did I really fall asleep in the middle of *Casablanca*?"

"You did."

"Wow."

"I know. You need to repent of that behavior."

"Cute." Just as she took her first sip of coffee, her phone went off and she tapped the notification. "Uh-oh."

Kenzie raised a brow at her. "What?"

"Fire at the Endurance Empire Gym."

"Oh no."

Jesslyn bit her lip and looked at Kenzie. "That's my gym."

"I know."

"I'm back on duty as of right now." Jesslyn raced to get ready, then hurried out to the rental that her friends had dropped off for her and loaded her gear into the back.

"You can't do anything yet, Jess," Kenzie said. "They have to get the fire out first. Why don't you wait until you—"

"No, I need to be there and I need Nathan and Andrew to be there. They should be looking for him."

"Yeah. Okay. Let's go. I'll follow you."

Jesslyn's heart pounded as she slid into the driver's seat of her rental and gunned the vehicle in the direction of the fire. Kenzie fell in behind her, and their lights and sirens parted the traffic like a hot knife through butter.

Within ten minutes, she parked in the vicinity of the fire engines. Close, but not in the way if the firefighters needed to grab something from one of the trucks. She climbed out of her vehicle and assessed the scene, starting with the facility.

The building, engulfed in flames, was located on a piece of property just off the main road through Lake City. Jesslyn tried to picture it as it normally was. In a shallow valley surrounded by tall oaks that separated the businesses on either side of it. The parking lot ran the length of the right and front sides of the fitness center with the main entrance off the right.

Flames and smoke billowed from the building while firefighters kept their gushing hoses aimed at the destruction. The heat reached her and she stepped back, continuing to sweep her gaze over the crowd.

Kenzie joined her. "So far no one has been reported injured even though people were in the gym at the time."

"How many?"

"Four."

"It's an off time during the day," she murmured. "Most of the early morning crowd is gone and the lunch breakers haven't gotten here yet."

"So, does this person want to hurt someone or not?" Kenzie asked.

"I'm not sure. Mr. Christie was at the church, but his van was around the back. He cleans at night, and if he was at the back of the church, the front would have been dark and looked empty." She shrugged. "And even at the back, if there was a light on, it wouldn't have been unusual."

"But the van?"

"Could have been mistaken for a church vehicle. He doesn't have any kind of identifying logos or advertisements on the side." She studied the building while she thought. "And here, it's an off time. The arsonist started the fire away from the main workout space. It's possible he's at least making an effort to avoid hurting people. Assuming the two fires are related."

"You think they are."

"Not just related, but maybe somehow connected to me? It was my church, now it's my gym. Once the fire's out, I'll look for other things that may connect them."

Like purple stains.

Brittany Brown, the gym's owner, detached herself from several members Jesslyn had seen but didn't know. Brittany and Jesslyn chatted on a regular basis.

With Kenzie at her side, Jesslyn met Brittany halfway. "Are you all right?"

Sweat and black ash coated the woman's normally fair skin and her friendly eyes were shadowed. "I'm okay. We all got out, thank goodness. The alarms saved us."

"Where'd it start? Do you know?"

"Several alarms went off at around the same time. One in the women's bathroom. One in the childcare area, which was empty at the time, praise the Lord, and one in the spare equipment room."

"Can you access the security footage from your phone or laptop?"

"Yeah. It should all be in the cloud or on the server."

"Great. We'll need a copy of that."

"Of course." Brittany rubbed a hand across her forehead, smearing the spot. "I can't believe someone would do this. I mean, why?"

"We're looking into that," Kenzie said, and Jesslyn nodded. It was too soon to flat-out state that the person might be targeting places Jesslyn frequented, but she was putting every other location she could think of on high alert—including her favorite grocery store, doctor's office, coffee shop . . . and the Cornerstone Café, of course.

Movement at the edge of the property shifted her focus. Someone stood there, heavy coat on, hat, gloves, long pants, and work boots. She wasn't sure why she noticed him. Maybe because of his stance. Arms crossed, head low, alone. Out of place. She started toward him, wanting a look at his face. He glanced up and caught her eye. Looked away. Then stepped back.

"Kenzie?"

"Yeah?"

"Can you detain that guy in the green coat and black hat?" She gave a subtle nod toward the man.

"The one looking ready to run?"

"That's the one."

"Consider him detained."

Kenzie got on her radio and officers gave chase. Jesslyn hurried behind them. "Catch him," she whispered, "please catch him."

They would. They had to. Because she had a bad feeling that this fire was all her fault.

NATHAN TRACKED THE FLEEING MAN.

"Got him in my scope," Cole said. Not to shoot, but to give them information as to the direction he was going. "Take a left at Collier's Drug Store and . . . I lost him. He could have gone inside. I never saw him come off the sidewalk. Catch him coming out the back. King has the store."

"I've got the back." Nathan changed direction, vaguely aware of the others behind him. Some in front of him. All with one goal.

Catch the guy.

He ran to the alley that would take him to the back of Collier's. Two other officers followed him. A helicopter buzzed overhead. Finally.

At the back of the store, he pulled up. The other officers stopped next to him. "He come out?" the tallest one asked. Tremaine, his badge read.

"I don't know. Kenzie? Anything?"

"Negative. Sending all customers in the store out. He could be hiding in here somewhere. Gonna need some backup."

"On the way." James's voice came through the comms.

"You guys stay here," Nathan said. "I'll go around the front and join Kenzie."

He entered the store to find it empty except for Kenzie, James, Sampson Greene, and his K-9, Otis. Greene eyed him. "Can't track a man without a scent article."

"I know."

Kenzie backed away from the storage room. "It's clear."

James lowered his weapon. "The whole place is clear."

"Well, he didn't just disappear," Nathan said. He took a step forward, then stopped and looked up. Walked a few more paces, then stopped again and listened. "Maybe he went up, not out," he said, his voice low.

Kenzie nodded. "Just thinking that. But from what access point?"

James went back to the storage room. "Start looking."

They fanned out and started the search once more. Nathan checked the restrooms, then the women's changing room. He hesitated. A black curtain drawn across the back was darker in one area. Because sunlight had faded the other part? Weapon ready, he stood to the side and whipped the curtain aside.

An open window. It exited to a hallway, not to the outside. "Found his exit point."

The others joined him and they all climbed through. Cold air hit him. It might be inside, but it wasn't heated. Cole nodded right. "Cross and I'll go this way."

"Kenzie and I'll take left." Nathan swept down the hallway, praying the guy didn't step out of a doorway and open fire. They were all sitting ducks at the moment.

But it was quiet, the doors to other businesses clear. When he reached the end of the hall, he paused. Stairs leading up to his right, the sidewalk in sight through the window at his front. Going with his gut, he took the stairs.

Footsteps darted, pounding just above him on the flat roof. Nathan shoved out the door at the top of the stairs and caught sight of the fleeing man. "Hey! Stop!"

The guy looked back over his shoulder, spun once more, and aimed himself toward the edge of the other side of the roof.

Nathan had a bad feeling. "Don't do it!"

Of course the dude ignored him. Nathan added speed to his steps and reached, grasping for a handful of the loose-fitting green coat, but his fingers scraped the material and the suspect leaped over the edge of the building.

Kenzie's gasp echoed in his ear. Nathan came to a skidding stop and pinwheeled to keep from vaulting over. He looked down, expecting the worst, but to his surprise, the guy's gloved fingers were attached to the gutter of the neighboring building. "Help!"

"Hold on!" Nathan gave the man's location and officers closed in, but Nathan could see his fingers slipping.

"Help me! I'm gonna fall!" The terrified screech echoed in the air.

"Great," Nathan muttered and backed up as far as he thought he might need. He'd jumped that distance before. Barely. When he'd been a lot younger.

One hand slipped off and the guy cried out, arm flailing. Nathan took two more steps back.

"Don't you dare," Kenzie said.

"I don't have a choice." He needed that guy alive.

With Kenzie shouting in his ear, Nathan ran and vaulted over the open space below, soaring for a brief second before he landed just beyond the suspect. Nathan hit hard, his left leg buckled, and he rolled, gasping at the pain that shuddered up his hip. Then he shifted, clamped down on the wrist of the dangling possible arsonist, and held on.

"Th-thank you."

"Shut up."

Nathan tuned into his surroundings. Officers were finally on the roof and heading toward them. James, Cole, and Andrew led the way, all with ferocious frowns on their faces. Cole dropped beside him and added his strength to haul the guy up and over. In seconds, he had him on his stomach, hands cuffed.

Andrew turned to Nathan. "Are you out of your ever-lovin' mind?"

"Absolutely." Now that they had the man in custody, he allowed himself to take inventory. His leg ached, but his hip hurt with a vicious bite. *Please, God, don't let it be broken.*

"Are you hurt?" Andrew asked.

"Yep."

"Then I'll spare you the lecture until after you're discharged from the hospital."

"Appreciate it."

His friend's sheet-white face betrayed his fear for Nathan. Nathan hated it, but if he hadn't made the jump, Mr. Potential Arsonist might be dead. And if he wasn't the arsonist, he might know who was. As well as who might be after Jesslyn and why.

Cole held up a wallet. "No ID." He jerked the guy to his feet. "Let's go, kid. You've got some questions to answer."

"I want a lawyer."

"I see you're not a complete idiot. We'll get you a lawyer." He looked down at Nathan. "Get medical attention."

"Planning on it." He really prayed his hip was still in one piece.

Cole shook his head, his lips tight. "What made you do a dumb thing like that?"

"I was channeling my high school champion long jump days."

"Dude . . ."

"I know. Dumb."

"*So* dumb." Cole's face softened. "But the guy's alive and so are you, so we'll focus on the positive."

"Yeah. That's a good idea. Let's do that."

"Can you get up?" Andrew asked him.

Time to find out. He started to rise and hissed at the stab of lightning. He stilled, then gathered a breath and held out a hand for Andrew to help him up.

"Well?" Andrew asked once he was on his feet.

"It hurts, but doesn't have that 'I'm going to puke from the pain' feel."

"Then it's probably not broken."

"Thank God."

"Might have cracked something, though."

He might have. "I'll get it x-rayed and we'll find out for sure."

"James probably has Lainie on standby at the hospital."

"Don't tell Jesslyn about this."

"Won't have to." Andrew pointed to the sky. A news chopper hovered, cameras aimed at them. "Time to wash your cape. I think your Superman impersonation is going to go viral."

"Fabulous."

NINE

Jesslyn had been otherwise occupied when she'd received word that Nathan had tried to leap a tall building in a single bound—and was on his way to the hospital. As soon as the ambulance left, she'd done what she needed at the site and informed Chief Laramie she'd be back once the fire was out at the gym. Then she climbed into her rental and headed to the hospital. She had to see for herself that Nathan was all right.

She entered the main emergency department doors and was taken aback by the absolute chaos. People and hospital workers everywhere. People in the hallways, and every possible spot. "What in the world?"

She spotted several people she and Nathan both knew, but no Lainie. Well, Nathan might not even be her patient. Then again, if she'd had a heads-up he was coming, she'd arrange for it to happen.

Where was everyone?

James and Cole had probably taken the suspect to the station for booking and questioning—assuming he didn't need medical attention—but Andrew would have come to the hospital with Nathan. She assumed.

Jesslyn walked to the triage station. "Carly, have you seen Nathan? He was brought in a few minutes ago."

"He's back there, but we're so busy, I think he's actually in one of the storage rooms."

"The stor—seriously?"

"I know. It happens sometimes and most people prefer it to have a modicum of privacy."

"Unbelievable. What happened? Where'd all these people come from?"

"Tour bus heading to Asheville crashed with an eighteen-wheeler, which caused a twenty-car pileup. You didn't hear it on the radio?"

Jesslyn rubbed her forehead. "No. I've been busy with a fire." And other stuff.

"We've pulled in everyone off duty including paramedics and EMTs to help triage people. On that note, I've got to go, but from what I understand, Nathan's not hurt too bad."

Relief flowed. "Thanks." Jesslyn started checking rooms and finally saw Andrew in the hallway. "How is he?" she asked, hurrying to his side.

"He's okay. Lainie's been with him. When he saw all the people needing help, he tried to walk back out the door, but Lainie convinced him to let her clear him. He's had X-rays, just waiting for the results. For what it's worth, Lainie doesn't think his hip is broken."

More relief. "Pain level?"

"Manageable. He let them give him something nonnarcotic and said it was helping. I stepped out while they did their thing."

"That was fast work on Lainie's part."

"Once he said he'd stay, she double-timed it."

Jesslyn huffed. "Afraid he'd back out and leave."

"I'm sure. We're both anxious to question the suspect, but he was calling his lawyer. He'll keep for a few hours. Oh, I called Nathan's parents to let them know and I think they're on the way."

Uh-oh. "Um, okay."

Andrew stilled and frowned. "What? Should I not have done that?"

"Guess we'll see. From what I understand, his relationship with his family is good for the most part, but . . . also complicated."

"Complicated how?"

"Not for me to say."

Andrew held up a hand. "I got it. I'll go tell him and hope I still have my head if I messed up."

"Maybe try groveling?" He grimaced and Jesslyn took pity on him. "It'll be all right."

"Guess we'll find out." He paused. "You want to go in first?"

"Get the lay of the land, so to speak?"

"Am I a coward?"

"Either that or just smart."

He chuckled and shook his head. "It's fine. I got this."

"How about I go with you?"

"God bless you."

He led the way to Nathan's makeshift room and rapped his knuckles on the door.

"Come in."

Jesslyn followed Andrew inside and let the door shut behind her. The space was bigger than she'd anticipated. And organized well.

Nathan was lying on a gurney on his right side, facing the door. He cracked his eyes open at their entrance. "Hi," he said.

Jesslyn gave a sympathetic smile. "How's the hip?"

"Fine. They gave me a muscle relaxer too. Forgot how dopey those things make me feel. I should have refused."

"Right. Well, while you're dopey and in no shape to kill me if I messed up . . ." Andrew cleared his throat. "I have a confession to make."

Nathan's eyes narrowed. "Okay."

"I . . . uh . . . called your parents and told them you were here."

"Oh."

Jesslyn raised a brow at Andrew's questioning look.

"Wait. You what?" Nathan popped into alertness, the fog in his eyes clearing.

"You gave me their contact info in case anything happened. Something happened."

"Dude, I meant if I died. Not if I bruised a hip."

"Oh, right. Sorry about that."

"'S'okay." He closed his eyes again. "Parents are good people. Eli's the one I gotta watch out for. No idea what his problem is, but . . ." He mumbled something she couldn't catch.

It was Andrew's turn to raise a brow at Jesslyn. "How much of that stuff did they give him?"

"Beats me."

A knock on the door sounded and Jesslyn opened it to find a couple in their late fifties. "Hi." She introduced herself and Andrew. "I'm guessing you're Nathan's parents?"

"We are," the man said and held out a hand. "I'm Blake and this is Connie."

"Nice to meet you." Connie's slightly furrowed brow clued Jesslyn in to the woman's worry despite the smile on her face. "He's fine. Come on in."

Blake turned to look behind him. "This is Eli, his brother, and Carly, his sister."

Carly, who looked very much like a feminine version of Nathan, rushed past them all and beelined for her brother. He'd rolled to his back. "Nathan, are you all right?" Carly leaned over and kissed his cheek.

"I'm fine, sis. Just a bruise."

His parents greeted Nathan with pats and his mother held his hand with no clear intention of ever letting go. Eli hung back near the door and shuffled his feet, his ill-at-ease hovering painful to watch.

Jesslyn's attention switched back to the parents. They looked younger than she knew them to be, and Nathan favored his mother but got his smile from his father.

She switched back to study Eli. The brother Nathan avoided. He looked like a slightly older version of Nathan. Anyone looking at them would pick them out as siblings.

She smiled at Eli, and he returned it while raking a hand over his head. He nodded and stepped into Nathan's view.

She thought she might have heard Nathan bite off a low groan.

"Glad you're okay, Natty," Eli said.

Natty?

She caught Nathan's glare at the nickname and vowed never to use it. Then wondered why Eli would. Sibling stuff or something more? It was awfully crowded and her earlier assessment of the room's size changed. It was getting smaller by the moment, and now was a good time to make her exit. She backed toward the door, not wanting to make a production of leaving. She gave Andrew a small wave and slipped out of the room.

He caught up with her seconds later. "Hey, you think it's okay to leave him alone with them?"

She smiled. "Yes, he's a big boy, he can handle it."

"No conviction to rescue him?"

"Nothing wrong with his voice. He can holler for help if he needs to. Besides, I'm not the one who invited them."

"Man, you're cold."

The words froze her for a brief moment. Was she? She'd really been teasing and hoped Andrew was as well. She just didn't know him well enough to read him like she could the others.

Before she could find an answer, Lainie appeared and hurried over. "Hey, are you okay?"

"I'm fine. Just here to check on Nathan. Speaking of checking in, I need to call the chief and see if there's anything I can do when I return to the scene." She turned to Andrew. "Can you let me know when you head to the station to question the guy? I'd like to listen in if possible."

"I don't mind."

She nodded. "Thanks."

A door slammed behind her and she spun to see Eli exit Nathan's room and lean against the wall, head back, eyes closed, pulling in measured breaths while he clenched and unclenched his fists. Carly stepped out next to him and placed a hand on his arm. He pulled away and walked toward the watercooler at the nurses' station. She followed, brows pulled in concern.

NATHAN LOCKED HIS JAW against the words he wanted to say and the pain shooting through his hip. Carefully, he leaned back and swallowed. Why did Eli continue to set him off every single time they were together? It was like his brother had suddenly made it his mission in life to be as obnoxious as possible.

He looked at his parents. His father's tight jaw and narrowed eyes and his mother's tear-filled ones sent remorse racing through him. Eli and he needed to keep their . . . argument? spat? whatever . . . to themselves and not stress their parents out over it. "Guys, thanks for coming, but it looks like Eli and I have a few things to settle before we're going to be able to be civil. Can you tell him to come back in here, then go get some coffee or something and let us talk?"

"Are you sure you can without . . ." His father didn't have to finish the sentence.

Nathan took a breath and shifted, then winced before he could stop it. Thankfully, the pain settled fairly quickly. "I don't know, to be honest," he said, "but I guess I have to try."

His mother nodded and took his dad by the arm. "Come on, hon."

He followed her out of the room, and Eli stepped in seconds later, arms crossed, eyes blazing. Nathan bit his tongue and willed his thoughts to settle down. It was not a great choice to do this while the muscle relaxant was still coursing through his veins. It might relax his filters too much.

Eli took a deep breath and pressed a hand to his lips as though physically restraining his words. Seeing his brother make that effort had a calming effect, and Nathan gathered his composure. "What is it with us?" he asked, his voice low.

"I . . . just . . . I worry about you. I love you and I worry about you.

And while I know everything I say is going to rub you the wrong way, even with all my training, I can't seem to not say it."

Nathan nodded. He could appreciate that. "Eli, you keep saying I need counseling, that I need to deal with the . . . incident. I *had* counseling."

"As a child, not an adult." Eli looked at his hands, then back to Nathan. "Do you still blame yourself for the fire?"

"Of course I do. The whole thing was my idea! I wanted the s'mores, I wanted to do what I wanted to do. And I wanted to hide so no one would find us and stop us. I stole the lighter and I got us trapped in a shed with a door that often got stuck." Eli flinched, but Nathan ignored him. "So, yeah, Eli. I still blame myself. I thought I'd left the door cracked, but I didn't, and as a result, Danny died. It's on me. I've learned to live with it. I've learned that kids do dumb stuff and sometimes that can have tragic consequences. I've learned not to hate myself anymore. But does it still haunt me? Do I still wake up with dreams of Danny's screams echoing in my ears? Yes. Will that ever stop? I don't know. Will I ever be able to move past that and allow myself grace? Again, I don't know. All I know is I'm sick of you bringing it up, so if there's any hope at all of us having a relationship, you need to let it go."

The rant had exhausted him, his hip throbbed, and he wanted nothing more than for Eli to leave before he puked. His brother stood there looking like he wanted to say something else, then tears flooded his eyes and his throat worked. "I don't know if I can."

"Then we have nothing more to say to each other. Get out."

"I was . . . I need—I—could we—"

"What, Eli? Why is this about what *you* need? It's always about what you want, what you need, isn't it? Nothing's changed in that regard, has it? Drop it, man. You weren't even there!"

His brother's face went concrete hard. "Right. Exactly. I wasn't there." He opened the door and disappeared.

Nathan stifled the yell he wanted to release and settled for a combination of a low growl and harsh groan instead. He pressed a hand to his pounding head. It almost hurt worse than his hip. He swallowed hard, dragging in ragged breaths, ordering the contents of his stomach to stay put.

The door creaked open. What now? Couldn't everyone just leave him alone for five seconds?

Jesslyn's head appeared. Okay, everyone except her.

"You okay?" she asked.

"How much did you hear?"

"Not enough to really understand what it was all about. You weren't shouting."

"This time."

"You said things were strained between you and your brother. Did he have something to do with the fire you mentioned? When you were a kid?"

He frowned. "No. It was all me. I was the one who . . ." Something blipped at the edges of his memory. Eli shouting at him and Danny. It faded as quickly as it appeared. What was that? Where *had* Eli been? "I mean, maybe he was inside the house? Or with a friend? He was sixteen when it happened, so he would have been driving." He leaned back and crossed his arms. "I don't know. I'm not sure it matters."

"So your parents left you alone at the age of eleven?"

Nathan thought about that. "I guess they must have." Why didn't he remember? Did it matter? Another something flickered in the back of his mind and he swiped a hand down the side of his face and froze. "Wait."

"What?"

"I just remembered that Eli was supposed to be watching us." Nathan swallowed hard. Where had that memory come from? "Yeah. He told us to go upstairs and play video games. I decided to disobey and the results were tragic."

"You were kids, Nathan."

"I know."

His phone buzzed and he glanced at it. "It's Lindsay."

"Go ahead."

He swiped the screen. "What's up?"

"I hear you're channeling Superman."

Nathan worked hard not to growl. "Haha. I assume you have something helpful to share with me?"

"Lots. But, seriously, are you okay?"

"I'm in one piece, which is something like a miracle, but yeah, so please go for it."

"Right. So here we are. The gun from the attack at the restaurant is registered to a George Harlow. He reported it stolen about two weeks ago. I had ballistics test-fire it and compare bullets, and there aren't any known crimes where this gun has been used in the system. Not to say they haven't been committed, they're just not in the system. I ran a background check on Harlow and he came back squeaky clean. He owns several other weapons and they're all accounted for. This one was stolen out of his car."

"That's good to know. Frustrating, but good to know." Another dead end, but . . . "I'll talk to Andrew and we'll see if we can run down Harlow's acquaintances. Close friends, but also people maybe not so close? His yard guy, cleaning lady, pool boy, whoever. Even the person who cleans his workspace. I want to find out who knew he had a weapon in his car."

"You think the person who stole it knew him?"

"Maybe. I'm not ruling it out. Might have just been a guy looking for a gun and got lucky. Or it could be someone who knew Harlow kept one in his car and acted on it. Where was the car parked when the gun was taken?"

"At the guy's office. He's a financial adviser with an office on North Main."

"Thanks, Lindsay. If you don't mind, pull footage of the parking lot from when he says the gun was stolen. I'm curious to see if there's anything there. Like a dark blue sedan."

"Sure thing. I'll be in touch if I find out anything else. Bye."

Nathan hung up.

A knock preceded the door opening and the doctor stepped into the room. Jesslyn rose. "I'll just wait outside."

"No, it's all right. You can stay."

The doc nodded and she settled back into the chair. "Just here to give you the results of your X-rays," the man said, "and let you know for sure nothing's broken or even fractured. You have a pretty massive bruise, though, that probably feels like it goes to the bone."

"Yep." Before everyone had arrived, he'd taken a look at the area that had gone from red to deep red and was no doubt heading toward a lovely shade of dark purple.

"So there aren't any physical limitations really other than to do your best not to injure the area again." He cleared his throat. "I saw the news footage of you jumping off the building. That was intense."

"A bit." Was there anyone who hadn't seen it?

"Take it easy, all right? When it hurts, take the meds. There are two different kinds. One for daytime that won't make you sleepy, but the other will. It's a mild narcotic."

"No narcotics."

"Fill it, and if you need it, you have it."

Nathan suppressed a grumble. "Fine." He'd say anything at this point just to get going.

"And, uh . . . you might want to put your cape away for a while. You're going to be sore for a good long time. Running and jumping, falling? Not a good idea. Let someone else chase the bad guys."

"I got it. Thank you." He paused. "But I'm not on desk duty, right?" His SSA would be here to talk to the doc to determine exactly what Nathan could and couldn't do. He'd require authorization from the doctor for Nathan to resume full duty.

The doctor hesitated. "It's just a bruise and you're going to be sore, but there's no reason to ride a desk if you don't want to."

"I don't."

He nodded. "I thought that might be the way you'd lean. I'll sign off that you're fit for duty, but if you find that's not the case or you develop any other symptoms, let me know."

"I will."

The man left and Nathan groaned, then gathered the strength he was going to need to get off the bed. His next stop was going to be the interrogation room at the station—after he hugged his parents and Carly and thanked them for coming. Hopefully Eli had made himself scarce.

Jesslyn eyed him. "I'll wait for you outside."

"Thanks." He swung his legs over the bed, then got to his feet and simply stood there.

"You okay?"

"I will be. Just gonna be moving slow for a bit."

"Right. Do you need— Never mind. I'll just be outside."

Nathan raised a brow, curious as to what she'd been about to say, but the door shut, cutting off his question.

TEN

Seeing the trouble he was having moving, Jesslyn had almost offered to help him get dressed but figured that might take things way past awkward. If he needed help, the hospital had workers for that.

He emerged from the room ten minutes later and bypassed the "mandatory" wheelchair. His face was pale and his limp pronounced, but at least he was walking. She waved to Andrew, who was texting, to join them.

He'd live. *Thank you, Lord.*

Three female hospital workers—two nurses and a doctor— spotted him, and their eyes went wide in unison. One pointed and said, "That's him." Jesslyn wasn't a professional lip-reader by any stretch, but caught the words. One of the nurses giggled and the other rolled her eyes but stole another look over her shoulder while walking away.

Another female worker approached them. "Excuse me, you're the agent who jumped the building, right?"

Nathan stopped. "I am. Not the smartest move in my career."

"Could I have your autograph?"

Jesslyn couldn't quite cover up her slight snort. He glared at her but smiled at the woman. "I don't think I'm going to be giving out autographs."

"Oh, right. Okay. Well, I'm glad you're okay."

"Thanks. I am too."

She hurried off, her cheeks pink, and Jesslyn felt sorry for her. Andrew smothered a laugh with a coughing fit, and Nathan transferred his glare to his partner. This time Jesslyn couldn't stop a soft chuckle from slipping out.

"Jess . . ."

The low growl almost sent her into peals of laughter, and only the sight of his sister and parents waiting anxiously doused her humor.

"We'll let you say goodbye to your mom and dad," she said and pulled Andrew to the side.

As soon as he was free, his parents rushed over to hug him gently, and while it took some doing, he finally convinced them to go home, that he was fine and not about to take it easy while he had a suspect in the interrogation room.

Once Carly had ushered them out the door with a fierce scowl at Nathan, he turned to Jesslyn and Andrew. "Anyone wanna give me a lift to the station? I'm very anxious to question this guy."

"Well," Andrew said, "you risked your life to save him, I guess you should have the opportunity to try and get him to talk. I'm sure there will be some officers there who'll have seen the footage. You might have to sign autographs for your adoring fans."

"Shut up."

Jesslyn bit her lip on yet another grin, and Andrew looked like he was doing the same.

"Guys," Nathan said, narrowing his eyes, "just remember I have a long memory."

Jesslyn cleared her throat. "I'll follow in my car. I need to check in on the status of the fire. I can do that on the way."

Twenty minutes later, after watching her mirrors and determining she wasn't followed, she pulled into the station and joined Andrew and Nathan as they climbed out. Nathan grimaced.

"Stiff?" she asked.

"Yeah. I can tell it's going to be a fun few weeks ahead."

"What made you do that?" she asked. "I can't imagine how scary that was."

He shivered and grimaced. "It was either jump or let him die. There's no way someone would have gotten up there in time to grab him."

"True. How long before you heal up?"

"Two to four weeks, the doc said. I'm aiming for one and a half."

"You're such an overachiever."

He gave a light snort and this time she smiled. Why was it she always felt like smiling when he was around? She needed to stop that. It was weird. And disconcerting.

But . . . nice too.

Good grief.

Andrew led the way into the station, down the hall, and to the interrogation rooms. An officer met them and eyed Nathan. "You're the one who went after this guy?"

"I'm the one."

"Glad you're okay, Superman."

Jesslyn snorted. Andrew coughed again.

"Oh for the love of—" Nathan sighed and chose to ignore the comment. "Does he have a name?"

"Not that he's sharing. Maybe you can get it out of him. He's in room three. He's also changed his mind about a lawyer and medical attention. I had him sign a statement to that effect."

"He say why the change of heart about the lawyer?"

"Nope. Good luck."

Nathan nodded, took a deep breath, and walked into the room with only a slight limp, but his face was two shades paler than normal.

Jesslyn watched from behind the mirror. The room had a rectangular table and two chairs facing each other. The prisoner sat in one, hands resting on the table in front of him, cuffed.

Andrew stood next to her. "All right, partner," he said, "scratch your nose to signal you can hear me."

Nathan complied, then after identifying himself, took a seat opposite the man. Jesslyn could tell it took a lot for him not to grimace in pain. He leaned back, hands gripping the seat on either side of his thighs. His pose said he was relaxed and had all the time in the world.

The prisoner sat silent, eyes downcast, his face made of stone.

"He's so young," Jesslyn said. "He doesn't look older than seventeen or eighteen."

He had a lean and agile build and was about five feet ten. His short, dark brown hair matched the scruffy beard that needed a good trim. His green eyes darted to Nathan, then back to his clasped hands. Hands that were rough with calluses and chapped from the cold weather. He wore an older watch on his left wrist that had a cracked face. She wondered if that happened when he jumped from the building.

She also noted the faded scar that ran from the corner of his left eye and disappeared under the mustache and was curious where he'd acquired that. He wore a faded black T-shirt under the worn-out green jacket, jeans that had seen better days, and scuffed boots.

"You're welcome, John," Nathan said.

The man blinked. "Um . . . what?"

"You won't tell us your name, so it's John Doe until we learn otherwise. And I saved your life, so, you're welcome."

"Oh. Thank you."

Nathan rubbed his lips. A sure sign he was holding back certain words and searching for substitutes. He finally lowered his hand. "What's your name, kid? Don't you think you owe me that?"

The young man shook his head. "I can't."

"You mean you won't?"

"You wouldn't understand."

"Try me. I mean, we're going to find out eventually. We have your DNA, your prints, your face. When we put you on the six o'clock news asking for an ID, how long do you think it's going to take for the phone to ring with your name, age, and address?"

The prisoner groaned and dropped his forehead into his palms. "Kenny," he mumbled.

"Kenny?" Nathan asked.

"Yeah."

"Kenny what?"

"Davies." More mumbling, but she caught the name.

Nathan closed his eyes for a short second as though gathering the shredded remnants of his patience—or trying to push past the pain he had to be in. "You asked for your lawyer but refused to call him. Or her. Would you like to do that now?"

Kenny shook his head.

"Let the record show," Nathan said, "the suspect responded with a nonverbal no." Nathan leaned forward. Carefully. "If you don't want a lawyer, that's your choice, but do you think you could look up and tell me how you know Jesslyn McCormick?"

The kid looked up as requested, but the blank stare was convincing. "Who?"

Jesslyn frowned and glanced at Andrew, who answered her with a frown of his own.

Nathan repeated her name and Kenny shrugged. "I've never heard of her."

"Then maybe it's all just a coincidence?" Jesslyn said to Andrew. "The fires with the personal connection, the attack at the church, and so on."

"You really believe that?"

She frowned. "No, not really. I mean, what are the odds?"

"Exactly. I think you're being targeted. It's just going to take some digging to figure out why."

The interrogation room door opened, and an officer entered with a soda and a bag of takeout food that he set next to Nathan. Then left without a word.

"Is this Kenny guy the one who snatched you from the restaurant?" Andrew asked her.

"I don't know. If I had to guess, I'd say no. His voice is different and I think he's shorter."

"Then he's working with someone?"

"Maybe." But why? "I've racked my brain about all of my cases. There were a few that could be angry enough to come after me for exposing their crimes, I suppose."

"Then we need to investigate them."

"Let me keep thinking and I'll give you some names later."

Nathan had pushed the soda in front of the young man, who licked his lips and eyed the bag.

"Drink up," Nathan said. Kenny obeyed and took a few sips, then set the can aside. "All right, Kenny," Nathan said, "here's where we are. As you may have noticed, no one's arrested you yet."

"I noticed."

"Wanna tell me why you asked for a lawyer, then changed your mind?"

"No."

"Okay, then how about you tell me who you're working with?"

Kenny blinked and straightened, his jaw dropping a fraction before he snapped it shut and dropped his gaze to his hands again. "No one. I'm not working with anyone. I mean I was just there to watch them put out the fire and then you guys were chasing me and here I am."

"He's lying," Jesslyn said.

Andrew shifted and crossed his arms. "Definitely."

"So, we're looking for two people? The question is"—she pointed to the suspect—"did he set the fires or was it the guy from the restaurant?"

"Or someone else altogether," Andrew said.

"Right." She rubbed her temples, a headache beginning to form behind her eyes. What a mess. And she still had a fire scene to assess. She dropped her hand. "What'll happen with our friend Kenny, there?"

"We'll hold him for forty-eight hours, and if we don't have enough to charge him, then we'll have to let him go."

"What if you just let him go anyway?" she asked.

"Sorry?"

"Let him go and follow him. See where he goes, who he talks to, and so on. Can you get a wiretap order for his phone?"

Andrew sighed. "That might be a long shot."

"He's burning buildings, Andrew. Mr. Christie still isn't stable enough to come out of a coma yet. I can't believe no one was hurt at the fitness center. But if he—or whoever he's working with—starts another fire, someone else could get hurt. Or die."

Andrew rubbed the back of his neck, but nodded. "All right. Let's talk to Nathan and see what we can do."

"Good. Thank you. Because I'm not just worried about innocent people caught in those flames, I'm also thinking about the people who fight them. *My* people risking their lives when they shouldn't have to. We need to stop him. Now."

NATHAN STUDIED KENNY, taking in every detail. The kid was nervous but not overly jittery. He didn't want to be here but was keeping his cool. Nathan wanted to keep pressing to see if he could break him. But he'd heard Jesslyn's idea through the comms and it also held merit. He cleared his throat. "Do you have a job? Go to school? What do you do with your days besides start fires?"

"I didn't start that fire!" Kenny shifted, twisting his fingers together. "I go to school."

"Where?"

"At the community college."

"Major?"

"Math."

"GPA?"

"3.9."

"Smart guy."

A smug smile crossed Kenny's lips. "I am."

"So why are you at L Cubed?" The nickname for Lake City Community College. LCCC was just too hard to say. "Why not Lake City University or UNC?" Nathan had no problem with students who went to the community college, but some people felt like it was "less than" the bigger universities. A lot of students complained about the stigma, but most in Lake City knew it was a good school. He wondered what Kenny thought.

Kenny's smile slipped. "That's none of your business."

"Come on, now. I'm not dissing community college. You can get a great education there. But you look like more of a university guy to me."

Nathan refused to look at the mirror. Andrew would be all over this new information and getting the details, including the class schedule and who Kenny hung out with.

"Mainly because of the shoelaces you're wearing. Lake City Bears? I mean, you could be a fan, I guess, but seems to me like you'd be a Cougar fan if you were at the community college."

"Shut up, man! Just shut up! Stop it!" Kenny lurched to his feet.

Nathan raised a brow. "Why don't *you* stop it? Sit down. Now." His voice, louder than normal but not quite a yell, had the desired effect.

Kenny sat, shuffled his feet, and rested his head on his hands.

"Stop playing games with me," Nathan said. "Quit lying and tell me why you ran."

Kenny's head snapped up. "Because you chased me!"

"Actually, the fire marshal just wanted to talk to you. So, technically, we were just walking toward you. We didn't chase until you ran." Nathan leaned in once again. "Look, man, I can do this all day and night. This is my job. I get paid to sit here. But I'll be honest. I'm hungry." He nodded to the unopened bag of food. "I'm guessing you are too."

"So you think you can bribe me. Withhold food until I tell you what you want to know? That'll really hold up in court."

"Oh? You're picturing this going to court? I hadn't really thought that far ahead, but okay."

Kenny let out a low groan. "No, I just . . . no." He gathered himself and shook his head. Then jerked at his shackled wrists. "Unless I sue you for false imprisonment. Then yeah, I guess we'll wind up in court."

Nathan shoved the food in front of the guy. "Eat."

"In exchange for what?"

"Nothing, man. Just eat." And hopefully talk. "Are you sure you don't know Jesslyn?"

"I'm sure." The kid grabbed the bag, opened it, and took out the burger.

"But you were at the fire."

"Yeah, I saw it from the street and went to watch with the other gawkers." He paused, took a bite, chewed, then swallowed. "What made you single me out anyway?"

"Instinct."

"Well, I can't say much for that. You got the wrong dude."

"We'll see. You didn't want a lawyer. Do you want to call your parents?"

"No!" The shout echoed and Nathan raised a brow.

That question had touched a nerve. "Why not?"

Kenny swiped a hand over his eyes. "I can't tell them about this. They'll cut off my school funds and I'll be forced to go home. No way. I'll deal with this myself."

"Let me guess. The reason you changed your mind about the lawyer is because he or she is actually your parents' lawyer and would tell them why you called?"

"Yeah." The answer was subdued.

"Eat," Nathan said. "I'll be back in a few minutes."

Nathan left the guy scarfing the food and stepped out of the room. Andrew and Jesslyn appeared seconds later. "Well, that was a bust," Nathan said.

Andrew waved his phone at him. "Not necessarily. As soon as you picked up on the shoelaces, I called Lake City U. His name is Kenneth Davies like he said."

"Guess he didn't want his face splashed across the evening news," Nathan muttered. "He's scared to death his parents are going to find out about this. That's what all the lies were about. Stupid." He huffed. "Do people really think they can lie and we'll just buy it? They don't think we're going to check on their story?"

Andrew shook his head. "I know, man. They always hope they're going to get away with it. As for the other stuff, he's a junior and majoring in math—again, like he said. The school is sending over his file—the warrant was provided quickly, thank goodness—but said he hung out with several other math major students. They're on the competition team. Got their names along with a couple of the professors' who travel with them to their competitions."

"Great," Nathan said. "Looks like we've got some old-fashioned footwork to do. Let's go knock on some doors and see if we can find out what Mr. Kenneth Davies is up to these days."

"And if he likes to play with matches," Andrew murmured. "And has access to pool supplies."

Nathan nodded. "Does he live on campus?"

"Yep."

"Excellent."

Jesslyn ran a hand over her hair, tucking stray strands behind her ear. "Right. Excellent. Good place to start."

Nathan's phone rang. "It's Lindsay." He tapped the screen. "Hey."

"Sending you some footage from George Harlow's business."

"That was fast."

"I asked nicely. But I don't think it's going to help you. Looks like the guy left his car unlocked. He simply walked up to the car and opened the door. The thief's got a beanie hat on, along with sunglasses and a heavy coat. He's just shy of six feet and probably in the hundred ninety, two hundred pounds range."

"Thanks." He hung up and the phone buzzed with the incoming footage. "Hold on, let me take a look at this and then we can go." He hit play. It lasted all of ten seconds. The guy was in and out. She was right. "That tells us nothing."

"Tells us the gun was stolen when Harlow said it was," Jesslyn said.

"True."

"Play it one more time and let me watch?"

"Sure."

Jesslyn watched again, brow furrowed. "I'm not saying it is, but it could very well be the guy from the restaurant. He has on the same beanie-type hat and his height is right."

"All right," Andrew said, "George reported it stolen that very day, said it had to be someone who had access to his key fob—to use it or clone it. He knows he locked the vehicle. He said he's super careful with the weapon, and this is his nightmare come true. Someone stealing his gun from his car. So while I recommend we don't waste time investigating that all over again, we can see if we can get some help digging into who would have access to the key fob. And have someone show this video to Harlow and his coworkers to see if any of them recognize this guy."

"That works," Nathan said. "You take care of that, then we'll go to the school and see what we can find." He cleared his throat and looked at Jesslyn. "I'm assuming you're headed back to the scene?"

Jesslyn checked her phone. "Not yet. The blaze is under control, but not ready for me yet. Do you mind if I tag along?"

"Don't mind at all," Nathan said. With someone targeting her, the closer he kept her, the better he felt.

He ignored the little voice that said he liked keeping her close for more personal reasons.

ELEVEN

Once in her vehicle and on the way to the school campus, Jesslyn called Chief Laramie, who was still in charge of the scene. He assured her that as soon as she could access the site, he'd let her know, but she had a few hours. Which she knew, she was just . . . impatient. Anxious to compare the two scenes. She hung up and glanced at the mirrors.

A phone call had arranged the delivery of Nathan's vehicle to the station, so he was ahead of her and Andrew behind her. Grateful for the distraction and the uneventful drive to the university, she unbuckled her seat belt and climbed out of the car.

Andrew and Nathan did the same and joined her. The imposing math and science building stood before them. If she'd gone to school here, as a chemistry major she would have spent a lot of time in those classrooms.

Andrew stepped to the side to take a call, and Nathan looked at her, forehead wrinkled in concern. "You okay?"

Were her feelings that obvious? Apparently. She forced a small smile. "I'm fine. Just thinking about what might have been had my family lived. Would I have gone to school here?" What she didn't say was her fear all those years ago that the person who killed her family was still in town. Yeah, there was that too.

He patted her shoulder, then narrowed his eyes. "You're exactly where you're supposed to be. God knew what was going to happen. It didn't take him by surprise."

"I know. What I don't know is why he didn't stop it."

"I can certainly understand that."

The quick flash of pain on his features said he understood more than most people. There was more to his story than he'd told her. Maybe one day he'd trust her enough to give her the extended version.

Andrew returned just as her phone buzzed. "Hold on a sec. It's a text from Pastor Chuck." They waited while she tapped the screen and read. "He said he's asked every single member of the church, excluding us, if they knew where the piece of jewelry from the fire came from and no one recognized it." She blew out a low breath. "Well, it doesn't surprise me, but I was rather hoping."

Andrew nodded. "Guess that's that then. Ready?"

"Wait," Nathan said. "Anyone mention recognizing the logo on the back?"

Jesslyn stilled, then texted Chuck.

> Did anyone say anything about the logo on the back of the piece?

They didn't. Should I ask specifically about that and see if anyone can tell what it is or where it came from?

> If you don't mind. I know it's a lot of work, but it would be helpful.

I'll see what I can do.

> Thank you.

"Now I'm ready," she said.

They walked up the steps and through the double glass doors into the building. "Dr. Byron Claymore should be waiting to talk to us in his office. He's the head of the math department and is one of the sponsors of the math club and goes to all of the competitions."

"Like a coach?" Jesslyn asked.

"Yeah, exactly."

"I did science competitions in high school," she said. "They were a lot of fun."

"Science competitions were fun?" Nathan asked with a raised brow. "Were you a nerd?"

She kept a straight face at his teasing. "No, just smart."

Nathan laughed.

Andrew cleared his throat and pushed the elevator button. "He's on the third floor."

They rode up in silence and found the man in his office as promised. Jesslyn studied him. He was in his early fifties, with salt-and-pepper hair cut short but in need of a trim. His dark brown eyes were friendly enough, and he waved them into the very neat office. No absent-minded professor here.

"Have a seat," he said. "My secretary said you were coming. That you had some questions about Kenny Davies."

"Yes, sir," Nathan said and then introduced everyone.

"I'm sorry I don't have enough seats. We can walk down to the conference room if you prefer."

Andrew leaned against the doorjamb. "This is fine. Hopefully we won't take up too much of your time."

Jesslyn motioned for Nathan to take the chair. She could tell his hip was bothering him. The fact that he sat without comment spoke volumes.

"What can I help you with?" Dr. Claymore asked.

"Right now, Kenny is sitting in an interrogation room at the local police station," Nathan said. "He was at the scene of a fire at the Endurance Empire Gym. When we tried to approach him, he ran. The fire is most likely arson. The fact that he ran raises red flags for us."

"Kenny?" The professor blinked away his shock and rubbed his chin while letting his gaze bounce between them. "Wow. I can't imagine it. Is he okay?"

"He's fine right now."

"Okay, well, what does it have to do with me?"

"Not much that we can tell," Nathan said. "We were hoping you could help us identify the friends that he hangs out with."

Jesslyn opened her notes with the names Andrew had already acquired, ready to add more if the professor came up with new ones.

Dr. Claymore scratched his nose. "Yeah, I can give you a few names." He grabbed a pen from his drawer and a Post-it from the stack next to his laptop. "Brad Granger, Toby Child, and Heath Peterson should be able to answer any questions you have. They're big buddies, hang out all the time, and are all on the math competition team." He frowned. "Speaking of competitions, we have one coming up next Friday in South Carolina. Will Kenny be able to go?"

"That depends on Kenny," Andrew said. "Thanks for the information. By the way, do Kenny and the other three live in the same dorm?"

"I believe they do. Chapman Hall, if I remember correctly."

"Perfect." He took the note from the professor.

"What's going on?" A voice from outside of the open door turned them all as one. A man in his late thirties with blue eyes and a salt-and-pepper military buzz cut stood with his hands in the front pockets of his green slacks.

"Ah," Dr. Claymore said, "this is Professor Derek Morgan. Derek, Kenny's gotten himself into some trouble and these three officers are here to talk to a few of his friends and professors."

Professor Morgan nodded. "Good to meet you. What's Kenny done to generate this kind of interest?"

"We believe he might be involved in two fires."

"Fires? What kind of fires?"

"Arson," Jesslyn said.

Morgan laughed, then frowned when no one joined him. "Oh, you're serious."

Jesslyn raised a brow. "Very."

"Well, I can assure you, Kenny is not an arsonist."

"I'm afraid we can't take your word for it," Andrew said. "Anything you can tell us about him?"

The man blew out a slow breath. "Well, he's smart, driven, keeps his grades up, is definitely extroverted, and has a wide community of friends."

"You sound like you know him well."

"I grew up here in Lake City. I know a lot of people well. Kenny's parents are friends of mine and my wife's."

"I see. How often do you see Kenny?"

"He used to be a student of mine, but I don't teach him this semester. My wife and I get together with Nancy and Gary, his parents, once a month or so to double-date, but other than passing Kenny on campus occasionally, I don't really see him that much except for math competitions."

"What about the friends that he hangs out with?" Jesslyn asked. "Brad, Toby, and Heath?"

"Yeah, they're all good guys. Good students, participate in a lot of school activities." He shrugged. "That's about it."

Nathan nodded, then he stood. Carefully. "Thank you for your time. We'll be in touch if we have any more questions."

Professor Morgan's phone rang, and he pulled it out of his pocket with a roll of his eyes to the others. "Hi, Sam. Yeah." He stepped out of the room. "Yes, I can do that." A pause. "I said fine. Chill, will you?"

Dr. Claymore shot them a small smile. "Sam is his sister. She's trying to get hired here. I guess she thinks volunteering with the math team will score her some brownie points. From what I gather, she's a piece of work." He shook his head. "Makes me glad to be an only child most days."

"Being an only child definitely has its benefits, I'm sure," Nathan said with a grunt. "Wouldn't mind experiencing that myself at the moment."

Jesslyn bit her lip on a smile, and the three of them said their goodbyes, then left the office.

In the hallway, Jesslyn said, "They both seemed genuinely shocked that Kenny would be involved in something like that."

"I noticed that too," Nathan said.

"Maybe Kenny really didn't set the fires," she said. "Could be innocent and ran just . . . because."

"Maybe," Andrew said, "but I'll feel better once we have a clear picture of who this guy is. Ready for a trip to the dorm?"

Jesslyn nodded. "Let's go."

Together, they walked back to their cars. "I can drive," he said to Nathan, then turned to Jesslyn. "You want to leave your car here?"

"Sure." She climbed in with the guys, and they drove to the designated dorm. Classes had been back in session for only a week since breaking for Christmas, but the place was a beehive of activity with students bundled in heavy coats, hats, gloves, and boots, rushing from one place to the next, backpacks slapping against their backs. "I remember these days," Jesslyn murmured. "Different campus, but same energy and vibe."

Nathan nodded. "I graduated from here, then explored the world a bit before coming back."

It didn't take long to find Kenny's room and knock on the door. "Roommate is Jeff Mitchell," Andrew said. They waited and Andrew rocked back on his heels, then knocked again. "Security said he got out of class an hour ago, but he could be anywhere on campus—or off. He's got a car."

A young man next door slipped out of his room and turned to lock the door.

"Excuse me," Jesslyn said, "you don't happen to know where Jeff Mitchell is, do you?"

"No. Did you try calling him?"

And giving him a chance to run? Not likely. "No."

"Then I can't help you. Sorry."

"Thanks anyway."

The kid headed down the hall and stopped next to a guy who'd just walked in the door. He pointed to Jesslyn and the others, and she waited for him to run. They always ran.

He nodded and walked their way.

Well, miracles still happened apparently.

"Hi," the young man said. He was nineteen or twenty with a five-o'clock shadow, green eyes, and dimples. "Guy said you're looking for me?"

"Yeah," Andrew said. "For you, Brad, Toby, and Heath."

"Brad and Heath live on the other side of Kenny and me. Toby's up one floor. You want to come into the lobby so we can talk? I'd invite you in the room, but it's a mess and no place for everyone to sit."

Truly? Or did he just not want them to see inside his room?

He turned and headed toward the lobby. Jesslyn raised a brow at Nathan and Andrew, and they wordlessly followed.

They found seats on the couches in the room that was set up for socializing. Jesslyn leaned forward. "What can you tell us about Kenny?"

"What do you want to know?"

"Everything."

THIRTY MINUTES LATER, Nathan stood and did his best not to wince at the pull on his hip. Jeff had been open and willing to answer questions. He and Kenny weren't close friends, they just shared a room. "We're on different academic tracks and rarely see each other, but he's a good friend to those he hangs out with." He eyed Nathan and Andrew. "You said you're partners. You'd take a bullet for each other, right?"

They both nodded.

"That's how Kenny is. Once you have his love and loyalty, he's got your back no matter what. He's a good guy. Not one to go around burning buildings. You're looking in the wrong place for your answers." He looked at Andrew, then Nathan and Jesslyn. "That's pretty much all I've got."

Nathan shook his hand. "Thank you for talking to us. If we need anything, we'll call you, and if you see or hear anything that's out of the ordinary or makes you wonder if something's going on, will you give us a call?"

"Sure."

"Assuming they don't answer the knocks on their doors, any idea where to find the other three guys?"

"No. Sorry. If they're not in their rooms, they could be anywhere. Although, sometimes—a lot of the time, actually—Brad likes to play pool in the student center. He's probably there."

"We'll check it out. Thanks."

Nathan handed him a card and they knocked on the other students' doors. And got no response. They exited the building and walked back to the car. "Guess it's the student center."

Jesslyn's phone rang and she snatched it to her ear. "Hey, Marissa, please tell me you have something."

She listened and Nathan wished he could hear the other end of the conversation. He turned to look at her while Andrew drove. She raised a brow at him and nodded. "Okay, thanks so much. I'll think about it, and we'll try to get to the jeweler before they close."

She hung up and Nathan found he was almost holding his breath to hear what Marissa had found. "Well? Don't keep us in suspense, pretty please?"

"Since you asked so nice, she discovered the jeweler that made the piece we found at the scene."

"Excellent. Who?"

"Tradition's Custom Touch on West Beach Street."

"That's some very high-end jewelry," Andrew said. "Like really nice custom pieces. I think my grandfather gave my grandmother one for their twenty-fifth wedding anniversary—that kind of thing. All that to say, they've been there for a long time. As long as I can remember anyway."

Jesslyn was on her phone. She tapped the screen. "Yep. Founded in 1955."

"All right, we'll put that on our list of places to visit."

"Student center?" Jess asked.

They agreed and soon found Brad at the pool table. Andrew approached while Nathan and Jesslyn hung back. Nathan was slightly jealous of how nice the place was. It had been expanded and was a huge improvement over the board games and vending machines when he'd been a student. Now they had a full-service café on one end, a large seating area in the middle, and pool tables, Foosball, and air hockey games on the other end.

Andrew stepped forward, showing his badge to Brad. "Hi, Brad, you got a minute?"

The young man froze for a split second before he forced a smile and set aside his pool stick. "Sure. Can I help you?"

Jesslyn nudged Nathan. "You catch the body language?"

"He's going to run, isn't he?"

"Just a feeling he might be considering it."

"I'll cover the side door."

"I've got this one."

Nathan made his way to the other exit, a wall of three sets of double glass doors, while Jesslyn stayed close to the one they'd entered. His phone rang and he glanced at the screen. Eli. He sent the call to voicemail.

Andrew motioned to an empty couch and Brad walked over to drop down on the edge of it. Nathan glanced at Jesslyn and she shrugged as if to say, *What do ya know? He didn't bolt.*

Twice in one day. Nathan was glad, because there was no way he could give chase. He moved closer to hear the conversation. Jesslyn did the same.

Brad's eyes bounced on each of them before settling back on Andrew. "What's going on?"

"We're talking to friends of Kenny's."

The kid schooled his expression into a questioning look. "Okay. What about him?"

Andrew explained the situation, and with each sentence, Brad's face turned a shade whiter, and his eyes widened, nostrils flaring. "You really think he set the fires? No way. He wouldn't."

Well, those who believed in Kenny's innocence were unanimous. He was even starting to think they were chasing a dead end.

He saw Jesslyn glance at her phone and frown, then tuck it away. Andrew continued questioning Brad, who was about as much help as a case of the flu. On purpose or was he hiding something? Then again, who liked a visit from the FBI, so could he really read anything into it?

Andrew finally stood and handed Brad his card. "Can you call me if you think of anything that might be related to the fires and Kenny?"

"Sure."

Which sounded more like, "Don't hold your breath."

Nathan's phone rang and he held up a finger for Jesslyn and Andrew to wait. "Hi, Lindsay."

"You have a minute?"

"For you? Always."

"I'll make this brief, I have a meeting I have to run off to. I checked the database of crimes matching the one perpetrated on Jesslyn at the restaurant. There's nothing that matches up perfectly in this area or a two-hundred-mile radius. The ones that kind of came close are six women attacked in the parking lot of various restaurants, two had someone waiting in their cars and were snatched, but they caught the guy when he tried to kidnap an off-duty female police officer. She put him in the hospital for a month."

Good for her. "Anything else?"

"A few more random attacks, but nothing about any women being taken from the bathroom of a restaurant."

"Okay, thanks for letting me know."

"Talk to you later."

Nathan hung up and they tracked down Heath. He had the same

reaction as his buddy. Complete surprise that Kenny was a potential suspect in the fires. Also about as helpful. Toby, it turned out, was in the hospital recovering from a ruptured appendix. It didn't mean he didn't know anything, but he wasn't the one setting fires. He'd ask one of the detectives to go by the hospital and talk to the guy.

"I don't know," Jesslyn said after they were out of earshot. "I'm not getting the vibe that they were involved, and I'm not getting one that they weren't. The only vibe I'm getting is that they're nervous about cops snooping around, and that could be because of any number of reasons."

"I'm with you," Andrew said.

Nathan nodded. "Agreed. We'll just keep an eye on them and see what shakes loose. If anything. Let's go."

They returned to Andrew's vehicle and Andrew drove them back to their cars.

"It's late," Jesslyn said. "I'm starving and exhausted, but first thing in the morning, I'm going to the jewelry store." She dug her keys from her pocket. "I'll call you if I find out anything."

"Do you need to head back to the fire scene?"

She checked her phone. "Not until the chief texts me."

"Okay, then why don't I follow you home, hang out, and then go with you when you get word?" Nathan said. He really didn't think she needed to go anywhere alone, considering they didn't know who'd attacked her yet. In fact, he was tempted to camp out on her curb to make sure nothing happened during the night.

"I mean, you can. It might not be until morning."

"I'm okay with that."

"Seriously, you don't have to do that. I'm just going to grab something to eat and then crash for the night." She swung the car door open. "I'll be fine."

He shook his head. "Stubborn. But I'm still going to follow you home." He glanced at Andrew as he opened his door. "What's your plan?"

"I can meet you in the morning," Andrew said. "Then we can

check in at the hospital on Mr. Christie and this kid Toby. See if either of them has anything they want to contribute."

"Fabulous," Jesslyn said as she got out, "we'll make it a full-on party."

Nathan glanced at his phone as he turned toward his car. And now he had to call his mom and let her know he wouldn't be there tomorrow. He didn't have time for a family brunch. He had a possible arsonist to catch.

TWELVE

Saturday morning, after a restless night of dozing and checking her windows, Jesslyn walked into the jewelry store with Andrew and Nathan on her heels. The door shut behind them, bells chiming before going silent. It was a small shop on the corner of West Beach Street, one street over from Main.

Glassed cases held a number of beautiful items grouped according to type and material. In one case, there were elegant necklaces of varying lengths, adorned with diamonds and other gemstones. Another case displayed an array of rings, from simple bands to intricate designs with sparkling stones set in gold or silver.

The section to her right caught her attention. It held stunning jewelry, showcasing pieces with unique craftsmanship. Beautiful pieces she'd never seen the likes of. Jesslyn wondered if those were custom pieces waiting for their new owners to pick them up. The walls were decorated with mirrors and paintings, creating a cozy yet sophisticated atmosphere. She walked to the nearest case and peered at wedding and engagement sets. They were remarkable in all different kinds of settings and stones. Would she ever wear one? Not if she kept going the way she was. She looked up and caught Nathan's eye. He shot her a small smile, then looked away. Heat climbed into her neck, and she pulled in a slow breath, willing the warmth to stop. She couldn't help looking at him once more, though. "You slept outside my house last night, didn't you?"

He raised a brow, looking all innocent, but joined her at the case. "What makes you say that?"

"I thought I saw your car out there."

"It was quiet," he said. "I caught a few hours of rest. Knowing you were safe helped make that happen. And I had a buddy, Sampson Greene, come by with his K-9, Otis, around two o'clock. He took a shift."

Jesslyn bit her lip. She should have known he would do that and offered her couch. Regret climbed into her heart. "Thank you, Nathan. I'm not sure what to say to that except thank you."

His shoulders relaxed a fraction, and she realized he had been prepared to defend his actions. "You're welcome."

"But let me know what you're doing in the future, will you? I probably would have slept better knowing all of that. And you have the comfortable couch or not-so-comfortable guest room bed."

His jaw swung slightly open, and she grinned and tapped it. He snapped it shut and his eyes narrowed. All of a sudden she wanted to kiss him. Like really wanted to—

Oh no. No, no, no, no, no.

She turned and squelched the unbidden thought. Where in the world had that come from?

A low chuckle from the man told her he might have very well read her thoughts, and the fiery heat that she hated so much started to climb again.

She fixed her gaze on a cabinet on the far wall and walked over to it. She'd seen it before. Nathan and his blasted attractiveness faded along with the burn crawling up her throat. She touched the wood surrounding the glass, and a memory flickered in the back of her mind, daring her to yank it to the forefront.

Before she could, a young woman came out of the back office with a smile on her face. "Hello. May I help you?"

Jesslyn walked over, introduced herself, and pulled her phone

SERIAL BURN

from her pocket. "We're investigating the church fire. We found this piece of jewelry in the debris and are trying to find the owner. I understand this is your signature?"

Again, that glimmer of a memory tried to grab her attention.

The woman looked at it. "Oh yes, that's one of ours." She frowned. "It's an older one, though." She zoomed in on the picture and took a closer look. "I'd say that was made about thirty years or so ago. Maybe slightly longer, but not much."

Jesslyn blinked. "Really?"

"Yes, it's one of the signatures the senior Mr. McElroy used. See, the *M* with the line through it is only a partial, so the *E* is turned on its side."

She took another look, with Andrew and Nathan looking over her shoulder. Why was she so aware of Nathan and wouldn't have known Andrew was even in the room? She focused. "Oh, that's really clever."

"Grandfather would be thrilled to know you think so."

"So the man who made this is your grandfather?"

"Was." A sad smile curved her lips. "He passed away four years ago. My father, who is on vacation this week, took over the shop, and I decided to join the family business as well." She held out a hand. "Isabelle McElroy Sims at your service."

"That's fabulous," Jesslyn said. "Is there any way to find out who purchased it?"

She tilted her head, studying the piece. "I don't think so. They didn't keep digital records back then. Grandfather was meticulous about paperwork and had a filing system, of course, but once we started with the computer system, the old stuff was stored somewhere. I know he wouldn't have tossed it, but I honestly don't know what happened to it."

"So they didn't upload the old records into the new system?"

"No, as far as I know, they didn't bother. I do know Grandfather kept all of the hard-copy records for years and years, but when we remodeled the space, it's possible those things were tossed."

130

Jesslyn's shoulders slumped as defeat wove through her. "Well, it was worth a shot. Thank you for your help."

"Of course."

The three of them walked back outside and Jesslyn glanced at her phone once more. "They're ready for me at the fire. I'll have to think about this jewelry stuff later."

"I have to head back to talk to Kenny," Andrew said. "Nathan can follow you."

"It's not necessary."

"It's necessary," Nathan said. The flat tone said he was coming whether she liked it or not, and she didn't have time to argue with him.

"All right, thanks. See you there."

When Jesslyn pulled up to the scene, the fire was still smoking, but out. Firefighters dotted the landscape, watching for any hotspots that they'd have to deal with.

Her phone buzzed again and she glanced at it. Her aunt. She'd have to wait. Nathan had followed her, of course, and while she appreciated his vigilance, she was annoyed at the need for it.

She waved, and he nodded, then pulled out his laptop to rest it against the steering wheel, clearly going nowhere anytime soon. Her very own bodyguard. She pushed the annoyance away. He cared and she was going to be thankful if it killed her. And besides, if she was honest with herself, she really didn't mind knowing he was there. The church shooting had scared her. A lot. On the way over, she'd checked on her bullet-riddled vehicle and learned it would be ready when it was ready.

The chief spotted her, and she made her way toward him, meeting him halfway. "Looks like it's pretty much out," she said.

"It is, but we found this at the edge of the blaze." He handed her a crime scene bag.

With gloved hands, she opened it and pulled out another piece of jewelry. "No way. Another one?"

"Yep. I knew you'd want to see it right away."

It didn't look anything like the one she'd found at the church fire, but gut instinct told her what she'd find when she turned it over.

And there it was.

The logo.

"Well, at least we know where it came from," she murmured. She had a feeling there was some meaning she should know behind the pieces, she just couldn't put her finger on it. "So, our arsonist has a signature. Expensive custom jewelry."

Chief Laramie frowned. "Sorry?"

"We know the store the jewelry came from. And we now know that the arsonist left it." She frowned. "Well, I guess we don't know for *sure*, but with this, I'm going to say odds are in our favor that he did."

"What's it mean?"

She huffed a short, humorless laugh. "I wish I knew."

Her phone rang and she let it go to voicemail. The piece of jewelry was once again tugging at her memories. Had she seen this piece before? For some reason, she thought she had. Or was it just that she'd seen the logo somewhere else?

Maybe. But where?

Frustrated with her inability to figure out what it was about the jewelry that bugged her so much, she restrained the urge to stomp a foot.

"Any progress on figuring out who's doing this?" the chief asked.

"Not really. I need to sit down and go through my cases to see if anyone pops out. I've been thinking about them during . . . everything . . . and there are three that I believe bear looking at a little closer."

"People you've put away?"

"Yes. Either because I found the evidence needed for them to do some jail time or I testified in court that their story was a lie and the fire couldn't have happened the way they said it did."

"Someone with a grudge."

"Hm. That's my thought, but the one I'd suspect the most is still sitting in prison."

"A family member then? Someone getting revenge?"

"Possibly. But why now? The most recent one has been in prison for two years."

"You never know what goes on in a person's head."

True.

She set aside the thoughts of the jewelry for now with hopes that her subconscious would work on it while she swept the scene. Dressed in her gear, she walked the remains and found her purple stains, evidence of multiple points of origin. She'd process the whole thing, of course, but considering all the similarities, she had no hesitation saying the arsonist for the church and the gym were the same person.

And she felt confident enough to say she was a target.

For the next several hours, she worked the scene, ignoring her buzzing calls from her aunt. Finally, she stopped and called the woman back.

Carol answered halfway through the first ring. "Thank you for *finally* calling me back."

"I'm sorry, Aunt Carol, I'm working."

"Oh dear. I figured. I'm sorry to be so persistent, but someone sent me a message that might affect the benefit. I've hesitated to tell you about it because it's just . . . hogwash."

"Hogwash?"

"Sorry, shades of your grandmother talking. Anyway, I just decided I needed to mention it to you in case there would be any danger to anyone who attended. I mean, I'm sure it's just something silly . . ."

Danger? "What kind of message?"

"It said that if I went through with honoring such a dishonorable man, there would be consequences to pay."

"What? When did you get that?"

"About four hours ago. I got home and it was attached to some flowers sitting on my front porch."

"I'm assuming your prints are all over the note."

"Of course. I opened the envelope."

Jesslyn's pulse picked up speed and she had to work to ignore it. "Okay, I'm going to ask a friend to send an officer to your house. That's a threat and it needs to be on file."

"I can't believe this. Utterly ridiculous. One tries to do a good thing and someone's always got to throw hate at it."

"I know." A memory flickered stronger this time.

"I told you, I'm sorry! It won't happen again!"

She flinched. "What do you think the sender means by dishonorable?" The line went silent. "Aunt Carol?"

"Oh, sorry, hon, I've got to go. We'll talk a little later, okay?"

"Um . . . okay." She had to go as well. "Right. We'll catch up later."

"You're working on your speech, right?"

"Of course." She'd thought about it. Sort of. That was working on it, right? "Bye, Aunt Carol. We'll talk soon."

She hung up and Nathan walked over. He'd been on his laptop for hours. Ever since they'd arrived. "Did you get some work done?" she asked.

"Yeah. I've got footage of a lot of the scene for you. Bystanders mostly. I watched for new people coming and people who left, trying to see if anyone stood out."

"Thanks. I didn't have a chance to do anything but scan the crowd." She should have just asked him to do it. "At least we know Kenny isn't here."

He chuckled. "Right."

She rubbed her nose. "I'm beat. How about you?"

"The same. How do you feel about letting me take you out for a steak?"

"That sounds amazing, but I think you should get some rest. You're still healing."

"I'm fine, I promise."

She hesitated, thinking about it.

He was handsome.

He made her heart yearn for things she couldn't yearn for right now.

And he was a distraction she couldn't afford. "Thanks, I really appreciate the offer, but I think I'll take a rain check. I really need to work on this arson case. And I want to visit Mr. Christie."

Hurt flickered in his gaze before he shot her a tight smile. "All right, I get it. I'll follow you to the hospital to make sure you get there in one piece. And I'll check in on Mr. Christie as well."

She nodded. "Sounds like a plan. See you there."

"Sure thing."

THE GYM WAS LOCATED halfway up the mountain, and as Nathan navigated his way back down, keeping her in his sights, his mind spun with thoughts of the pretty fire marshal.

What was he going to do? He was attracted to a woman who wanted nothing to do with him. Had asked him for a *rain check*. Which meant "go away, I'm not interested," and he still was trying to figure out a way to spend time with her.

What in the world? He didn't *chase* women. He pushed them away. Not to be cocky or anything, but he did so quite frequently. He might enjoy a night out with a date every so often, but as soon as someone wanted more, he went the other way without looking back.

So what was he doing now?

If he didn't take a few steps back, he was going to be in trouble. Relationships required a willingness to be vulnerable, to open up and allow another person to know his deepest, darkest secrets. And that wasn't happening.

Not that she was interested.

No was no. So, fine.

He'd keep his romantic emotions in check, but he wasn't leaving her to fend for herself when there was a possible killer after her.

Once they were on the road, he stayed a car length behind her, his thoughts tangled in the complexities of the case. It was like he had several different puzzles dumped together on the table. The pieces were there, he just couldn't figure out which ones went to the right puzzle. He shuffled through the fragments of evidence, theories, and dead ends, wishing he could at least get the right border pieces put together.

He voice-texted Lainie.

How's Mr. Christie? Any change?

Her reply was instant.

Not for the better. He's really fighting for his life.
I'm sorry.

I am too. Thanks.

So there really was no point in going to see the man. But Toby might yield some answers. Maybe. A quick call to his hospital room turned out to be less than helpful, and the kid dozed off midsentence. His mother's voice came over the line. "Is there anything else you need?"

"No. Tell him thanks for talking to me. I'll check back if there's anything else I can think of."

"Perfect."

He hung up and started to voice-dial Jesslyn when his phone rang once more.

Andrew. "What's up, partner?"

"The police chief let Kenny go."

"What? When?"

"About two hours ago. I came to ask him a few more questions and he's gone. The chief was getting antsy with nothing to hold him on. Apparently, the kid's parents are high up on the food chain and he didn't want to tangle with them."

"But they don't even know about him."

"Which is another issue. He's worried about what's going to happen when they find out."

"He's not a minor and the law says we can hold him for—"

"I know what the law says. The chief knows what the law says.

And he made an executive decision to let the kid go. Said when we have some actual evidence, we could bring him back in." Andrew sighed. "He's not a bad guy, Nathan. He's been easy to work with up to this point, and when he was telling me about all this, while he was firm, he was apologetic. I say we let this go and keep an eye on Davies ourselves."

"Right. Okay." A headache started to drum behind his eyes. "Thanks."

"I'll check in with you later."

Nathan hung up and called Jesslyn's number to fill her in, but before she answered, a flash of light to his left caught his attention.

He braked and turned slightly for a better look just as a bottle, ablaze with angry flames, arced through the air and smashed through the rear window of Jesslyn's vehicle.

THIRTEEN

Jesslyn jerked the wheel while the smell of gasoline enveloped her and flames erupted in her back seat. She had no time to scream, only react. Her car spun like a fatally wounded beast, swerving, then skidding, tires screeching a desperate protest against the asphalt.

She saw the edge of the road coming, jammed the brakes, and prayed she'd stop in time. But reality punched her. She was too close to the side and gripped the steering wheel in disbelief when she slid over and started down the embankment.

Gravity won.

The car rolled, a tumble of metal and glass, each impact a brutal assault. Her body jerked with each jarring movement, her seat belt the only thing that kept her from crashing from window to window. The flames that had started in the back crept toward the front, the temperature climbing, the smoke swirling.

And then her car came to a stop with one last gut-wrenching crunch. She hung suspended and dizzy, choking on the smoke. "God, please," she whispered. "Help."

The world had finally stopped spinning and she heard someone calling her name. The sound of harsh gasps filled her ears, and it took her a moment to realize the breaths were coming from her. She sucked in another gulp of air and discovered that was a bad move. She choked and coughed, the fumes and smoke suffocating. She blinked and tried to take inventory. Her shoulder and hip hurt, but surprisingly, that was it.

Adrenaline.

She dreaded how she'd feel when that wore off.

But she was alive. For the moment.

And it was time to get out of the vehicle.

She fumbled for the seat belt release with trembling fingers and it let go. She collapsed onto the driver's side door, now her floor.

A sharp pain grabbed her leg when she stood and she had to use precious seconds to pound out the flames licking her pants. Then she stood on the edge of the seat and pressed the power button for the passenger window. A sob escaped her when it rolled down. *Thank you, Jesus.* She started to haul herself out of the vehicle.

Weakness gripped her, blackness swirled around the edges of her vision, and she started to slide back into the now burning inferno. If she dropped, she'd die.

A sob ripped from her throat, and she clung, clawing for a grip while her dangling right foot sought a place to find purchase.

And then a strong hand clamped around her right wrist and yanked. "Come on, Jesslyn, hold on!" With Nathan's help, she moved up enough to plant her elbows on the side of the door and push, lifting herself out while he pulled. One moment, she was seconds from certain death and the next she was tumbling out of the passenger window and over the side to land with a hard thud on the ground. Nathan let go of her hand while she coughed and gagged, the smoke in her lungs greedily sucking all the oxygen from them.

Nathan lay on the ground next to her, having landed beside her when they fell from the vehicle. His white face scared her and she rolled toward him. "We have to move, Nathan. The car could explode."

"Yeah, I know." He spoke through gritted teeth, and she suspected he'd landed on his hip or maybe the rescue had caused him a massive amount of pain. Or both. With a half grunt, half groan, he pushed himself into a standing position. She did the same and took his hand.

Thankfully, the little roll down the embankment wasn't much, although it had felt like it lasted a lifetime. She'd done a three-sixty and a quarter in the car and hit a part of the ground that sloped upward. That slope had stopped her. She coughed, her lungs protesting the smoke inhalation. She was going to need an inhaler for the next year if she kept this up.

Together, she and Nathan made their way up the incline, with him leaning against her and her encouraging him that he could make it. At the top, several bystanders waited, many on their phones. That meant help was on the way.

"You can make it. Just one foot in front of the other."

His answer was another grunt.

Hands reached for them as they crested the top, and Nathan went to his knees. "Sorry," he said with a gasp, "gotta sit a minute."

Jesslyn rested a hand on his shoulder while she tried to cough more smoke from her lungs. She looked at the burning vehicle, her stomach twisting into one big knot. How had she survived that? She glanced at the man beside her. "You saved my life, Nathan."

"It was a team effort."

Sirens sounded and Jesslyn lowered herself to the ground, her knees turning weak and her adrenaline starting to fade. "I think someone wants me dead," she said.

"Really? What gave you that idea?"

She chuckled, only to go into another coughing spasm which led to tears that streamed down her cheeks. She wiped her face and sniffed, then coughed again.

She hadn't inhaled that much smoke, had she? While everything seemed to happen in slow motion, it had actually been relatively quick.

Hadn't it?

She honestly had no idea.

Nathan grabbed her hand and pulled her to him. She winced at the sting in her fingers and palms and held them up to look at them. They were raw, burned, and bleeding. Her leg joined the pain party, and she gave in to lean against the man who'd literally risked his life to pull her from a burning car. "Thank you," she whispered.

"Any time."

NATHAN WALKED . . . okay, *limped* . . . down the hospital hallway to Jesslyn's room on the fourth floor, trying to contain his rage. Kenny had been released and two hours later, Jesslyn—and he—almost died. That was a bit of a coincidence for him. And yet, how would he know where Jesslyn was going? With enough time to arrange to be lying in wait to attack her? He wasn't sure but figured Kenny could supply those answers.

Nathan had already requested Kenny be picked back up and held for questioning, influential parents or not—and the chief had agreed. The timing couldn't be denied. It would take Nathan a minute to get to the station to question the kid, because honestly, that wasn't his priority at the moment. First, he was checking on Jesslyn.

She'd been admitted for observation against her protests that she was fine and could go home. Lainie put her foot down, and when Jesslyn's aunt Carol showed up, that was the end of the argument.

Nathan had managed to avoid the same fate by promising he planned to stay close to Jesslyn—with the exception of the visit to the station to talk to Kenny Davies. Lainie could check on him when she checked on Jesslyn. He had some cuts and bruises, but surprisingly no burns. Jesslyn had some first- and second-degree burns on her hands, but the one that hurt the most was on her right leg.

Thankfully, shockingly, the smoke inhalation had been mild. Enough to irritate her lungs once more, but she should heal with meds and breathing treatments.

His phone buzzed with an incoming text, and he glanced at the summary notification. Something about Jesslyn's vehicle—he'd check it in a minute. He knocked and pushed the door open at the call to come in. Jesslyn sat up in the bed, her laptop open on her lap. While her hands were wrapped in bandages, most of her fingers were free. Her aunt Carol sat in the chair by the window reading a book by someone named Elizabeth Goddard. She put it down—reluctantly—at his entrance.

He smiled. "Hello. I'm Nathan."

"Oh hi," she said, eyes crinkling at the corners. "Jesslyn's mentioned you." Her dark hair was pulled into a ponytail. Her jeans were torn at the knees and her Gamecocks sweatshirt about two sizes too big. She might be in her midfifties, but she looked about twenty years younger. "I hear you're quite the hero," she said, her voice soft.

Heat crept into his cheeks and he wanted to duck his head in an "aw shucks" kind of way. Instead, he simply shook it. "I did what needed to be done. So did Jesslyn."

"I couldn't have gotten out of that car without your help, Nathan," Jesslyn said. Her voice was soft, raspy, low. "Just so you know. If you hadn't been there . . ." She shuddered.

Carol stood and placed her book on the table. "I'm going to grab a coffee while you two chat. I'll be back in a bit."

She left and Jesslyn burst into tears. Sobbing as though she'd lost her best friend—or her entire family. Feeling helpless, Nathan wondered if he should go after her aunt or track down Lainie.

He decided to man up. If he could handle a burning car, he could handle her tears.

Hopefully.

He thought he might prefer the car, though. Not because he didn't want her to cry, but he didn't know how to stop her pain—and he wanted to. Just about more than anything else on earth at the moment.

He sat on the bed next to her and slid an arm around her shoulders, unsure if it would comfort her. He braced himself for her to push him away, but instead, she leaned into him and he pulled her into a full embrace. She wrapped her arms around his waist and went silent.

After about five seconds of quiet, he asked, "You okay?"

"Yes. Sorry. I've needed a good cry for hours and I couldn't in front of Aunt Carol."

But she could in front of him? Interesting.

She pulled back and dried her face with the sheet, then let out a low sigh. "Sorry to blubber all over you. I couldn't hold it in any longer." She shrugged. "I'm only a crier when things have built up and I feel like I'm going to explode. This latest thing was the dead man's switch, I guess."

He held up a hand. "No apologies necessary."

"How's your hip?"

"It's fi—" The words froze on his lips at her look. "Okay, it's not fine. It hurts."

"Did you do more damage when we fell from the car?"

"No, it wasn't far and I actually landed on the other hip, so at least that was a blessing." She raised a brow at him. "And yes," he said, "I had it x-rayed again. It's just going to hurt a while."

"I'm sorry." A pause. "What am I going to do, Nathan?" she blurted. "This guy is serious about killing me, I do believe."

He told her about Kenny, and she gaped, then snapped her lips shut. "So, it could be him."

"Could be."

"But how did he know where to find me? How would he know the route I'd be on?"

"One sec. I got a text—something about your car." He pulled out his phone and read the message that had come in earlier. He pursed his lips.

"What?" she demanded.

"Well, we know how he found you. There was a tracker on it. One of the guys who loaded it on the wrecker spotted it."

She swallowed. "Okay. That makes sense. I should have been checking, I guess."

"Yeah. We all should have been checking. And will do so going forward. And as soon as Kenny's located, we'll bring him back in for questioning. A lab tech will look for any kind of residue on his hands to show he handled the Molotov cocktail ingredients, but the problem is, unless we can place him there with a witness, we still won't have much to hold him on. And he still has to be found." He glanced at his phone, hoping for a text saying Kenny was at the station, but so far, nothing.

"Right."

"Why don't you talk to Lainie and Kenzie and see how they mentally handled having someone after them?" He hadn't been around during those times in their friends' lives, but he'd sure heard about them.

"Maybe. I mean, I was right there with them through most of it. I'm not sure what they could tell me now that they didn't tell me then."

"But maybe you have different questions now?"

She hesitated. "I'll think about it."

The door opened and Lainie entered, followed by James, Steph, and her boyfriend Detective Tate Cooper, then Kenzie, Cole, Andrew, and Kristine.

Jesslyn coughed and laughed, then coughed some more. "Whoa, guys, this is a bit much. I'm okay."

Kenzie walked over and narrowed her eyes at Jesslyn. "You know, we've had some adventures over the last year or so and you were right there with us, supporting us and watching out for us. We're here to do the same for you."

Nathan thought she might burst into tears again. Instead, she sucked in a ragged breath, coughed . . . and nodded. "Thanks," she whispered.

"All of your firefighter buddies are outside too," Kristine said. "Well, probably not all of them but a good many."

"That's nice. Tell them to stick their heads in on your way out if you don't mind."

"Sure thing."

"When did you get back?" Jesslyn asked. "Thought you were gone for another few days."

"I caught an early flight to deal with some family stuff." She didn't elaborate, but the look on Jesslyn's face said she didn't have to.

There was a story behind that, and he couldn't help but be a little curious about it, but he could ask Jesslyn later. Right now, they needed to leave so she could rest.

The other firefighter buddies came in small groups to wish her well and stayed only a short time. He was relieved he didn't have to kick anyone out. Not that it was his job to do so, but Jesslyn's fatigue was obvious. And besides, if she slept, he could too.

He settled himself in the cushioned chair as comfortably as his hip would allow.

"You're sticking around for a while?" she asked, eyes drooping.

"At least until your aunt returns. She stuck her head in, left me her number"—he lifted the Post-it that Lainie had passed to him—"and said she'd be back later this afternoon."

"Good."

"You said you grew up with your aunt and two cousins. How old are they?"

"Ginger's twenty-four and is getting married in June. Sandy's twenty-two and working as a vet tech while she decides what she wants to do with the rest of her life."

"Do you get along with them?"

"Sure. I'm three years older than Ginger, and Sandy was two when I moved in. They've never really known life without me. They're not the sisters I lost, but they became the sisters of my heart."

"What about your uncle?"

"A loser. We don't talk much about him. He left us."

Her voice drifted off and her eyes closed. They'd probably given her something for pain. He wouldn't mind something himself. He dug in his pocket for the ibuprofen the nurse had given him and swallowed them dry. Then leaned his head back and closed his eyes, wanting to know more about the uncle, but that would have to wait. He'd just rest until Carol came back. He hoped she took her time because he wasn't sure he could move.

FOURTEEN

The buzzing of her phone woke Jesslyn from a sound sleep. The first thing she noticed when she opened her eyes was that her hands hurt, but the pain wasn't unbearable. There were burns in small patches and they stung, but she could live with it. Her leg, on the other hand, was really uncomfortable. The buzzing had been a text from Lainie checking on her.

Jesslyn, grateful someone had retrieved the device and her surprisingly intact purse, answered with a simple *I'm fine. Talk later.*

She glanced at the clock and figured the nurse would be coming in any minute to check on her and take her vitals. Again. Jesslyn shifted and spotted Nathan asleep in the chair. His soft snores filtered through the room.

And into her heart. He'd stayed despite his own discomfort. His hip had to be killing him, but he'd found a way to sleep. She'd have to ask him his secret.

Someone knocked on the door and it opened slowly.

The nurse. Gwen. A friendly redhead with dimples as deep as the ocean. Laugh lines crinkled and the freckles across her nose danced when she smiled. "Hi there. I'm back."

"No problem. Thanks."

Gwen did her thing and left.

Nathan stirred and straightened, his face pinching at the movement. But he swiped a hand across his eyes and blinked a few times.

Jesslyn smiled at him. "Have a good nap?"

"Yeah. You?"

"Too short."

"Same." He smiled and her heart lurched. He was really adorable. Not that she was interested. Okay, she was. Why bother to deny it to herself? For a moment, she let herself dream about what it would be like to be a part of Nathan's life in the role of girlfriend. And maybe one day more.

But her family . . .

What about them and getting justice for them? Could she juggle both? And what if she allowed herself to fall in love with him and the killer caught up with her? Or worse, Nathan?

She shivered and turned those thoughts off. Better to be alone than have that happen.

"You sure you're okay?"

She nodded. "I'm just sore."

He stood with a grimace and walked over to squeeze the tips of her fingers very gently. "This will pass."

"I know."

He walked to the sink and picked up the pen and pad of paper sitting next to it, then handed both items to her. "Can you write down any cases that you've thought of that bear looking into? Someone who would have a grudge against you?"

Jesslyn nodded. "I've already thought of three."

"Good."

She picked up the pen, wondering if it would hurt or be too awkward, but managed.

A knock on the door sounded just as she wrote the last name.

"Come in," she called.

Andrew stepped inside. "Hey, I just wanted to give you two a little update." His eyes landed on Jesslyn. "How are you doing?"

"Better. I think. I hope."

"Good."

"So what have you found out?" she asked. Maybe listening to him and concentrating on the case would take her mind off her throbbing leg.

"The officers scouring the local sources for the chemicals—pool supply companies and hardware stores—came up with seven possible suspects in a thirty-mile radius who bought both items in the last three months," he said. "I've got their names and addresses. If it's not one of them, we may have to expand our search and/or our time. Maybe go to a hundred miles and six months. And bring in other departments to help because that's a big undertaking."

Nathan raised a brow. "Well, it's a start. Between that and the list of names Jesslyn just wrote down, we'll have our work cut out for us."

Andrew nodded. "But if our arsonist already had the stuff in his garage for a while—say someone who has a pool—we're just chasing our tail."

"Or he ordered from an online service."

"Yes, we covered that possibility once." Andrew groaned and dropped onto the built-in seat under the window while Nathan rolled his eyes and shook his head.

He pulled out his phone. "I'll get Lindsay on that too with all of the big distributors." He tapped the screen for a few seconds, then looked up. "All that is well and good, but there has to be another way to track this guy down before he strikes again. He's going to have time to burn the whole town down at this rate."

Yes, there had to be another way. Guilt slammed her. She shouldn't have poked the bear. What if someone died because she'd said what she said? But what if this gave her the opportunity to take a killer off the streets and possibly save someone else by doing so?

It was a Catch-22.

"Did anyone find a connection between Kenny and my family?" Jesslyn asked.

"We looked," Andrew said. "His parents are about ten years younger than yours would have been. They're well off, well thought of, and are active in the community, their church, and various charitable organizations. If your parents were still alive, it's possible your families would run in the same social circles, know some of the same people, et cetera, but with you? There doesn't appear to be an obvious connection."

"Okay, then let's focus on something else for a minute." Jesslyn rubbed her eyes, then picked up her phone and scrolled to her pictures. "I keep coming back to the jewelry. If he's planting it, it means something to him. He picked those pieces for a reason. Maybe it has to do with the store."

"But why?" Nathan asked. "If he's got a grudge against the shop, why not just burn it down instead of other local businesses?"

"I don't think he has a grudge against the store per se, but . . ." She googled the store and noticed it had a blog. "Oh, this is interesting. They just did a renovation about two years ago. The woman we met, Isabelle Sims, put up simple posts so customers could follow the progress." She noted the excitement in the comments. "Wow. Who knew people were so passionate about their favorite jewelry store? I have about three pieces of jewelry to my name and those belonged to my grandmother." She jerked as a memory surfaced.

"Just because, darling," her father said, handing her mother a slim rectangular box.

Her mother opened it, stared at it a moment, then snorted and tossed it on the counter. "You can't buy forgiveness, Owen. At least not mine." Her mother's voice caught on a sob, and she ran from the room while her father stood there, his face like granite, nostrils flaring. He spotted Jesslyn in the doorway and walked over to pick her up.

"Jess?" Nathan snapped his fingers in front of her eyes and she blinked the image away. "You okay?"

"Yes, um . . . just a memory. A very *strange* memory."

"Anything you want to share?"

She frowned. "It was just a moment when I was five or six and my parents were arguing in the kitchen." She gave a shake of her head and shoved the past away. "I have no idea why I'd remember that now. I mean, I do remember arguments, but that one really stuck with me."

Another memory that had to have been shortly after that floated to the surface.

Her father slammed the door behind him. Sobs came from the den. She walked over to the couch to find her mother swiping tears from her eyes while Gabby and Maria argued over a toy. Jesslyn marched over to her sisters and snatched the item. "Stop it. Both of you. Stop it!"

The girls looked at her wide-eyed, then Gabby burst into tears and fled. Maria moved on to another toy, shooting a scowl at Jesslyn over her tiny shoulder. Jesslyn went to her mother and climbed up beside her. "What's wrong, Mommy?"

Her mother sniffed. "Nothing, baby. I'm sorry. I should have stopped the girls arguing. That wasn't your responsibility."

"You're sad. Why?"

"It's nothing for you to worry about. I'm fine." But she pulled Jesslyn into a tight hug and held on for a long time.

"No you're not. Daddy was mean. He's a meanie."

"He doesn't do it on purpose, Jessie-girl. He'll apologize later. You have to understand, mommies and daddies argue sometimes, but never think that your daddy doesn't love you and your sisters. You're all so very precious to him. You know that, right?"

Jesslyn blinked again. And again. Where were these memories coming from? And why now?

She shoved aside the images and continued scrolling the blog. She stopped when she came to the "before" picture of the store. There were six pictures and the post was titled "A bold step out of the past and into the future."

But what interested Jesslyn most was the cash register in the image. It was distinctive, with the gold dragon design on the side. "I've been in that store," she said. "Before this morning, I mean. I went there with someone."

Andrew leaned forward. "Who?"

She shook her head. "No idea. My mom maybe? Or my dad?

Probably my dad since he's the one who bought the jewelry for my mother. I don't know, but I do recognize the interior of the store and know I've been there because of that cash register. The man, probably Isabelle's grandfather, let me push the buttons on it and ring up the sale." Why couldn't she remember who she'd been with?

Her phone rang and it was her chief. She glanced at the guys. "I need to take this. I'm sure it's about the fire."

Nathan nodded to Andrew. "We'll just step outside. I want to check in and see if there's an update on the wreck."

"The wreck. Yes." Jesslyn pressed fingers to her temples. "I need to call the rental car company. Thank goodness I got all the insurance available on it."

NATHAN LEFT JESSLYN at the hospital under the watchful eye of two Lake City police officers. They were men he'd worked with as a detective and he trusted they would keep her safe. And Tate promised to keep an eye on her as well.

"I'm going to head to my parents'," Andrew said. "I have a family dinner thing I promised to attend."

"Have fun. I'm going to the scene of the fire and then I'm going home too."

"Let me know if you find out anything new."

"Of course."

The fire at the gym had been out for a while, and Charles Alexander, a fire marshal from Asheville, had come over to work the scene. He'd update Jesslyn with his findings and she'd take it from there if she was able.

When Nathan stepped out of the hospital, the rain was coming down in buckets. His first thought was that at least the arsonist wouldn't strike in this kind of downpour. If that was the case, maybe they could catch a break while he waited out the weather.

The problem was, they really didn't have any viable suspects.

151

A few maybes, but no one who really stood out. Which was odd. Usually—okay, *most* of the time—someone did.

He was stumped.

He drove out to the scene of the gym fire. Well, it wasn't so much a fire now as a burned-out shell, thanks to the downpour that had now slowed to a misty drizzle.

He grabbed his umbrella and walked over to the man who he suspected was the fire marshal for this scene. "Nathan Carlisle, FBI."

"Nice to meet you, I'm Charles Alexander. How's Jesslyn?"

"She's still in the hospital for observation, but they'll probably release her tomorrow."

"Good. Scared me to death when I heard about the wreck."

Try witnessing it, he wanted to say. "Anything else you can tell us about this fire?"

"It was a doozy. Permanganate and antifreeze. Sound familiar?"

He nodded. Just like the other fire, but Jesslyn had already figured that out. He handed the man his card. "I know you're going to loop Jesslyn in on everything you find, but do you mind calling me too?"

"Of course not." Charles pocketed the card, and on a whim, Nathan pulled his phone out and tapped the screen to show the man Kenny's picture. "Have you ever seen this guy before at any other fires you've investigated?"

Charles shook his head. "No, don't recognize him."

It was a long shot. "Thanks."

"But I did have a fire with this same accelerant. I'm guessing whoever set this one set the one I covered."

"Really? Where and when?"

"Last week. The bank on Shady Oaks Drive. First Credit about thirty minutes from here on the outskirts of town, so it would normally have been her fire, but I covered it because she was gone."

"Jess never mentioned that one."

"No reason she'd know about it."

"It wasn't entered into AEXIS?" The Arson and Explosive Incident

System was a database of information from federal, state, and local law enforcement agencies. It provided information about the nature of incidents, devices used, and other relevant details.

The man grimaced. "We're backed up, so no, it hasn't been entered yet."

And while it was mandatory for federal agencies to do so, it wasn't for state agencies. Most did, just sometimes not in a timely manner. Jesslyn would want to know this ASAP. "Thank you. Do you think you could get that entered since we have two other fires that seem to be connected?"

"Yes. Absolutely. I'll do it myself before I go to sleep tonight."

"Appreciate it. One other question. Do you know if they found any jewelry at that fire?"

"Yes, they did. It was weird because it didn't suffer any damage. Just needed a good cleaning."

Because it had been dropped after the fact? "Do you happen to have a picture of it?"

The man pulled up his phone and within seconds showed Nathan a picture of two beautiful black pearl swans' necks curved into a heart. "A brooch?"

"Yes."

"Send it to me?" Nathan gave him his number and waited until the picture showed up on his phone. "Thank you, sir. Have a good night."

Nathan went back to his car, stashed the umbrella, and called Andrew. He briefed him on his meeting with the other fire marshal. "Any word on picking up Kenny?"

"Nope. The guy is in the wind, but we've got a couple of officers watching the entrances to campus and one on his dorm. If he shows, we'll nab him."

"Anyone check his parents' home?"

"Yep. Nothing there either, and according to his cell records, he hasn't called them. Could have used another phone, but the officers on his house said the parents left yesterday with overnight bags and bicycles mounted on the back of their vehicle. There's been no sign of the kid before or after. If he doesn't show up in the next few hours, officers will have to talk to them, but honestly, I'd rather not tip them off that we're looking for him."

"Because they could tip him off."

"Exactly."

"Okay, just text me if you catch him. I really would like another go at him."

"You got it."

"In the meantime, I'm going to go back to the hospital and let Jesslyn know this latest. She'll want to see the picture of the jewelry."

"You could just call her, you know. And text her the picture."

"I could."

"So why don't you?"

Because I want to see her. "Because she may want to talk out strategy, thoughts on capturing this guy."

"Oh, that's why. Riiight."

"Shut up."

"See you later, partner."

When Nathan returned to the hospital, he found Jesslyn asleep and her aunt Carol had returned, occupying the chair he'd used earlier. She waved him back out the door and followed him into the hall.

"How's she doing?" he asked.

"Not much change from the last time you were here."

He flushed and tried to ignore it. "I guess not."

The woman took pity on him and smiled. "I'm glad she has you in her corner."

"She's a very interesting person. I like her."

Carol narrowed her eyes at him. "That surprises you."

"Yeah, I guess it does a little."

Grief flashed for a brief moment before she lowered her lids and covered the emotion. "She needs someone like you," she said, her voice soft. "Just understand that she's a very driven person."

"I do understand that. We've talked about it."

Her eyes went wide and locked on his. "You have?"

"Yeah." He cleared his throat. "I don't know if it's my place to ask this, but what do you make of the fact that she believes the arsonist—murderer—was in her bedroom watching her sleep shortly after her family's funerals?"

"She told you about that?" Carol couldn't have looked more shocked if he'd punched her in the nose.

"She did."

"Wow."

Nathan fell silent in case she didn't want to talk about it, but after several seconds, she shifted. "It was a terrible time for her. For all of us who were left to deal with the aftermath. But for Jesslyn, it was . . ." She waved a hand. "I don't have the words to describe it, really."

"I can't imagine." Well, he could. A little. But not really. He'd lost a friend. She'd lost her entire immediate family in one night. However . . . grief was still grief. Loss was still loss.

"She insisted the man was there, but I shudder to think how he got in the house, much less managed to get to her room without waking anyone. It's honestly easier to believe he wasn't real."

"But what if he was?"

She grimaced. "What if he was? He left without hurting anyone. I don't have answers and I prefer not to add questions to the ones I already have."

"Understandable."

"She's so dedicated to her job," Carol said, then frowned. "Actually, dedicated isn't a strong enough word. Obsessed is more accurate. She's had men interested before, and she's pretty much chased them all away because none of them could understand her fixation with catching her family's killer—or if they did actually sympathize, it didn't last long."

"Okay." What was he supposed to say to that?

Tears formed in the woman's eyes. "I wish she could let it go. As much as I want justice for my sister and her family, I want Jesslyn to move on more. I want her to find happiness and settle down with someone, but she . . . won't. Not until she's exhausted every avenue and concludes that she'll never know who killed them."

"Do you think that's even something that could happen?"

She hesitated. "I'd like to think so, but I just don't know. Only God can answer that one." A pause. "There are a lot of questions that only God can answer."

She wasn't wrong.

FIFTEEN

Jesslyn was released from the hospital shortly after eight Monday morning. They'd kept her to be sure she'd have no adverse reactions to the smoke inhalation. She was well armed with instructions on how to care for her wounds and the supplies to do it. And of course, she had Lainie to rely on if she needed to.

At home she took off most of the hospital bandages from her hands and simply used large Band-Aids. Much easier to navigate the laptop keyboard and phone.

With two off-duty officers on her house thanks to Cole's connections, and Lainie and Kenzie in her kitchen, she was well covered. Aunt Carol had wanted to come, but Jesslyn was antsy about having the woman around her outside the hospital. All precautions would be taken. No one was assuming Kenny was the arsonist. If he was, great, they had their guy, not just a scared kid running from the scene.

And if it *wasn't* Kenny, she didn't know if her attacker would take out his anger on others close to her. This was one situation where she'd err on the side of caution and keep Aunt Carol away. She didn't want to risk her law enforcement friends either, but at least they all had guns.

Kenzie, laptop in hand, walked into the den and settled into the recliner across from the couch where Jesslyn had made herself comfortable. "So that piece of jewelry Nathan showed you Saturday. What did you think of it?"

"I've definitely seen it before."

When she'd awakened this morning, Nathan was there in the hospital room, snoozing in the chair Aunt Carol had been in when Jesslyn had fallen asleep. She wasn't sure what noise she'd made to indicate she was awake, but he'd blinked and met her gaze while her heart nearly set off the machines at how handsome he was. Like a mussed little boy waking from his nap.

Then he blinked again and the little boy was gone, the look in his eyes going from sleepy to smoky hot at the speed of light. Heat crept up from her throat and into her neck, heading for her cheeks, and she buried her face in her hands under the pretense of wiping the sleep from her eyes.

Nope, he was all man for sure.

While she was trying to rein in her runaway attraction, he talked some more about the other fire and they looked at the picture of the piece of jewelry again.

"I just wish I could remember where I saw it." She paused. "The fire at the bank is confusing, though. I'm not connected to it, so I don't understand the relevance."

"If it wasn't for the Molotov cocktail thrown into your car, I'd say maybe it's time to rethink whether this is about you. But . . ."

"Right."

"You're definitely a target."

"But how does the bank fire factor into my life, that's the question."

"You don't bank there."

"No."

"Have a safety deposit box there?"

"Nope."

"Know anyone who works there?"

"No." She shrugged. "I don't think I've ever set foot in that branch."

She blinked away the memory and pulled her laptop from the end table, intending to do some research after she made a phone call.

Lainie walked into the room, tucked her phone into her back pocket, and dropped into the matching recliner on the other side of the fireplace. "What'd I miss?"

While Kenzie filled her in, Jesslyn stretched out on the couch and made a phone call to her aunt.

Carol answered on the last ring, sounding out of breath.

"Are you okay?" Jesslyn asked.

"I'm fine. Was just doing my exercise video. Are *you* okay?"

"Yes, I'm settled at home with all of my babysitters in attendance." From the recliner, Kenzie stuck her tongue out, then went back to whatever she was doing on her laptop. Jesslyn smiled. "Anyway, I have a question. Do you know if I ever went to the Tradition's Custom Touch jewelry store with Mom or Dad?"

"I . . . um . . . I don't really remember. Why?"

"It's just a memory I have. At least I think it's a memory. I found some pictures of the store before they renovated it and I remember being there."

"Well, it's possible. Your dad gave your mom a few pieces of jewelry during their marriage. I guess he could have gotten them from there."

Jesslyn frowned. "Do you still have some of those pieces or did they get destroyed in the fire?"

A low breath reached her through the line. "She kept a lot of her jewelry in a safe deposit box, so yes, I have everything in that. She put my name on the box in case . . . well . . ."

"And you haven't taken them out in all these years?" And why hadn't she offered them to Jesslyn?

"No. I haven't."

There was something she wasn't saying, but she could address that at another time. "Okay. Do you mind if I go look at them?"

"Why the sudden interest in the jewelry?"

"It's a long story. I can explain later. So, do you mind?"

A pause. "No. Of course not."

Memories flickered at the back of her mind and she wanted answers. "Aunt Carol, I remember my parents fighting quite a bit before the fire. I don't know how long before, but I just remember bits and pieces. Like Dad storming out of the house and slamming the door. Mom crying. When I asked her what was wrong, she just shook her head and told me not to worry about it."

"You remember that? You couldn't have been more than six or so."

"I know, but yes, I remember that."

Her aunt fell quiet, and Jesslyn wondered what she was thinking. "Oh, hon," she finally said. "I don't suppose it will hurt to tell you that your parents' marriage was in a really bad place before the fire. It was getting better, but for a while there, it was bad. You must be remembering some of the bad parts."

She didn't know why she wasn't more shocked. "I suspected. Do you know why?"

A pause. "Yes."

"Will you tell me the reason?"

"It's not pretty, Jesslyn. I know you have this picture of your family in your head. Your heart. And I've not wanted to do anything to . . . damage that."

"Carol . . . please . . ."

"Do you really want to know? Because once I tell you—"

"I want to know. I . . . need to know."

Carol went silent once more. Jesslyn waited. "Okay then," Carol said. "Your father was cheating on your mother. Had been since shortly after they were married."

Jesslyn closed her eyes and let the words sink in. "I'm sorry. What? You mean . . ."

Carol's answer was short. "Yes."

"Whoa." It was a good thing she was sitting down. Her heart thundered. *Focus. Process later.* She gulped in air and finally found her voice. "Well, that explains the fights, I guess."

"I'm really surprised you remember so much."

"I do. Some in detail. Some just by the tension that was there. I knew something was wrong between them. Of course, I had no idea what it could be, but now it makes more sense than they just didn't like each other anymore."

"I'm sorry." Her aunt's voice caught and she cleared her throat. "I didn't want you to know. I wanted you to go on believing you had the perfect family."

Jesslyn scoffed. "I never believed my family was perfect, but they *were* my family and I loved them."

"I know, sweetie. But your dad had a lot of issues stemming from his childhood and it made living with him hard sometimes."

"Then why encourage me to develop the youth center? Why agree to help with everything that will honor him like that?"

"Because it's the right thing to do." She blew out a long breath. "It's a fairly long story. I'll tell you later, but if you truly want to see the jewelry, then I need to go."

"Fine. Sounds like we both have stories to share."

"Yes. Sounds like. I can meet you at the bank and open the box for you."

"Which bank?"

"Second National."

Surely, meeting her aunt at a bank would be all right, wouldn't it? They'd enter at separate times. If anyone was watching Jesslyn, there wouldn't be any way to put the two of them together at the bank. And someone could watch the street to see if anyone followed her. But what if someone had been watching them at the hospital? Then they'd already know who Carol was. The thought chilled her. "When?"

"I have a pretty full day today since you sent me packing and wouldn't let me stay with you."

"Aunt Carol—"

"I can do it in a couple of hours if you can wait that long." She paused. "Or I can just go by the bank and pick up the pieces and bring them to your house."

No way. She bit her tongue on the words. "I don't think that's a good idea." It was a very, very bad idea for more reasons than one. "How much is the jewelry in the box worth?"

More silence. Then another sigh. "Today? Probably forty or fifty grand."

Jesslyn choked. "What?"

"Your father had a lot of groveling to do, Jesslyn."

She flinched, glad her aunt couldn't see her reaction. She just realized Kenzie and Lainie had moved back into the kitchen to give her privacy. Tears pricked at her eyes. How she loved her friends and their thoughtfulness. "I'll meet you there, but don't leave your house until I text you, okay?" The extra caution might be the equivalent of shutting the barn door after all the horses were out, but with the threat she'd received and Kenny on the loose, Jesslyn didn't figure it would hurt.

"Sure."

She hung up. "You guys can come back in."

They returned and took their former seats while she sent a group voice text to James, Cole, Nathan, Kenzie, and Andrew.

> I need to run an errand related to the case. It's about the jewelry found at the scenes. But I need help. Are any of you free?

Kenzie looked up and Jesslyn smiled at her. "You don't have to answer to the loop."

"Okay."

The thumbs-up emojis started coming in. The only one not available was Andrew. And he sent a sad face with a tear on his cheek. It was fine. With the others, her plan should work.

> Cole
>
> Do I need to bring any of the other guys?

The SWAT team? It was probably a little too much for this. She responded with a negative, then outlined her plan by voice text again. Kenzie nodded and Lainie frowned. Clearly she wasn't a fan.

But it was the only thing she could think of that would keep her aunt—and herself—safe while doing a necessary part of the investigation. Which was her job.

NATHAN GOT THE TEXT while he and Andrew were scouring security footage from the homes and businesses around the Endurance Empire Gym. "What is she up to now?" he muttered.

"Sounds like she's got a plan about something," Andrew said, even though Nathan hadn't expected an answer. "Sorry I can't help."

Andrew had already told him he'd promised to help his folks with their bookstore and would be leaving as soon as they were done with the footage. Nathan tapped back that he was available and turned his focus back onto the screen. One person had caught his eye a few seconds before he stopped to check his messages. He used the cursor to drag the footage back to the part where he thought he recognized someone. "Hey, check this guy out. He looks familiar to me. What about you?"

Nathan enlarged the frame as much as he could without distorting the image, and Andrew narrowed his eyes. "Kenny?"

"That's him, yes, but we knew he was there. What about the guy standing a little bit back from him?"

His partner leaned in and took a closer look at the area where the cursor pointed. "Is that the other guy from the student center? Brad Granger?"

"Pool Table Brad." He nodded. "That's him."

"Interesting he and Kenny were there at the fire together."

"Isn't it, though?"

"I'm guessing you want to talk to Brad again?"

"I do. Kenny's phone might be offline, but that doesn't mean he's not finding a way to communicate with his friends."

"The officers who went to pick him up said all his friends denied hearing from him but also said it wouldn't surprise them if they were lying."

"Me either." Nathan hesitated, then glanced at his watch. "I have time to go talk to Brad before I have to head over to Jesslyn's. Let's go."

It didn't take them long to reach the campus and wind their way around to the student center. When they walked in, only a small somber crowd gathered on the sofas and chairs around the fireplace. No one played pool or any of the video games lining the wall. The café was quiet.

The door opened and Nathan turned to the young woman who'd entered. Her puffy eyes said she'd been crying. "Miss?"

She looked at him. "Yes?"

"What's going on? Why is it so . . ." He waved a hand. "Quiet."

"One of our friends died."

Nathan exchanged a look with Andrew. He was thinking the same thing. "I hate to ask, but could you tell us who?"

"Brad Granger."

Nathan stilled. "No. I'm so sorry. What happened?"

"He jumped off the roof of his dorm, which is completely unbelievable." She swiped a tear. "Brad wouldn't jump."

"When did this happen?"

"Late last night—or early this morning."

Nathan exchanged a stunned look with Andrew. He didn't surprise easily, but he had to admit, he hadn't expected this. "Did anyone see him jump?"

"I don't know. I don't think so."

"Heath is his roommate, right?"

"Yes."

"You know where he is?"

She shook her head.

"Right. Well, thanks for letting us know."

She nodded and moved on to the group near the fireplace. Two female students made room for her on the nearest couch and she sank onto it.

"All right then," Andrew said. "First move. Find Heath and have a chat with him? Ask him why Brad was at the fire?"

"Yes, then find out who's investigating this and ask to be updated on anything they find out."

"I sure would like to ask Kenny about his friend being at the scene with him."

"And see his reaction when we tell him Brad is dead."

"You think he doesn't know?"

"I have no idea." Nathan clapped his partner on the shoulder. "Let's find Heath."

It took them thirty minutes to track the young man to the math and science building. He was in Professor Derek Morgan's office. When Nathan rapped his knuckles on the open door, Heath jumped to his feet. It was obvious the kid had been crying. He palmed his eyes, then shot them a glare. "What do you two want now?"

Professor Morgan rose to his feet. "Hey, Heath, don't."

Heath settled back into his seat with a scowl, and Morgan rested a compassionate gaze on him before turning to Andrew and Nathan. "Special agents, right?"

Andrew nodded. "Yes, sir. We'd like to speak to you, Heath, about your friend, Brad, if you don't mind."

"I mind. I've already talked to the detectives who were here this morning and I'll tell you what I told them. Brad wouldn't have jumped. There's no way he killed himself."

Nathan raised a brow. "Then would someone want to cause him harm? Because if it wasn't suicide, then it was—"

"Murder. That's exactly what it was. He was always going up to the rooftop at night. Almost every single night. To study or just talk on the phone, whatever."

"Heath, stop." Professor Morgan walked around the desk to rest a hand on Heath's shoulder. "Son. Don't do this to yourself."

Nathan ignored the professor and looked the young man in the eyes. "So, what you're saying is that there was a pattern and someone who knew it could have . . ."

"That's exactly what I'm saying. We even called it Brad's roof." Heath shook his head and stood. "It's not right. He wouldn't have jumped."

"Do you mind sharing with us why you feel like that?" Nathan asked.

"We were making plans for the summer, talking about graduation." He threw his hands in the air. "Why make all those plans if you're just going to end it?"

People usually didn't, but it wasn't unheard of.

"Derek, I need your hel—" The woman's voice came from the door. Nathan turned to see a blond woman with green eyes and flushed cheeks. She stopped when she saw them and blinked. Then grimaced. "I didn't realize you had visitors. I thought you were going to introduce me to the dean."

Morgan looked from Nathan to the woman. "Sorry, Sam, just give me a few more minutes." He waved his hand at Nathan and Andrew. "This is my sister, Samantha. Sam, this is—"

"Nice to meet you," she snapped with a quick glance at Nathan and Andrew. She turned back to Morgan. "I don't have all day." She was gone as fast as she'd appeared.

"I-I'll be right there." He rubbed a hand over his lips. "I'm sorry about her. She's kind of a menace. I have to go. Is there anything else?"

"Was he seeing any kind of doctor for mental health issues?" Andrew asked, looking at Heath. "Taking any meds?"

"No. And before you ask, yes, I would know. He wasn't."

Morgan confirmed Heath's answer as he backed toward the door.

Nathan made a note to ask about any drugs—prescription or otherwise—found in the dorm room. "Where are you staying right now? I'm assuming your dorm room is off-limits?"

"Yeah, the detectives let me grab some of my stuff before they locked me out. Said I can come back tomorrow." He sniffed. "I'm staying with Jeff and Kenny." He frowned. "When is Kenny coming back?"

Nathan shot a look at Andrew, then back to the student. "He was released a while ago. You haven't seen him?"

"No. I mean, those other cops came around asking about him, but I haven't talked to him in a couple of days."

So he probably wasn't back on campus.

"Will you let us know if you hear of anyone who may have witnessed Brad's death?"

"Derek?" Samantha was back at the door. "Seriously?"

"I'm coming. I'm coming. I promise."

She huffed away and the professor gave a slight shrug. "Sorry. I promised to introduce her to Dean Fitzpatrick. There's a job opening she's interested in that she doesn't have the slightest hope of getting, but she insists that I . . ." He waved a hand. "Never mind. Sorry."

Heath's gaze turned back to them. "To answer your question, I-I'll ask around to some of the others and find out if he really had a death wish and I didn't see it."

Poor kid. "All right. Thanks for your help." Nathan nodded to the professor. "What about you, Professor Morgan? You were pretty close with Brad, weren't you?"

"Yes." His jaw tightened and a sheen covered his eyes. He blinked. "Very. Look, I have to go." He motioned to the door. "When she gets upset, she can be . . . difficult."

Nathan was starting to think Eli might not be so bad after all. "Did he confide in you about any suicidal thoughts?"

"No." Morgan frowned. "He did seem preoccupied lately, but when I asked him about it, he just said he was fine."

Andrew nodded. "What about Kenny? Still haven't heard from him?"

"No. I haven't. Now, I have to—"

"Right. You have to go. Thank you."

"Of course." He practically ran out of the office. "Sam—"

"All right, Heath," Andrew said, "thank you for your time. You know how to reach us if you have anything else to add."

They left and walked to the vehicle. "What do you think about that?" Nathan asked.

"I think something fishy is going on, but I can't determine where the smell is coming from."

"Yeah. Same."

"We'll keep after it. Something's bound to rise to the surface before too long."

Nathan just hoped it was before another attempt was made on Jesslyn's life.

His phone buzzed. A text from the chief of police.

Picked up Kenny Davies. He's in interrogation
room number one.

He showed it to Andrew, who raised a brow. "Let's go."

SIXTEEN

Jesslyn's phone buzzed with a call from a number she didn't recognize, but she swiped the screen anyway. She often got calls without any ID. "Hello?"

"Hi, is this Jesslyn McCormick?"

"It is."

"This is Isabelle Sims. From Tradition's Custom Touch. You left your card with me the day you visited and asked about my grandfather and his recordkeeping system."

"Oh yes, hi. What can I do for you?"

"I was talking to my grandmother and asked her what happened to all of the old files, and she said she has everything in her basement. She never got rid of them."

What she was saying sunk in. "You mean you have all of the files from the old sales?"

"Exactly. I thought you might want to come look at them."

"That would be incredible." She chewed her lip for a second. "But let me see if I can arrange to have everything transported to the police station."

"Oh. Okay. I don't mind you coming to her house. The basement has a separate entrance."

"It would be a real pain for her to have us there for as long as it's

going to take us to go through the files. Trust me, it's better this way."
And if Jesslyn was at her home, there was always the possibility of
her attacker following.

Isabelle laughed. "I guess you have a point. That's fine. Just text or
call when you're ready to come get the files. Her house is only about
five minutes from the store so I can meet you any time."

"A team of officers will come and make quick work of moving
them. But I'll let you know when they're on the way. Thank you so
much."

Jesslyn hung up and made the calls to arrange for the files to be
picked up and delivered to the local police department. Nathan and
Andrew had a small office there that they'd been given permission
to use for the duration of the investigation, but she had a feeling it
wouldn't be big enough to hold the files. They'd probably have to
use the conference room. She called the police chief to verify if that
was all right and he agreed. She then left messages with Nathan and
Andrew about what she'd done and sat back with a huff.

Her hands had started to throb and her leg was about to make her
loony. She wasn't sure how much longer she could ignore the pain.

Lainie walked over and held out a hand with a dose of pain meds.
In the other hand she held a bottle of water.

Jesslyn raised a brow. "So, you can read my mind now?"

"I'm observant. It's part of the job description."

"I can't take anything that will make me sleepy, Lainie. I've got
too much to do."

"This isn't a narcotic. It'll cut the pain but won't knock you out."

"Oh. Great." She checked to make sure she had all the information from the gym fire that Charles, the Asheville fire marshal, had
covered for her, then popped the pill with a swallow of water. She
set the bottle on the coffee table and closed her eyes. "Wake me
when everyone gets here?"

"Of course. Rest. You need it. Your body's been through a big
trauma."

"I know. I'll try."

Jesslyn shut her eyes, worried she'd dream of the attack or the man in her room, but found herself dozing, aware of the others near her, knowing she was safe—for the moment.

NATHAN AND ANDREW HAD A CHAT with the chief before they walked into Kenny's interrogation room, garnering the facts of how they'd found him. When they walked in, the smell hit them first and Nathan winced. Andrew grimaced and shook his head.

Kenny was dozing, head cradled in his arms. At their entrance, he blinked and looked up, eyes bleary and bloodshot but hard and angry. "I haven't done anything wrong and I'm missing classes. You can't keep me here." He picked up the towelette next to him and rubbed his hands with it. Nathan was glad to see they'd already swabbed them for residue, although it might be too late at this point to get anything from them.

"You didn't seem too concerned about missing classes when you were passed out drunk behind the gas station." One of the attendants had stepped outside to take out the trash and found him. Thinking he was dead, the guy called 911. Officers arrived and recognized him about the time Kenny started to wake up. Once they discerned he wasn't hurt, merely drunk, they brought him in and the chief had texted Nathan.

The door opened and a young officer handed Andrew a folder. "Results."

Andrew flipped it open and drew in a breath before shutting it and shaking his head at Nathan.

No residue on his hands. Great. Andrew passed him the folder. The chief had included a note. *Sorry, but ask him questions and let him go. We've got nothing.*

Nathan wanted to pound the table with a fist. Instead, he looked Kenny in the eye. "We just wanted to ask you a few more questions, then you can go."

Triumph flickered briefly and Nathan wished he knew why.

He set the surveillance picture on the table and slid it over so Kenny could see it. "Take a look at that, will you?"

Kenny raised a brow but leaned forward to look. He frowned and glanced up. "We all know I was at the scene of the fire. What's the big deal about this picture?"

"The big deal is the guy standing behind you to your right. Recognize him?"

Kenny looked again. "Whoa. What? Brad? What was he doing there?"

"That's what we want to know," Andrew said.

"I don't know. He didn't come with me. I had no idea he was back there."

Nathan scoffed. "Right, nice try."

"I'm serious, man. Ask him."

Nathan hesitated. "We can't."

Kenny frowned. "What do you mean?"

"Kenny, I'm sorry you have to hear it from us, but Brad died early this morning."

The boy paled and shook his head. "Died? No. You're lying."

"We're not lying," Andrew said. "The word is he jumped off the dorm's roof."

"No! It's not true! This is really cruel, even for the FBI. Why would you tell me that?"

Nathan's heart ached for the guy's potent grief, and he hated to be the one to have to break the news to him this way. "He was your friend. I'm sorry. I've lost someone I was close to and I know your grief."

At the kind words, Kenny nodded. "It's really true?"

"Yeah, man, I'm so sorry. Really."

Tears spilled over the young man's lower lashes to stream down his cheeks. Andrew grabbed a box of tissues and placed them on the table. Kenny grabbed a handful and shoved them against his eyes. "It's not true. Brad wouldn't jump. He wasn't suicidal. No way you'll ever convince me of that."

LYNETTE EASON

Nathan glanced at Andrew. Three denials of any suicidal tendencies. True? Or just clueless friends?

"Okay, if Brad didn't jump, can you think of someone who'd want him dead?"

He hesitated, then sputtered, "No, of course not. We're just college students, trying to figure out life. Did you ask Heath?"

"Yes. He said the same thing you did."

"This is wrong," Kenny whispered. "So messed up."

"Kenny, if you're hiding something, protecting someone—"

"I'm not."

He was lying. Every instinct shouted it at Nathan, but if the guy wasn't talking, there wasn't much more they could do about it. He rubbed his temples.

The chief—and their SSA, who was in agreement with the chief—might make them let him go, but they could keep an eye on him.

"You can call someone to come get you," Andrew said.

"Give me my phone and I'll call an Uber. I'm going back to campus. I need to be there. The guys will need my support." He looked from Nathan to Andrew back to Nathan. "Can I go now?"

"Yeah. You can collect your stuff from the officer at the end of the hall. The one behind the window," Nathan said.

Kenny shot them an open glare and left the room.

Nathan's phone rang and he glanced at the screen. Eli. For crying out loud. He sent it to voicemail and followed Kenny out the door, thankful to see an undercover unit watching from a distance. An Uber arrived and Kenny climbed in. The unmarked unit followed and would report where Kenny wound up.

Nathan checked the time.

Jesslyn was waiting. He texted the group he was on the way, said goodbye to Andrew, and hurried to his car.

173

SEVENTEEN

Once Jesslyn texted her aunt that it was okay to leave home, she and the others arrived at the bank ten minutes after her aunt did. It didn't take long to get the box, which Carol opened while the others stood guard outside the vault.

Carol reached in and pulled out a black velour bag and set it on the table. "Here you are. Each piece is in another bag just like that one, just smaller. There are twelve of them. Each of them was worth between two and four thousand dollars if I remember correctly. No telling what they'll appraise for in this day and age."

Her father had been a very successful commercial real estate agent and developer, but . . . "I know we lived very comfortably and our house was lovely, but I don't remember Mom and Dad really being big spenders like this."

"They weren't. It was just your dad, and he had his reasons for forking over the big bucks for those."

"I see." She'd get to that in a minute. Jesslyn eyed the bags, her throat working. "Did Mom ever wear these?"

"No."

She looked up and met her aunt's gaze. "Never?"

"Not once. She didn't want them."

"But I don't understand. Why keep them then? What was the purpose?"

Aunt Carol's gaze slid away.

"Carol?"

The woman huffed a soft sigh. "They were her escape plan."

Jesslyn's jaw dropped. "Her *escape* plan? Things had gotten *that* bad?" Well, her father *had* cheated on her mother. What did she expect?

"Yes."

The simple one-word answer punched the air from her lungs and it took her a moment to recover. Finally, she dragged in a breath. "And that's why she kept them in the safe deposit box." Jesslyn paused. "Did my dad not notice she wasn't wearing them?"

"Oh, he noticed, but your mom loved jewelry, and I believe he thought she'd eventually cave and wear them."

"But she didn't."

"No. Not this stuff."

"Well, all right then. I guess we'll do this." She reached for the first bag with her right hand and dumped the piece into her left palm. It was a cold but beautiful brooch. A diamond-studded poodle about three inches in width and two in height. The ears and eyes were black pearls and the nose a pink diamond. "Wow. It's beautiful. And Mom's favorite dog."

"He had that crafted for their first anniversary. She actually did wear that for a while, until she learned of his infidelity and the reason for the other pieces that came home with him."

Jesslyn's heart squeezed against the pain of knowing her father cheated. Her poor mother. "I can't believe he did that."

"I know it's a tough pill to swallow. I wish I didn't have to tell you, but I can't lie to you."

"Which I appreciate." Jesslyn ran shaky fingers over the piece. "You never let on. Never said a word against him."

"What would be the point? He's gone—and your mother had forgiven him before the end."

Jesslyn snapped her head up. "She did?"

Carol nodded. "She wasn't going to wear the jewelry because of what it represented, what it was a reminder of, but she wasn't going to be angry with him anymore either. He was a good father to you girls, he just . . ." She shook her head. "I don't know. I can't explain it. He had a pretty traumatic childhood and your mother knew that going into the marriage. But she loved him and she never stopped—not even when he betrayed her. She was hurt and angry and thought about leaving him more than once, that's true"—she motioned to the jewelry stash—"but each time she'd pray and pray some more and told me she never got the green light from God to leave him."

"Like some modern-day reverse Hosea story? Even though he was unfaithful?"

"Even though."

"If she'd left him, she and my sisters might still be alive," Jesslyn murmured.

"I can't say I haven't thought of that more than once." Something deeper than grief flashed in her eyes.

"What is it? What are you not saying?"

Her aunt pressed her fingers against her eyelids. "This is really hard, Jess."

"I know, but please, don't hold anything back."

Carol nodded and lowered her hands. "Look, I'm not saying I understand her choice. Every person in that situation has to decide for themselves what to do. Leave or stay? Your mother stayed because she believed he truly *wanted* to change. And, by the time they died in the fire, they were going to counseling. He wasn't sneaking out at night. He was being accountable to Linda and to a support group he'd joined without Linda having to ask him. He was putting in the effort like never before and your mom was the happiest I'd seen her in years." She paused. "No, 'happy' isn't the word. She was at peace. She truly felt like God had answered her prayers and this time was it. Your dad was different. And I'll admit, I noticed it too. He had a stillness about him that I'd never seen before. I think not only was your mother at peace, but your dad was too." Another pause and tears filmed her aunt's eyes. "And I am too. It took a while, but I got there. If she could forgive him and plan to move on with him, then I can do the same. Which is why I agreed to help you build a building in his—and their—honor."

"Really? Because if you don't want to, then I'd understand."

Her aunt heaved a sigh and paused a moment, seeming to gather her thoughts and pick her words. Jesslyn wanted to tell her to just spit it out, but she held her tongue.

Finally, Carol spoke. "He wanted to do this before he died. He was excited about it. I never told you that he grew up with alcoholic parents who neglected him terribly. He was in and out of the foster care system before he landed in the Millers' home. They were good people and he kept in touch with them until he died."

"What?" Jesslyn gaped. She hadn't realized what "troubled childhood" had meant for her father.

Carol nodded. "That's what I'm saying. Your father had his issues, but he wasn't a horrible, evil man or anything—although, I have to admit I thought so at the time. But, over the past twenty years, I've come to realize he was simply a flawed man. A hurting man who overcame a lot and had more to overcome. A man in need of forgiveness and redemption like every other soul on this planet." She closed her eyes a moment, then offered a wry smile to Jesslyn. "You wouldn't believe how hard it was to finally admit that. Anyway, the youth center was his dream and your mother supported it. They were going to build the building from the ground up and even had the blueprints drawn up." She clasped her hands to her chest. "I'll show them to you and maybe you can incorporate some of their ideas for the different areas in your plan."

Jesslyn's knees were weak and she wondered how much more she could take. But she couldn't help herself. She pressed on, wanting every little detail. And now that Carol had started the telling, she didn't appear to be in any hurry to stop. In fact, she seemed almost relieved to unload. "I'd love to see them," Jesslyn said. "Who was the woman? Or was there more than one?"

"I think in the beginning there were a few, but then your father seemed to settle down with your mother and they were happy again for a while. He stopped giving her jewelry and she was thrilled with that." She shook her head. "Imagine being happy your husband doesn't bring you jewelry."

"Right. So, every time he had an affair, he'd bring her something from that store and she knew why. A psychiatrist would have a field day with that one."

"I know. It didn't make sense. But then they'd have an argument or a disagreement and he'd disappear into whatever mental place he went to deal with that. And he'd give her more jewelry, and of course, she knew."

"That there was someone else."

"Yes. The last time, I think it was someone who may have been in the neighborhood."

Jesslyn frowned. "Why do you think that?"

"Your mom said your dad would leave at night. Like after he thought she was asleep, he'd get up and walk out the door. Never took the car, so wherever he went was within walking distance." Carol fell silent for a moment. "Linda brought you girls over one night, you know. I pointed out the fact that your father was walking wherever he was going and obviously meeting someone. I asked her if she was going to continue letting him do that to her. She said no, she wasn't. Said she was going home to confront him and tell him it was the last time. That if he didn't stop and get back into counseling with her, she was walking away."

"And was she going to?"

"I think so. I don't think she meant it to be a permanent thing, just until he got it together. She told me she hated to leave, that she couldn't walk away for good, but she couldn't let him believe she wouldn't. He broke down and begged her forgiveness, bought her another piece of jewelry that went in the safe deposit box, and then went back to counseling, begging her not to give up on him. And she didn't. But . . ."

"But what?"

"So, she went home, they talked, and all was well. Until the night of the fire. They had an argument. She'd intercepted a phone call from one of the women he'd had an affair with. He promised her he'd cut off all contact, reminded her that he'd changed his phone number and everything. Your mom knew this but was still hurt. Terrified all of their progress was going to come crashing down on her. Your dad swore he'd made it clear that everything was over, but that the woman just wouldn't stop contacting him, begging him to come back to her. Your mom was furious. More so than I'd ever seen her. She didn't know what to believe. That's why she brought your sisters over that night. She was planning to stay, but then your dad called and begged her to come home. So she went. She called me and said everything was fine, that all was well, that she believed him." Her aunt sighed. "And she sounded happy again."

Jesslyn rubbed her eyes. Her head hurt. If only her mom and sisters hadn't gone home. She bit her lip and pushed the thought aside. *Focus on something else.*

She turned the poodle over and gasped. "It's there," she said. "The mark." She looked up at her aunt. "You're right. He bought this at the store involved in our investigation." She checked the other pieces, examining each one and silently marveling at their beauty—and still blown away that the logo indicated it came from the same store as the pieces from the fire. Finally, she sat back. "So, what do we do with them?" Jesslyn asked.

Carol reached over and gave her hand a short squeeze. "They belong to you. I've just been their guardian. I'll let you decide that."

"Okay." She'd have to think about that one.

Carol frowned. "You're not upset with me for not giving them to you sooner? When you turned eighteen? I just didn't know how to explain them, and you didn't need the money they would have brought."

On Jesslyn's eighteenth birthday, she'd inherited her parents' estate. It had been enough money to ensure she never had to work a day in her life if she chose not to. But she wanted to work. Had been desperate to excel in school, learn her craft, and graduate.

So she could have a job that would enable her to catch a killer. She reached for her aunt's hand. "I'm not upset with you."

WITH HIS HIP TWINGING PROTESTS, Nathan stood outside the vault while Jesslyn and her aunt conducted whatever business they had going on in there. Kenzie and Cole hovered near the windows, watching for anything that might indicate they were followed.

As of now, there was no sign of Kenny. The officers who'd followed him reported he'd returned to campus just as he said he was going to do and joined his friend group in the student center.

With Kenny taken care of, Nathan should feel a lot more at ease than he did, but he couldn't help asking himself, *If not Kenny, then who?*

He had no idea.

They were getting a few curious looks from the bank's patrons, but Nathan simply shot them a reassuring smile and kept his gaze on the activity in the parking lot.

Again, no one concerning. Customers entered and left. A few he knew and exchanged pleasantries with, but no one that sent his "bad guy" alert chiming.

But if not Kenny, then who?

They'd checked his financials, and no deposits or withdrawals had garnered attention. No red flags. So why had the kid felt the need to run? A knee-jerk reaction to having police approach him? Possibly. But Kenny's unwillingness to talk, his whole evasive attitude, said he knew more. Knew something.

His shoulders twitched and he shot a glance at the vault. What was taking them so long?

Just as the thought passed through his mind, the door opened and Carol emerged, then Jesslyn stepped out, her face set in a frown.

He walked over to her. "Are you all right?"

"Yes. Yeah. Carol filled me in on some family history and it's a lot to process, but I'm fine and I've seen the jewelry." She met his gaze. "The mark on the back is the same as the ones from the fires."

"You thought they might be."

"I know, but to have it confirmed . . ." She shook her head. "It's just weird." She pulled out her phone and showed him a picture of one of the pieces with the little logo. "I mean . . . what are the odds?"

He pursed his lips and thought about that. "I don't know. It's a well-known store, they've been in business forever, and they sell a lot of pieces. I don't think the odds are *that* great. But . . . I'll admit, it does make you kind of wonder."

"Yeah. A lot."

Carol walked over to them, and Kenzie joined them while Cole peered out the window once more. "What are you going to do with the pieces?" Kenzie asked.

Jesslyn hesitated, then gave a short nod. "Sell them. We'll put the money into the youth center."

Carol's eyes went wide. "You're going to what?"

"From everything you've just told me, I think that's what Mom would want." Jesslyn eyed the picture she'd just shown Nathan. "She'd want something good to come from something . . . not so good."

Nathan couldn't help but wish she'd elaborate on that statement, but he wasn't about to ask. Maybe later.

His phone buzzed and he scanned the email. "Got an update on the names you gave us for investigation into your old cases."

"And?"

"Two really stand out. Officers are going to question them. Let's get you back home and settled."

"I'm not going home. I'm going to your office where the files are waiting."

"Files?"

"In the conference room? From the jewelry store? I told you Isa-belle found her grandfather's stash of old store purchase files. I plan to go through them and see if we can match up the jewelry with who bought it." She shot him a tight smile. "You're welcome to help."

Nathan eyed her. "You sure you—"

"Yes, I feel like it, thanks. Can someone make sure my aunt gets home?"

"I can get home fine," Carol said.

Jesslyn caught his eye and he gave a subtle nod. He'd make sure Carol had an escort home—whether she realized it or not. Jesslyn smiled her thanks, kissed her aunt goodbye, and walked out of the bank and to his vehicle. He followed her, sent a short text to make sure Carol had protection, then waited for her to climb in and shut the door. When he slid into the driver's seat, he did his best to cover his wince.

Stupid hip. Stupid Kenny.

His phone buzzed and he glanced at it. Eli yet again. He sent it to voicemail but made a vow to put an end to this nonsense once and for all.

"I won't listen if you need to talk to him."

"There's nothing I need to say to him that I can't say in front of you."

"Oh." She shot him a sideways look. "Okay."

But if he could avoid doing so, he would. "Wanna tell me what had you so shook when you came out of the vault with your aunt?" he asked.

She hesitated, then gave a little shrug. "I learned a few things about my father that I never would have guessed him capable of. I also learned he grew up in and out of foster care, that my paternal grandparents were alcoholics."

"Uh-oh. That doesn't sound good."

"It's not. But it's also a long time ago." She frowned. "I remember him, but I don't. I mean, I can picture my mother a lot easier than my father. I've seen family photos, of course, but it's hard for me to find many memories of him."

"But you must have some."

"Of course. I remember he used to take me over to the neighborhood park and push me on the swings. And he'd pick me up so I could reach the monkey bars. He taught me how to ride a bike, and I remember making pancakes with him sometimes on Saturday mornings. But that's about it." She chewed her bottom lip, and Nathan could almost feel the sadness coming from her.

"What about your mother's parents?"

"They were killed in a car wreck two weeks before I was born."

"Oh my. I'm so sorry, Jesslyn."

He reached over and squeezed her hand, a little surprised when she flipped her palm up and threaded her fingers through his. "Thank you for being so caring, Nathan. I really appreciate it."

Nathan glanced at her and the look in her eyes made him swallow. And remember it was just gratitude. Nothing more. She'd made that clear. He slipped his hand from hers and gripped the steering wheel.

And until she indicated otherwise, he'd respect those wishes.

EIGHTEEN

Jesslyn's mind was on Nathan when they walked into the conference room of the Lake City Police Department. He'd offered comfort and, when she'd accepted it, had pulled away. Of course, she'd made it clear she wasn't interested in anything other than a friendship, but still . . .

No. There was no "still."

He was doing exactly what she'd not so subtly asked him to do. Picked up on her wishes and was honoring them. Because that's the kind of man he was. She needed to be less confusing, stop sending mixed signals.

Not that she meant to. It just seemed like her heart wanted to stray from a lifetime of focus while her head was telling her she needed to stay on track to do what it took to find the person who killed her family. The arsonist she might very well be chasing even now.

Letting romance enter into the picture wasn't part of the plan. She ignored the disappointment that swept through her at the thought, but acknowledged the fear too. The question that she'd not been brave enough to ask herself. Was it possible for her to simply be Jesslyn? A woman in love? Could she leave what had become her mission? Her very identity?

A cold hand squeezed her heart. She had no idea.

Which meant she couldn't have a relationship with anyone until she had time to figure that out. It really *was* that simple.

Kenzie and Cole entered and settled on the other side of the table, leaving the side closest to the door for her and Nathan.

Chief Badami stepped inside the conference room and Jesslyn forced her personal issues to the back burner.

"Good to see you guys here," the chief said. "Let me know if you need anything. Water bottles are in the mini fridge. Think there are some protein bars, chips, and crackers in the cabinet next to the fridge."

"Thanks," Jesslyn said. "Hopefully this won't take too long and we can clear all this out."

His dark eyes were kind, and his skin glowed with good health. She often saw him at the gym with his wife and two children. He played well with other agencies, and while everyone liked him because of his personality, the fact that he excelled at his job made it easy to respect him. Even when he had to let suspects like Kenny go. It wasn't his fault the evidence wasn't there to hold Kenny. It was on the officers and agents to find the evidence.

"It's not a problem," he said. "We don't have any meetings scheduled for a couple of days."

Her phone buzzed with a text from Lainie.

Mr. Christie is awake. Sort of. He's in and out. I'm not sure if he'll be able to talk yet, but his daughter said if he could identify the person who set the fire, he'd want to try. Give him a couple of hours to see if he becomes more alert then stop by if you want.

Jesslyn tapped back a thanks, then read the message aloud for everyone else. Nathan's brow rose. "Well, that's good news."

"Indeed. In the meantime . . ." She passed out hard-copy pictures of the three pieces of jewelry. "This is what we're looking for. Isabelle said her father took a picture of each piece sold and stapled it to the receipt." She pulled the first box of files labeled "A–B" toward her. "Let's see what we can find."

It didn't take her long to go through the first few boxes, even though she had to force herself not to stare at the exquisite, hand-crafted pieces. Mr. McElroy had been an incredibly talented man.

Nathan moved quickly as well, flipping through the pictures and setting boxes to the side. Kenzie and Cole started at the other end of the alphabet and worked backward.

"Man, this place did a *lot* of business," Cole said. "I recognize a lot of wealthy Lake City citizens. Some of these pieces are worth a fortune. Like more than my car." He glanced at Nathan with a smirk. "Not more than yours, though."

"It's not mine."

"Right."

"Shut up."

Jesslyn chuckled. Then they fell silent and continued to work until Kenzie gasped. They all looked at her as one. "What?" Jesslyn asked. Kenzie's face had lost some color and her wide dark eyes were on the paper in front of her. "Kenzie?"

Cole touched her hand, and she swallowed, then met Jesslyn's gaze. "I found the buyer."

"Who?"

She pushed three photos with receipts attached across the table toward Jesslyn. "Your father."

NATHAN WANTED TO OFFER comfort at the shock that froze Jesslyn for a brief moment, but she reached for the papers, her brow furrowed. "My father."

"Owen McCormick, right?"

"Yes."

Nathan looked over her shoulder, breathing in the scent that was only hers, and focused on the receipt and photos. Photos that matched the jewelry pieces from the fires, just as Kenzie said.

Jesslyn rubbed a hand down her face and stood, causing Nathan to shift back so she didn't knock into him. She paced from one end of the conference room to the other. Then again. Nathan glanced at Kenzie and she shook her head. In other words, *Be quiet.* He nodded.

Finally, Jesslyn stopped. "My father is the one who bought the pieces that have shown up at fires?"

Kenzie nodded.

"I'm so confused. Bumfuzzled. That's a word, right?" No one said anything. "All right then," she finally said, tapping her lips, "that opens up a whole new Pandora's box, doesn't it?" She held up an index finger. "Who did he buy them for? My mother? I don't think so or else they would have been in the safe deposit box with all the other pieces he bought her. So, who? Obviously, the woman he was with at some point. So, again, who was that?"

"Wait a minute," Kenzie said, "what are you talking about?"

Nathan wondered too.

Jesslyn hesitated, then seemed to make up her mind about something. "My father cheated on my mother," she said. "Whenever he was feeling guilty, he bought her a custom piece of jewelry, which she never wore because of what it represented."

Kenzie's face dropped into compassion and Cole's jaw tightened. "I'm so sorry, Jess," Kenzie said.

"I am too. I realize this is old history, but it's new to me, so I'm just going to have to process all of this."

"Of course," Cole murmured.

"At a later time. Right now, we need to figure out the next step in all of this. My father bought pieces of custom jewelry over twenty years ago. Those pieces have shown up at various fires connected to me."

"Except for the bank," Nathan said. "How's that fire connected to you?"

"I have no idea, but a piece of jewelry was there, so I'm sure if we dig deep enough, we'll figure it out."

He nodded and Kenzie pursed her lips.

Jesslyn leaned forward and put her palms on the table. "But I've got another question. Why is he buying another woman the same kind of jewelry he bought my mother? For the same reason? How many women did he have on the side? Is there even a way to figure that out?"

She was asking the same questions Nathan was thinking when his phone buzzed again. He checked the screen. A text from Eli.

Can you stop by later? I really need to talk to you.
Or I can come to your place.

Nathan hesitated, then tapped,

Yes, I'll let you know when I'm on the way.

It was time to get to the bottom of whatever was going on with Eli. But he'd go to Eli. If things went south, he didn't want to have to kick his brother out of his house. He wanted to be able to walk away.

Where are you?

Mom and Dad's.

Fine. See you in a bit.

It just dawned on him that he might have Jesslyn with him. Well, he'd just have to leave her with his parents while he and Eli had a chat. Because this whole thing was getting ridiculous.

"Everything okay?" Jesslyn asked him.

He just noted she'd stopped talking and everyone was looking at him. "Fine. Sort of. I can explain later. Right now, I'm thinking we need to figure out who your father's friends were, people he may have confided in, and see if they recognize these pieces."

She nodded. "I'll talk to my aunt about that." She rubbed her head and winced.

"What is it?" Kenzie asked.

"Nothing. Just where I got conked. It's still sensitive."

He frowned, wishing she would take it easy, but was quite sure his suggestion wouldn't be welcomed. Not that she would ignore him, but after a moment of consideration, she'd politely decline.

So he kept his mouth shut. At least she wasn't coughing and her hands didn't seem to be bothering her. If her leg was, it didn't show. Maybe she wasn't as uncomfortable as he would have thought.

Or she was just good at hiding that kind of thing. Probably that. "So, the next steps are for Jesslyn to talk to her aunt about her father's friends and see if she actually knows any of the women he might have been seeing. I need to go see my brother and take a moment to deal with some family stuff."

"Brad's funeral is Wednesday," Cole said. "I think we should plan to attend and see who else is there."

"Agreed," Jesslyn said and Kenzie nodded. Jesslyn's phone rang and she grabbed it. "Hello?" She listened without expression, then said, "Thanks," and hung up. "Well, all of the investigations into my past cases have turned up empty. Every single person has some kind of alibi. Either they're dead, in prison, or have witnesses who are willing to testify where they were. And no, it's not just family willing to say so."

"Okay," Kenzie said, "that's not a bad thing. It saves us time chasing a dead end. Knowing your father bought this jewelry allows us to turn our focus in a different direction."

Nathan nodded. "Now, I've got two places I need to hit. The hospital to see Mr. Christie, then my parents' home to talk to Eli. Jesslyn, you want to come with me? If you feel like it. Or Kenzie and Cole can take you home."

Kenzie's phone went off.

And so did Cole's. "Got a call," he said. "We've got to go."

Jesslyn looked at Nathan. "I guess that answers that question. I just have to change the bandage on my leg and the Band-Aids on my hands and I'll be ready. I'll be very interested in what Mr. Christie has to say."

"You and me both."

Cole and Kenzie left, and after she emerged from the bathroom, Nathan escorted Jesslyn to the car, noting she did favor her leg slightly. "I can take you home if you want and fill you in on what Mr. Christie tells me. Could be a wasted trip."

She shook her head. "I want to see him. My leg is just sore because of me cleaning it and changing the bandage. It'll be fine. I'll just go with you, unless you don't want me to."

"Wouldn't have offered if I didn't want you with me." It was much easier to keep an eye on her when she was within reach. Obviously. "I won't worry about you if I can see you."

She snorted, then huffed a laugh. "Wow. Okay then. How can I refuse?" Just as quickly, her humor faded and she lasered him with a narrow-eyed look. "But when you need to talk to your brother, I'm vanishing, okay?"

"Unless you want to run interference."

"Um. I think James said something to that effect to Lainie a while back. He wanted her presence while he faced off with his father. Thought she would have a calming influence on him."

"Did it work?"

"Yes."

He nodded and started the car. "Good to know."

NINETEEN

Jesslyn called her aunt as soon as she was buckled into the passenger seat and rolling out of the station's parking lot, with Nathan in the driver's seat.

Carol answered on the second ring. "Hi, Jess."

"Hi, Aunt Carol. So, I have a couple of questions for you if you don't mind."

"Don't mind at all."

"Did Mom and Dad have certain friends that they hung around with, did things with? Like couples things? Vacationing, eating out, having dinner parties? I seem to vaguely remember some of that but have no recollection of names."

"Oh sure, they had the Marshalls over a lot. They had a couple of kids your sisters' ages. And I know they were in a small group at church where they became good friends with the Nelsons. Your dad used to golf on Saturdays quite a bit with Bob Nelson."

"Okay, great. Thank you. Could you text me their names and last known contact information if you have it?"

"I'm not sure I have it, but I can look for it. The Nelsons lived two doors down from you. You all were number 9 Wedgewood Lane and the Nelsons were number 5."

"Oh, okay. That makes things a little easier." Jesslyn took a deep breath. "Now for a harder question."

"All right."

Jesslyn grimaced at the wariness that had entered Carol's voice. "Did you know any of the women Dad was . . . um . . . seeing?"

Silence.

Jesslyn stayed quiet, giving the woman time to think. Or maybe try to decide whether she wanted to answer.

A sigh filtered through the line. "I know he was seeing a woman he worked with. I don't know her name."

"How do you know that?"

"I came into town to see your mom. I was supposed to meet her at a restaurant. I got there early and your dad was eating with another woman. I confronted him and let him know your mom was on the way. He left in a hurry, and the woman was mortified to learn he was married and stalked out of the restaurant. Your dad was furious with me, but later apologized and promised it wouldn't happen again."

"But it did."

"Yes."

Jesslyn was already mapping a plan to figure out who the woman was. Surely there was a way, right? "Anyone else?"

"I know there was a woman named Felicia. A friend of your mom's filled her in on that one."

Jesslyn closed her eyes. "Who was the friend?"

"Her hairdresser. Pam Silver at Hair Care and More on Main Street."

Jesslyn had driven past the salon more times than she could count. How did she not know her mother had gone there? "Is Pam still there?"

"I have no idea. I don't go there."

"Okay, thanks, Carol. If you think of anything else, will you let me know?"

"Of course."

Jesslyn hung up, then checked her email. "I've got Charles's report. The gym fire was started with the same chemicals used at the bank and the church."

"Yeah, that's what he said. I'm not surprised."

"I'm not either." She sighed. "I need to make another phone call. You mind?"

"Not at all."

Jesslyn looked up the number for the beauty salon and dialed it. A woman answered identifying the salon. "Hi," Jesslyn said. "Is Pam Silver available by any chance?"

"Sure, sugar, hold on."

Sugar? Jesslyn laughed and Nathan shot her a questioning look, but before she could explain, a woman's low voice said, "Pam speaking."

Laughter fled and a rock lodged itself in her throat. "Hello, Pam. I was wondering if you'd have a few minutes to chat in person."

"What's this about?"

"I believe you were friends with Linda McCormick years ago."

The woman gasped. "Yes, I was. Who is this?"

"Her daughter, Jesslyn."

Another gasp. "Oh, my word, are you for real?"

"Yes, ma'am."

"Well, I'll be. I knew you went to live with Linda's sister, but always wondered what happened to you after that."

"I'm back in Lake City and would love to ask you some questions about my parents. Would you have time to meet with me today?"

"I got a full schedule this afternoon but could talk to you first thing in the morning."

"Well, see, here's the thing, I'm now a state deputy fire marshal, so I'm helping investigate the recent fires. I really need to connect with you fairly quickly."

"Oh my . . . those fires. It's just terrible. And you think I can help?"

"I'm not sure. That's why I want to talk to you."

"Hold on a sec." Jesslyn did. Seconds later, Pam returned. "All right. We close early on Mondays. If you can get here in about forty-five minutes, we'll have time after my last client. Will that work?"

"Can you hold a second to make sure?" Jesslyn muted the phone.

"Pam can see us in forty-five minutes. Should we head to see her first, then Mr. Christie, then your brother?"

Nathan glanced at the clock on the dash. "I think I need to head over to talk to my brother first. Get it over with. It's only a few minutes from that salon, and this will keep it quick."

Jesslyn unmuted her phone and confirmed their meeting. As she hung up, a wave of fatigue hit her, but she did her best to push it aside. Her hands were itching and her leg was throbbing. She ignored those too.

"Okay. I'm just going to close my eyes for a few minutes." She was tired. Very tired. She closed her eyes and leaned her head back to think.

Her next moment of awareness was Nathan's hand on her shoulder. "Hey. Jess. We're here."

She blinked up at him and her heart stuttered at the gentle look in his eyes and slight frown of concern on his face. "Oh, man. I must have passed out."

"Sort of." He smiled and she let her gaze drop to his lips. What would it be like if she—

She rubbed her eyes to break the moment and cleared her throat. "Sorry about that."

"It's fine. You needed to."

"Should I stay out here?"

"No. I want you close by. Inside is safer. Besides, Mom will enjoy talking to you."

She checked her appearance in the visor mirror to make sure she didn't have sleep in her eyes or drool on her chin. She didn't. "All right. I'm ready when you are."

He led the way out of the car and the wind whipped her hair around her face. She shivered and shoved the strands aside and admired the traditional ranch home. It had been updated with a white coat of paint over the brick. Black shutters graced the windows and the landscaping was absolute perfection. "Who's the green thumb? Winter has muted it, but I can tell it's probably beautiful in the spring and summer."

"Mom. She loves gardening and yard work." He wrinkled his nose and shook his head.

"I'm guessing you don't."

"Nope. My sister Carly does, but Eli and I never learned to love it. Dad helps Mom, but just because he loves her, not because he loves the work."

For a moment, Jesslyn's world darkened and she couldn't help the flash of sheer fury that zipped through her. She could have had a family like this. *Should* have had a family, period. *Should* have worked in the yard with her mother, played in the park with her sisters, had her dad teach her how to drive. Her uncle Sean had taught her, then walked out of their lives the next year. They'd all been devastated.

"Jess?"

She took a deep breath. "Sorry, was just thinking." She forced a smile, grateful he didn't push her about her thoughts.

He rapped his knuckles on the door and pushed it open. "Mom? Dad? Eli?" The hardwoods in the foyer gleamed with a recent polish. The living room to the right was done in neutral colors with the exception of a light blue sofa that offered a splash of color. Footsteps sounded from the den area straight ahead, and the man she recognized from the hospital stepped into view.

Eli.

He smiled and she noted a dimple exactly like Nathan's in his left cheek. They were definitely brothers. Eli nodded to her, his smile slipping into a slight frown. "Hi."

"Hello."

"Jesslyn and I are on the way to another appointment. She can visit with Mom and Dad while we talk."

"Mom and Dad aren't here."

Nathan paused. "Great."

"Hey," Jesslyn said. "I don't want to be in the way. Just point me in the direction of a comfy couch or chair and I can work on my phone."

Once she was settled in a very comfortable recliner with a bottle of water and a pain pill in her system, Nathan kept his coat on, Eli grabbed a blanket, and they walked out onto the back deck and shut the French doors behind them. She sent up a silent prayer that the brothers could work through whatever was causing them division, then she pulled her phone out and began reading through the bank's fire report one more time.

What was the connection with her?

Or maybe it wasn't a direct connection with her, but something else?

Someone who banked there that she knew? Good grief, that could be anyone. She should have asked her aunt Carol, but she'd been so thrown by the story of her parents' marriage and everything they'd been going through, it had slipped her mind.

She yawned. She was so sleepy. The physical and mental fatigue were taking a toll on her and she was making mistakes. Mistakes she couldn't afford to make if she was going to catch the arsonist before he struck again. She could see Nathan and Eli sitting opposite each other at a brown wicker table.

But they didn't seem to be talking.

She frowned. It looked like they might be a while, so she called her aunt Carol and got her voicemail. "Hey, call me when you get a chance. Thanks." Then she closed her eyes once more.

NATHAN REFUSED TO BE the first one to speak. A little voice whispered that he was being immature, but at the moment he didn't care. Okay, he cared. A little. But Eli just sat there, head down, eyes on the table.

Nathan checked his phone. Okay, enough was enough. He'd be the mature one. "What are you doing here at Mom and Dad's? Why aren't you at your place?"

Eli finally lifted his head. "I don't have a place anymore. I sold it and moved home until my other house is built."

"What other house?"

"I bought a piece of land out near your friend James's lake house. Figured it would do me good to get out of the city and be somewhere peaceful."

Whoa. Nathan really was out of the loop. "No one told me that."

Eli shrugged. "It was kind of a recent thing. I just signed the papers last week. Closing on my old place and buying the new."

"And they're your friends too, you know."

"Not really. Sure, y'all let me hang out occasionally, but I'm not a part of that group."

Nathan couldn't refute that, and all of a sudden he was sad about it. "Maybe we can do something about that, but first, what's this all about? Why do you keep bringing up the past? Why can't you just let it be and move on?" Taking the direct route seemed to be the quickest way to reach the end.

"Just rip the Band-Aid off, huh?" Eli said. "Speaking of Band-Aids, how's your hip?"

"It hurts. Quit stalling. You got me here, now let's talk."

"Right. Okay. Then, here's another Band-Aid rip. It was my fault," Eli said, his voice so low, Nathan almost missed it.

"What was your fault?"

"Danny's death."

Nathan blinked, having trouble processing the words. When it finally registered what Eli was saying, he scoffed. "Really? How was it your fault? Because if I remember correctly, I was the one who wanted to make the s'mores. I was the one who suggested to Danny that we sneak out to the shed that had no ventilation with a lighter and some wood kindling. I even lit the wood. I did all that. So, tell me, Eli, why would you say that it was your fault?"

Eli met his gaze. "Because I was the one who blocked the door so you couldn't get out."

Nathan had never been stunned speechless before. Not in all his years in law enforcement or any other time that he could think of, but today, he found himself in that moment.

Eli shuddered. Two tears tracked his cheeks and he looked away.

Nathan continued to stare at him. After several more seconds, Eli palmed his eyes. "Say something."

"What in the world should I say?"

"Ask me why?"

"I know why. You were put in charge of a younger brother and his friend and you resented it. So you thought you'd be cute and lock us in."

Eli swallowed and nodded. "Yeah," he whispered. "I guess you do know."

"You always hated having the responsibility of Carly and me."

Eli nodded again. "Especially when there was a party up the street I wanted to go to. I saw you sneak into the shed after I told y'all to play video games upstairs. I figured I'd teach you a lesson."

Nathan flinched, then let the anger rise. "How'd that work out for you?"

Eli gasped and a sob escaped as he dropped his head into his hands. Conviction pierced Nathan right through the heart, but he couldn't seem to bring himself to apologize. Or block his own tears.

He stood and paced to the railing to look out over the backyard. His mother had been working. Her flowers were still blooming despite the cold weather. And why did he even notice that?

"I'm sorry," Eli whispered, breath shuddering. "I'm so sorry. I don't even think words exist to express how sorry I am."

It had been eighteen years since that horrible night. Eighteen years of self-blame, guilt, shame, and nightmares.

"I didn't know what you were going to do," Eli said. "I didn't know you planned to build a *fire*. I just thought y'all were being little brats and deliberately doing the exact opposite of what I told you to do. If I had known, I'd have never—"

Nathan turned to face him. "Why are you telling me this now?"

"Because I'm selfish." Eli laughed. A sound without an ounce of humor in it. "I think about it every day. Lately, it's worse. I can't sleep. I can't focus at work. I can't . . . live. I was . . . uh . . . hoping you'd go with me to counseling so I could drop this bomb with a professional there to help walk us through it, but . . ." He ran a hand over his hair, then dropped it to fiddle with the cuff of his sleeve. "It became obvious that you weren't going to go along with that, so this is it." He swallowed and let out a shuddering sigh while Nathan simply stared. "I have no life because of the guilt," Eli said. "And I don't know how to make it right, get my life back, except to tell what really happened and face the consequences."

"You can't make it right. The consequences are Danny's dead and he's never coming back."

"Don't you think I know that?" Eli's shout was carried away by the wind, but it echoed in Nathan's head. And heart. His brother had been suffering too.

But Nathan was struggling. Making himself feel something besides disbelief and . . . hate? resentment? yes, all of those . . . was difficult. Eli had been a selfish teenager, argumentative, disruptive, wanting only to do what Eli wanted to do and no one and nothing else mattered.

But . . . deep down, even as angry and shocked as he was at this confession, Nathan believed Eli never considered that his actions would result in the death of Danny. He'd wanted to scare the boys, maybe even terrify them.

Nathan looked at his broken brother.

He hadn't meant for anyone to die.

And yet, someone had. So, where did they go from here?

TWENTY

Jesslyn jerked awake at the shout that had come from the deck. She sat up to see Nathan standing at the railing. Eli had his face in his hands and his shoulders trembled. Oh dear. Something was going down and it didn't look good.

Nathan turned on his heel, strode past his brother, and stepped inside. He gazed at her, and his features softened a fraction. "Are you ready?"

"Sure. I had a nice little nap." She'd keep her throbbing leg to herself. "Are you okay?"

"No, not really. I can't be here a second longer."

She frowned and glanced at Eli, who still sat at the table on the deck. He still had his face in his hands and his shoulders still shook. The man was sobbing. "Nathan—"

"Leave him. I'll . . . I need to cool off and think before I can talk to him anymore. He'll be all right."

"You can't leave him like that."

His eyes hardened. "It's better if I do, Jesslyn. Trust me. If I don't walk away, I'll say something that will only make a bad thing worse."

She bit her lip and let her gaze bounce between the men. "All right. If you're sure, then let's go."

"I'm sure." He glanced at the clock on the mantel and Jesslyn snuck another look at Eli. He'd stopped crying and was staring out over the backyard. Maybe he *would* be all right, and having some time apart would be the best thing for both of them.

"Let's go see Pam," he said. "I think she might actually be more help than Mr. Christie at this point."

"All right." She led the way out of the house, and he followed her to the car.

They climbed in, and within seconds, he was backing out of the drive and heading toward the salon. He drove with clenched hands and a tight jaw. His hip didn't seem to be bothering him that much at the moment, which meant his adrenaline must be flowing pretty good.

She bit her tongue on all the questions she wanted to ask. He was in no mood to talk, so she'd just give him some space, and when he was ready, he'd tell her what was going on.

By the time they reached the salon, Nathan had relaxed some. Enough that she didn't think his teeth were going to shatter. The salon was just closing up when they walked in, and a woman in her early sixties was sweeping the floor. Her classy, styled shoulder-length hair swung around her face. She straightened and turned at their entrance, and Jesslyn's first thought was how good she looked for her age. She had green eyes and wore understated makeup that made her appear younger than her years. She was the only one left in the place.

"Hi," Jesslyn said, "are you Pam?"

"The one and only, hon." She smiled. "And you're Jesslyn. You look just like your mama. Wow."

"Thank you. And this is Special Agent Nathan Carlisle with the FBI. He's a friend of mine and we're working on the arson case together."

"FBI, huh?" Pam's perfectly arched brows rose into her bangs. "All right. Now you got me curious how all this fits with your mother. This is going to call for a sit-down." She set the broom aside, locked the entrance, and motioned for them to follow her. She led them to a small break room that held a table and chairs for four. "Y'all need any water or a snack?"

"I'm fine," Jesslyn said, and Nathan echoed her.

They sat and Pam clasped her hands in front of her. "Wow. Last time I saw you was just before the fire." She blinked away a sheen of tears. "I still miss your mama."

Jesslyn blanked, wishing she could remember the woman.

Pam leaned forward. "All right, I'm listening."

Jesslyn sent up a silent prayer for answers and took a breath. She let it out slowly while she gathered her words. "All right. So, I'm the new deputy fire marshal. I vowed to one day catch the person responsible for my family's murder and I feel like I'm getting closer to doing so."

More tears gathered in Pam's eyes, and once more, she blinked them away. "Some days I still can't believe she's gone. I was a couple of years older than her, but we were friends since high school. The age difference never mattered to us. And if we didn't see each other for a while, that didn't matter either. As soon as we were back together, we picked up where we left off."

This time a memory surfaced. Sitting in a stylist's chair and this woman spinning Jesslyn around until she nearly fell out laughing. "Wait, I *do* remember you. You used to cut my hair."

She nodded and a smile glimmered. "And your sisters' too."

"And did you babysit every so often?"

"I did. You remember that?"

"Just vaguely, but yes, I think I do." She glanced around the shop. "This store is different."

"Yep. We renovated a few years back, but I know you're not here for small talk. Why don't you tell me how I can help you."

"My aunt said you told my mother about a woman named Felicia. A woman my dad was . . . um . . ." She rubbed a hand over her eyes, then clasped her fingers together in front of her. "Seeing."

Pam swallowed. "Oh. She told you about that, huh?"

"Just recently and only because of some things that have come to light."

"I see. So you want to know . . . ?"

"Who is this woman, Felicia? What's her last name and how do I find her?"

"Why do you want to find her?"

"I have questions for her. Please, it's important. I don't want to cause her pain or bring up any bad memories. If this wasn't a matter of life or death, I'd never ask."

"Life or death. Wow. Okay. Well, her last name is Smart and I still cut her hair every month like clockwork." She pulled her phone out of her back pocket and tapped the screen. "Here you go." She rattled off Felicia's information. "As far as how I discovered your father was being unfaithful, whew, honey, I remember the day like it was yesterday. Felicia came in for her monthly cut and was all excited. She started telling me about this man she'd met and then showed me a picture of him. They'd done one of those goofy booths at some event one night. You know where you get a strip of four black-and-white pictures? This was way before selfies. Anyway, she showed them to me and I was stunned. I was like, that's my best friend's husband. Felicia didn't believe me at first, but I finally convinced her and she was furious." She crossed her arms and shook her head. "Ran out like her pants were on fire after I finished drying her hair. She was so mad and in such a hurry, she forgot to pay me that day. Next time she came in, she said she'd given Owen his marching papers and if he ever contacted her again, she'd tell Linda."

"Part of me wishes she had," Jesslyn murmured.

"Well, she probably figured I'd take care of that. And I did. After much contemplation and a few sleepless nights."

"What did Mom say?"

Pam pressed her fingers to her lips and shook her head. "She didn't react at first. Then after about thirty seconds, she thanked me for telling her and said she'd talk to Owen. The next time I saw her, I asked her how things were and she simply said they'd worked out the issues and everything was fine. And I think it was for a while."

"Thank you for telling her. I know that had to be one of the hardest things to do, but thank you."

"You're right. I didn't want to say anything," Pam said. "But I couldn't *not* say something. She was my friend. If the situation was reversed, I'd want to know."

"You were caught between a rock and a hard place."

"Yes, but I think she knew there was someone before I told her. She never said, but I got the feeling she wasn't surprised."

"Felicia wasn't the first."

"Right. I suspected either she wasn't the first or your mom already knew there was someone, she just didn't have a name. I gave her the name so she could use it when she talked to Owen."

"Do you know if my dad gave Felicia any jewelry?"

"He did."

"Do you recognize any of these?" Jesslyn pulled up the collage of pictures of the jewelry from the fires, then turned her phone so the woman could see the screen.

Pam looked at it and her eyes narrowed. "Well, I know Owen gave Felicia a bracelet because she showed that off to me before she showed me his picture, but I don't recognize any of those pieces. He wouldn't have had time to give her anything else. He'd just given her the bracelet the night before. She later told me she went to him and threw it in his face, then regretted not keeping it when she calmed down. Said she could have sold it for a nice sum."

Jesslyn tucked her phone away with a flash of disappointment. When she looked up, her smile was in place. "Thank you for meeting with us."

"I'm sorry I couldn't help more."

"You've been more help than you know. Thank you again."

"Of course." Pam hesitated. "Do you mind if I hug you? You look so much like your mother that I think it might be like giving her one last hug."

"I don't mind a bit." They stood and Jesslyn wrapped her arms around the woman and received the sweetest, tightest, yet most gentle squeeze she'd had in a while. A hug from someone other than Aunt Carol who'd known and loved her mother. It was a blessing.

Nathan had remained silent during the chat, but shook hands and murmured his goodbyes.

Pam locked the door behind them, and they walked out to his vehicle, his limp more pronounced.

"Hip bothering you?" she asked. She'd rather bug him about his hip than think about confronting a woman her father had dated while married to her mother.

"Nah, it's fine."

"Sure it is."

He cut her a sideways look and laughed. "Okay, yes, it's bothering me. I've got some pain pills that'll help in a little bit."

He slid behind the wheel with a soft grunt and she rolled her eyes. Men.

THEY SAT IN SILENCE FOR A MOMENT. Nathan popped two little pills that would hopefully ease the ache in his hip, and Jesslyn stared out the window, lost in her thoughts.

He let her think.

After several seconds, she turned to him. "I guess we should confirm with Felicia that the bracelet was the only piece of jewelry my father gave her."

"Might be a good thing to do, though it sounds like he didn't have time for more than that one piece she threw in his face."

"True. But just to be sure? And I have another idea," Jesslyn said.

"What's that?"

"Aunt Carol said Mom thought my dad was having an affair with someone in the neighborhood. That he would leave the house and be gone all night, then return just before everyone got up. But he never drove. He always walked."

"Okay."

"I want to find out who was living in that neighborhood the same time we were. It's a narrow timeframe so it shouldn't be too hard.

Then we can narrow it down by age and gender. I'd say women ten years on either side of my dad should be a good range."

"What are you going to do? Track down each one and ask them if they knew your father?"

"Yes. Basically. I guess."

"Lindsay should be able to find them, but it might take a while."

"We can start questioning people as the names come in. Starting with the Nelson family—assuming I can find them. They lived a couple doors down."

"That works for me. In the meantime, why don't you reach out to Lainie to see if Mr. Christie can talk."

"I'll do that right now." Jesslyn got on her phone.

Nathan's buzzed with a text from Eli.

> I'm sorry. I can't make it right. I can't ever make it right and I don't know how to express how sorry I am. I don't know how to deal with this kind of all-consuming pain and guilt. I just don't know.

Nathan groaned. He shouldn't have let his emotions rule him. He definitely shouldn't have walked away from Eli. He tapped the screen.

> Give me some time to absorb everything and we'll talk again. I know you're sorry. I am too. We'll work it out.

"Nathan?"

He looked up. "Sorry. Eli was texting me and I needed to answer."

"It's fine."

He texted Andrew, asking for an update from him. *Nothing to report*, came his reply. *Stay tuned.*

Jesslyn looked up and shook her head. "Lainie said Mr. Christie is unconscious again. She'll let us know if anything changes."

"All right then, let's get this taken care of."

Ten minutes later, he pulled to a stop in front of Felicia Smart's home and glanced at Jesslyn. "You okay?"

"No. Not really."

She'd thrown his answer back at him. The same thing he'd said just before walking out of his parents' home.

"Want me to take over?" he asked.

"No. I've got this."

She knocked on the door and stepped back to wait. Finally, footsteps approached and the door opened. A woman about the same age as Pam looked out at them. She was slender and had friendly blue eyes beneath the stylish dark hair streaked with gray. Growing old gracefully? "Hello," Jesslyn said. They introduced themselves and showed badges. "Pam Silver gave me your information. I hope you don't mind."

"Pam? I guess not. What can I do for you?"

Jesslyn glanced at Nathan. "Well, I don't want to go through the whole spiel of why I'm here, but I believe you knew my father, Owen McCormick."

The friendly eyes turned hard. "I knew him. Briefly. It wasn't a good experience."

"I understand you may not want to talk about it, but if you could just answer a few questions, I'd really appreciate it."

"What kinds of questions?" She stepped out onto the porch and let the door shut behind her. Then she crossed her arms.

"We know he gave you a piece of jewelry. A bracelet."

"He did and I threw it in his face when I found out he was a cheater."

Jesslyn gave a subtle flinch and Nathan placed a hand on her lower back before he thought about it.

"Stupidest thing I could have done. I should have kept it and sold it, but I was angry."

"I don't blame you," Jesslyn said. "Is that the only piece he gave you?"

"Yes."

"Do you know of any other women he might have been . . . with? Besides you?"

"No. I never spoke to him after that day, and he certainly never said anything about other women in our short three weeks of dating—or whatever you can call it when one person is married."

"I see. Do you mind looking at some other jewelry to see if you recognize any?"

"Sure."

Nathan held out his phone and Felicia leaned in with a squint. She studied the three pieces and frowned. "No. They don't look familiar."

"Do you know what happened to the bracelet?" Jesslyn asked.

"I assume he took it back to the store or gave it to some other poor unsuspecting woman."

Jesslyn glanced at Nathan, silently asking if he had any questions. He rubbed his chin and shook his head. She'd done a good job and he couldn't think of anything else to add.

"Do you mind if we call you if we have more questions?" Jesslyn asked.

"I don't mind." She huffed. "You'd think I'd be over that experience, but it broke something inside me to realize there are men like that in the world. And I hear they're having some sort of shindig to honor him. A building with his name on it, of all things." She rolled her eyes, then frowned. "Sorry. I know he was your father, but a man like that doesn't deserve to have his name on a building."

"I know it seems like that," Jesslyn said, her voice low, "but he changed before he died. At least that's what my aunt says."

Felicia stilled. "Well, he did send me a note saying he was sorry and hoped I could forgive him someday, so maybe he did change. And truly, I'm not really angry anymore. I've moved on. Your questions were just a shock and brought back old feelings that I let go a long time ago." She paused. "At least I thought I had."

Jesslyn blinked. "Wait a minute, he sent you a letter?"

"Came in the mail about a week before he died. I didn't know if he was sincere or not, but from what you say, then maybe he was."

"I want to believe that."

For the first time since they arrived, Felicia offered a small but genuine smile. "You know what? So do I."

Once they were back in the car, Jesslyn's phone rang. "It's Lainie." She tapped the screen and turned on the speaker. "Hello?"

"Hey, shortly after we talked earlier, Mr. Christie woke up. He was still in and out, but he doesn't remember much. I asked him about the fire, and he said he was working in the kitchen area when he smelled smoke. Went to investigate and saw someone bent over a bucket that I think was the accelerant. Mr. Christie walked over and asked what he thought he was doing. Then said the person turned so fast and knocked him in the head. The next thing he remembers is waking up in the hospital."

"Wow."

"Right."

"So, he never saw the person's face."

"That's what he said."

"Thanks, Lainie," Nathan said. "I'll let Andrew know. He'll want to come by there and confirm the story."

"You're welcome. Stay safe."

Nathan called Andrew and filled him in on Lainie's report and what they'd learned from Pam and Felicia about the jewelry, then hung up.

"That poor man," she whispered. "This guy knew Mr. Christie would likely die in that fire and he left him there. That's a whole other level of evil."

"I know."

TWENTY-ONE

As soon as Jesslyn buckled up, her phone buzzed with a call from Carol. "Hello?"

"Hey, sweetie, you needed me to call?"

"Yes, good timing, thanks. So there was a bank that burned down a few days before the church fire. I was out of town at a conference, and no one realized there was a connection to the other two fires until recently." She told her the name of the bank. "Can you think of any connection I might have to that bank?"

Silence.

"Aunt Carol?"

"Jesslyn, your mom almost took a job at that branch just a few days before she died."

A taser hit couldn't have shocked her more. "What? Why? I didn't think she needed to work."

"Money wasn't an issue. It was more her wanting some independence. She had the jewelry, of course, but the job was her safety net in case . . ."

Jesslyn swallowed. "Right. In case she wound up leaving Dad. What did Dad say?"

"He wasn't happy when she told him she'd taken the job. He put two and two together and said if she was planning a future without him, then why were they even trying? She didn't have an answer for that. He disappeared that night like he'd done so many times, and she packed up you kids and came over and cried on my shoulder a while. Then she pulled herself back together and said he was right and she was going to tell them she wasn't going to be able to take the job."

"But that's not fair," Jesslyn said. "What if she really wanted to work it?"

A sigh filtered through the line. "I think she wanted to, just for something different in addition to it being more security for her and you girls. But her marriage was her priority, and if staying home was what it took to keep it together, then that's what she'd do."

"Sounds like Dad was really good at gaslighting people."

"Well, yes. He was. In fact, I pointed that out to your mother that night and asked her if she was going to let him do that to her."

Jesslyn pinched the bridge of her nose. "And?"

"She said she recognized the ploy, but just in case it was real and he really meant what he was saying, not just trying to manipulate her, then she had to give it a shot. She went to the bank the next day and asked if she could delay her start date. They told her no."

"I see." Jesslyn bit her lip, thinking, processing, trying to keep her emotions out of it. "It's almost as if the fact that she *could* leave made her try harder to keep their marriage together."

It made sense in some weird way.

Her phone buzzed and she glanced at a text message. "Oh boy," she muttered.

"What?"

She covered the speaker on the phone and said, "Head to the Lake City General Store. It's on fire."

"What?" Nathan gunned the engine.

"Thanks, Carol. I've got to go. If I have any more questions, I'll call."

"I know you will. Your cousins are coming home for a visit next week. We'll put them to work on the benefit."

"Sounds good. I look forward to seeing them." She hung up, and five minutes later, Nathan pulled into the back of the parking lot of the Lake City General Store. Smoke billowed from the log cabin–type structure with flames shooting out from the windows.

Her heart shuddered. She shopped here on a regular basis.

She stared at the blaze, the conversation with her aunt lingering in the back of her mind, but her focus on the scene before them. "He knows I shop here," she murmured. "Often. This is my go-to store."

Nathan nodded. "Yeah. Unfortunately."

They climbed out of the car, eyes on the fire. Nathan's presence beside her offered more comfort than she wanted to admit. "I go a lot of places," she said. "I have a connection with just about every place in Lake City. How do I warn them all? How do I . . ." She waved a hand at the enormity of the idea.

"There's no way."

There really wasn't, but . . . "I feel like I need to try."

"Who else would you call?"

"The fire station for starters."

"Oof," he said, "yeah. Tell them to be on the lookout for anyone hanging around and showing unusual interest in the place."

Fire trucks screamed into the parking lot and Jesslyn waited for them to stop a safe distance from the blaze. Firefighters she knew and respected spilled out of the trucks and went to work in their fast-paced, well-practiced choreography of courage.

To anyone else it might look like chaos, but to Jesslyn it was poetry in motion. Familiar. Safe. "Do you know if anyone is in there?" she asked a bystander.

"No, I don't think so," the woman said. "There were about ten of us, and as soon as we realized smoke was coming from the back area, we all ran out."

Jesslyn motioned to one of the firefighters. "I know this store has a gas fireplace. Has the gas been shut off?"

"I don't know, but I'll make sure. Thanks." He trotted off and Jesslyn turned to Nathan. "I'll be back." She had duties to attend to.

He nodded. "I'm going to walk through the onlookers and see if

I spot anyone I recognize." He glanced at his phone. "Andrew is on his way too."

Jesslyn found the chief and waited for a break in his spiel of orders to approach. "Chief Laramie."

"Jesslyn. What are you doing here? Thought you were taking some time off."

"I am, but . . ."

He raised a brow. "Right."

"You'll let me know if you find a piece of jewelry?"

"ASAP."

"Thanks." She spent the next two hours talking to people at the scene, questioning if they'd noticed anyone hanging around, looking suspicious. She didn't get much to work with, but wrote everything down. She'd return when the fire was out and safe to walk through. When she finally took a break, Nathan walked over and handed her a bottle of water. She chugged it. "How'd you know I needed that?"

"I've been watching."

He had, huh?

"Listen, I've got to run. I got a weird text from Eli. I typed out a response, but never sent it. I just realized that and called him, but he's not picking up his phone."

"What kind of weird text?"

"I'm not sure, but it doesn't sound like him."

"You're worried."

He nodded and she patted his shoulder. "All right. Go find him. I'll text you when I'm done here and ready to head home."

"Thanks. Just don't go anywhere unless you have someone with you. Someone who can use a gun."

"I have a gun and I know how to use it."

He narrowed his eyes. "I know. I just think it's best if you're not alone right now."

"I know. I feel safer with someone watching my back, so don't worry, I'll make sure to stay with people I trust."

"Good." He hesitated. "Jesslyn, I like you."

She blinked. "I like you too, Nathan."

"No, I mean, I *like like* you. I want to ask you out on a date, but I've picked up on your 'keep your distance' signals and I'm trying to honor those." He glanced around. "I know this isn't the best time to bring this up, but I've been thinking about this awhile and just wanted *you* to think about it. Think about going on a date with me. I won't ask you for anything you're not ready to give, I just want to get to know you more. Spend time with you away from all of this."

It was all Jesslyn could do to keep her jaw from swinging. He was right. This wasn't the time. "Nathan—"

"Nope. Not right now. Focus on the fire. We'll talk about us later."

Us?

He squeezed her fingers and then he was gone.

All righty then. She had some thinking to do.

Her phone buzzed. Lindsay from the bureau. "Hello?"

"I've got some interesting information for you. You know how you wanted a list of all the people who lived in the neighborhood the same time you did?"

"Of course."

"I've got that. I'm sending it to your email."

"That was incredibly fast."

"I pulled in reinforcements."

"Awesome. Be sure to send it to Nathan and Andrew too, will you?"

"Already done. Check your inbox."

She would just as soon as she was done with this fire. She'd use it as a distraction from obsessing over the fact that Nathan *like liked* her.

NATHAN DIDN'T WANT TO LEAVE HER, but he had a bad feeling in his gut about Eli. Some internal warning was telling him to go find his brother. Before their conversation and the last text from Eli, he'd never have believed his brother was suicidal but had to admit that thought was in his head. He could only pray it wasn't in Eli's, but . . .

His parents were out of town for the week with friends at Hilton Head. Carly and her husband, Kip, had left yesterday while Brandon, his nephew, stayed with friends.

Eli was well and truly alone, and if he was planning to self-harm—he had a hard time thinking "kill himself"—this would be the time to do it.

Please let me be wrong, God. Let me be wrong.

He gunned his vehicle toward his parents' home and his mind went back to Jesslyn and the look on her face when he'd told her to think about going out with him. He was an idiot. That had not been the place or time to do that. What had he been thinking? Obviously, he hadn't. But she was a professional. She wouldn't let that little moment of his weirdness interfere with what she had to do at the scene. Comforting himself with that thought, he pressed the gas a little harder.

The drive took only fifteen minutes, but he tried Eli's phone four times and each time it rolled to voicemail.

Eli never turned off his phone. Ever.

Nathan turned into his parents' driveway and spotted Eli's silver sedan in the third parking spot. He climbed out and pressed a hand to the hood. Stone cold.

He jogged up the front porch steps and knocked on the door. "Eli? You here?"

No answer.

He found the key under the little porcelain bunny in the mulch, opened the door, and stepped inside. "Eli?"

All appeared well in the house. Nothing out of place. He cleared it quickly, then stopped in the den to look out on the deck. The exterior lights were on and Eli sat on the top step facing the backyard.

Nathan walked back into the kitchen, grabbed two bottles of water out of the fridge, then went back to the sliding glass door. He rapped his knuckles on it, and Eli started so bad, Nathan was glad his brother had a healthy heart. He slid the door open. "You okay?" he asked. Eli turned, his face ravaged with a sorrow so deep Nathan almost fell to his knees. He set the bottles on the table and walked toward him. "Eli, man, what's going on?"

"What are you doing here, Nathan?"

"You sent me that weird text so I came to check on you." He walked to the steps and sat next to his brother.

And then noticed the gun in Eli's right hand. Nathan stilled, doing his best not to react. His heart thudded and he couldn't help drawing in a steadying breath. "What are you doing with that?"

"I don't know yet."

"I answered your text. I just got distracted and didn't hit send until about thirty minutes ago."

Eli looked up, the dark circles under his eyes giving him a haunted appearance. "I thought you were ghosting me."

"So you were going to kill yourself?"

"Maybe. Thought about it."

"You're holding a gun. That's more than thinking about it. Can you put that thing down, please?"

"No."

A chill swept through Nathan and he was more certain than ever if he hadn't come now, Eli very possibly wouldn't be alive to see tomorrow.

"Why not?" Nathan asked. He sent up a silent prayer of thanks for the divine nudging to come check on his brother.

"Because I'm not completely sure I don't want to use it."

"You have it aimed at the ground."

"Well, with my luck, I'd change my mind and the stupid thing would go off anyway."

"You really want to die?"

A hefty sigh escaped Eli's lips. "No. I really don't. I just don't know how else to make the pain stop. I don't know how to move on from the past. I don't know how to repair the damage to us." He swiped a sliding tear. "It's ironic, isn't it? I talk to clients all day long and

LYNETTE EASON

offer words of advice and what I hope are wisdom, but I can't seem to put into practice those words for myself. I don't know how to heal—or forgive—myself."

Nathan wanted to press his palms to his burning eyes but couldn't bring himself to take his gaze off the gun. Should he address the whole idea of self-forgiveness now or save it? Maybe just talking would help. "A lot of people think they should be able to forgive themselves, but that's not really a thing."

"What?"

"After Danny died and after a couple of years of counseling, I finally started doing research on how to forgive myself for what happened."

"What'd you find, because it must have worked."

"I figured out that forgiving yourself just isn't something you can do."

Eli huffed. "Well, that's just great news."

"The better news is all forgiveness comes from God. The need to find a way to forgive ourselves comes from the need to be released from the guilt we feel about something."

"Yep, that guilt is a real killer."

"But guilt isn't from God. There's no condemnation in him, re-member?"

"I feel condemned. Condemned to a lifetime of pain and guilt. I can't get away from it."

"Eli, the issue isn't you forgiving yourself, but accepting the for-giveness that God offers you. In doing that, you'll find that he gives you the ability to release the guilt and shame that's got a strangle-hold on you." He sighed. "Once I realized that I have no power of forgiveness over my own sins, that it was up to God, then because I believe he is who he says he is—which is a loving, forgiving God who has a plan for my life—then . . ." He rubbed both hands down his cheeks. "I chose to grab on to that and hold it tight. Some days it's more tangible than others. But I feel it. I feel his forgiveness. And even when I don't feel it, I still know it because I know him. That's why I know you can too."

Eli had been hanging on every word. His eyes started to glow with a fragment of hope. "You really think so?"

"I know so. One hundred percent." He eyed the weapon. "We've gone years, Eli, without all of . . . this. Why now?"

"You know, Mom and Dad never once accused me or blamed me for not watching out for you guys. They never said a word. And they never looked at me with accusation in their eyes. And because they didn't, it helped me bury it all." He flicked his gaze to Nathan. "That and the fact I could tell you didn't remember that I was supposed to be there, that there were some gaps about some things. Like my best bud came by to hang out and we had the music going so loud, I didn't hear the screams until it was too late." More tears swept down his cheeks and he swiped them away with his sleeve. A shudder rippled through him. "Anyway, I'd buried it for so long that I figured it would stay there. But then I had a client who was responsible for the death of her brother. She'd done something similar—played a mean trick on him—and he died. She was devastated. Turned to drugs and alcohol to dull the pain. In rehab, she had to face it, and one of the things she's supposed to do upon leaving the inpatient facility is to get counseling three times a week. Guess who was assigned to her?"

"You."

"Of course. When she was telling me about it, you can imagine the memories that dredged up for me. I tried to stuff it all back down, but it wouldn't stay there. I wake up in the night from nightmares of trying to break into the shed to get you and Danny out. I can't eat. I can't focus at work. I can't do anything but grieve and try to figure out what I need to do to fix it. The only thing left was to come clean."

"That explains a lot." Nathan hesitated. "We'll work through this, Eli. You didn't mean for anything to happen to Danny. I know that."

"You can't tell me you don't blame me."

Be honest or say what his brother needed to hear? Eli would see through anything less than honesty. "Yeah. I blame you. But the truth is, you're not completely to blame. I was a dumb kid too. We both were. Unfortunately, sometimes stupidity has tragic consequences. We can't change that, but we can make sure we do our part to help other kids going through the same thing. You in your counseling and me"—he lifted a shoulder—"however I can do that in my role as an agent. Even though I despise public speaking, I speak to schools and other groups, and I think sometimes my words make a difference."

"I'm sure they do."

"Can I have the gun, Eli?"

Another harsh breath left his brother, but he handed the gun over to Nathan, who unloaded it, noting with relief no bullet had been chambered. "Any other weapons I need to know about?"

"Just in Dad's gun case and I don't have the key."

But that didn't mean he couldn't find a way to get the case open if he really wanted to. "Why don't you come stay with me for a while at the Airbnb? At least while I'm in town. When this case is over, we'll figure something else out."

"So you can keep an eye on me?"

Nathan met Eli's gaze once more. "Yes."

Eli hesitated, then nodded. "Okay."

"You know you can't be alone for a while. You need counseling. Help to work through this."

His brother fell silent. "I know that's the protocol and we can follow it, but honestly, the fact that you thought something was wrong and came here to check on me is more than . . ." His throat worked and he cleared it. "More than enough. I have hope now. Whereas before, I didn't." He paused. "I mean, I just didn't know I did. Never mind."

"There's always hope. You're my brother and I love you. I don't ever want anything bad to happen to you." The words were hard to say. He meant them and he knew they were true. And Eli needed to hear them.

"Even though I did what I did?"

"Even though."

"So you forgive me? That's biblical, right? Forgiving those who've wronged you? 'Forgive us our debts, as we also have forgiven our debtors,'" he whispered. "Can you forgive me for what I did?"

"I . . ." Could he? "Yeah. Yes, of course it's biblical, and yes, I forgive you." His hands fisted, but he forced the words out. "I'm making the decision to forgive you. My heart might not be completely behind it yet, but it'll get there. You know as well as I do that forgiveness is a decision, not necessarily a feeling. The feeling will come. But we will get through this. We will. I want that and I need you to believe that."

Eli nodded and more tears coursed. He sniffed and used his sleeve to scrub his face. "I haven't cried since that night," he said. "I was afraid if I started, I wouldn't stop." Another tear leaked out. "Looks like I was right."

Nathan refused to let his own tears fall. "One more thing."

"What?"

"I need you to forgive me."

Eli gaped. "What for?"

"For being a dumb kid and being selfish. For wanting my own way that night and not caring what anyone else said. Including you."

More tears tracked his brother's cheeks, but he nodded. "Of course," he rasped.

Nathan squeezed Eli's shoulder. "We'll get through this," he said again, "but you have to swear you'll talk to me if you feel like picking up a gun again—or any other weapon."

"I will. I don't know what came over me. I know ending things isn't the answer. I wouldn't want to do that to Mom and Dad or Carly. Or you. I wasn't thinking clearly, obviously. I don't want to die, Nathan, I just want things to get better."

"And they will. From this moment forward. Okay?"

Eli sniffed again, but nodded. "Yeah. Okay."

"I still want you to see someone."

"I will."

"Good. Make the appointment."

"Now?"

"Yes. And put the phone on speaker."

Eli's eyes glittered with more unshed tears, but he actually barked a short, humorless laugh. "Okay." He made the call, and Nathan listened as his brother told his friend and fellow psychiatrist what had happened. The fact that he held nothing back gave Nathan hope that Eli was serious about getting help. He hung up. "He can meet with me tonight after his last client."

"Good." He patted his brother's shoulder. "Now, for the next step. We need to tell Carly about this."

Eli frowned. "Why?"

"You need the support of the family. I understand if you don't want to tell Mom and Dad, but Carly and Kip need to be a part of your support system. What would you tell one of your clients?"

After a few seconds of silence, Eli said, "The same."

"Exactly."

Twenty minutes later, Carly was informed and, while shocked at the news of Eli's current mental state, promised to be there for him. Eli's shoulders had loosened and he looked to be in a better place. But there was one last thing.

"Danny's parents and siblings don't need to know any of this," Nathan said.

"I thought about telling them."

"I figured you did, but I think it's better if you don't. I keep in touch with them. They're doing well. Let's not bring it all up again for them."

"You think that's best?"

"What purpose would it serve? Yeah. I think it's best not to say anything."

"I'll think about it."

Nathan patted his brother's shoulder. "All right. Come on. Pack what you need. The spare room is yours for as long as you need it."

"I don't know what to say." More tears slipped down Eli's cheeks and Nathan wrapped his brother in a tight hug. Seeing Eli's desperation and deep pain had snuffed out his anger like water on an open

221

flame. He snorted at the analogy, but it was accurate. Maybe God would give him the ability to forgive completely and there could be healing all around.

His phone buzzed with a text from Jesslyn.

Heath is here.

TWENTY-TWO

Jesslyn kept an eye on the young man at the edge of the onlookers. He had on a green sweatshirt, a baseball cap, jeans, and sneakers. She caught his eye and he frowned but didn't look like he was in any hurry to leave. She walked toward him.

"Hello, Heath."

"Hi."

"What are you doing here?"

He shrugged. "I saw the newscast and figured I'd see what Kenny found so fascinating that he had to show up to these things."

"I see. Any answers?"

"Nope."

"And you still don't think Kenny could have anything to do with setting them?"

He rubbed his nose and looked away from her. "I don't know."

"What's changed your mind?"

"Brad's death."

Yeah, that could make one think hard about things. "I'm sorry for your loss."

His eyes reddened and he looked away for a moment. When he turned his gaze back to her, he shook his head. "I don't get it. Why?" He waved a hand at the blaze. "What's the point?"

"That's the foremost question in all of our minds."

"I thought if I came, I might see something. Or someone. And then I'd somehow know why Brad died. Why someone wanted him silenced. Miraculously know what he knew." He laughed. A harsh, humorless sound. "But I got nothing."

She believed him. He was hurting at the loss of his friend. "Kenny can't tell you?"

"Can't or won't. I'm not sure which. I've asked him a couple of times and he just shuts me down."

"Right."

He let the conversation pause, so she did as well.

"Brad's funeral is Wednesday," he said after a few seconds.

"I know."

They fell silent once more, and Jesslyn started her mental check-list of everything she had to do before she could leave while she waited to see if he had anything else to add.

Heath finally huffed. "This is ridiculous. I don't know why I thought coming here would help. It obviously doesn't."

"Sometimes we do stuff out of desperation or just because it feels like we're doing something. Being proactive."

He nodded. "Yeah. Exactly. Just sitting around talking about him, wondering what was going through his mind in his last moments, and being sad is getting old. We need to be doing something to figure out what happened to him." He met her gaze and jutted his chin. "Figure out who pushed him."

"And you still don't have any idea who might have done that?"

"No." He shoved his hands in his pockets and kicked the ground. "I don't. If I did, I'd tell you."

"I think you would." She bit her lip. "Look, I'm not asking you to snitch on your friends, but if you want to keep pushing Kenny to tell you what he was doing at the last fire with Brad, then you might be able to move things along in figuring out why Brad is dead."

Heath frowned. "Brad was at the fire?"

"Yeah. You didn't know that?"

"No."

"And you can't think of any reason for that?"

"No, sorry. It's definitely weird." He glanced at his phone. "I gotta go."

"Wait, um . . . I don't know what's going on or what Brad and Kenny were into, but if you do start asking questions, be careful." She hesitated. "In fact, never mind. I shouldn't have suggested that. It might not be safe. Just let it go and let the investigators do their job."

"I'll see what I can find out."

She placed a hand on his arm. "No, I'm serious. Let it go."

"I've already asked Kenny what was going on. What he and Brad were into, and he just told me to back off, that it wasn't any of my business."

"But?"

"But I think he's scared."

"Scared of what? Or who?"

"No idea."

Jesslyn chewed her bottom lip debating whether to ask her next question, but finally decided to. "Do you know if Kenny owns a gun?"

"A gun? No." Heath snorted. "No way. Kenny definitely doesn't own a gun. And before you ask, neither did Brad. They're not allowed on campus, much less in the dorms."

Didn't mean one wasn't there, though. She nodded. "Thanks."

Heath kicked the ground and hung his head for a minute. When he looked up, he met her gaze, a firm resolution in his. "I'm going to go. This is a waste of time. I'll let you know what Kenny says."

"Be careful, Heath. Seriously."

"I will."

Nathan came into her line of sight, and she waved him over, filled him in on her conversation with Heath, and narrowed her eyes at him. "What's going on with you? Is Eli okay?"

"He is. For now. I'll tell you about it later. Are you about done here?"

"Yes."

"Anyone in the crowd stand out to you?"

"No one." She ran her gaze over the bystanders one more time while she told him about her conversation with Heath. "I don't think he knows anything helpful. Kenny and Brad kept him in the dark. But Heath said he thinks Kenny's afraid of something. Or someone."

"I'm guessing he didn't know who that might be?"

"Nope."

"Jesslyn?"

She turned to see the chief heading her way. He held an evidence bag in his hand. "You found another one?"

"We did."

She took it and studied it. A beautiful piece. Diamonds, pearls, and emeralds in the shape of a butterfly. She rubbed her thumb over it. It was just dirty. No sign it had been touched by fire. "Someone dropped this here at the edge of the scene."

"A bystander," Chief Laramie said with a nod.

"Most likely." Jesslyn bit off a scream of frustration. "Why can't we catch this person?" Then again, it would be so very easy to let something this small fall to the ground without anyone being aware.

"We'll get him, Jess." He shook his head. "You know, I remember when this place was built thirty years ago. Your dad even showed me the plans."

"Wait, what? My dad did?"

"Yeah. He and his architect buddy, Bob Nelson, had the plans all laid out on the dining room table one night. He was so proud when it was finally finished."

"I don't remember that," Jesslyn said.

"No reason why you would. You were real little." A firefighter waved to him and he patted her shoulder. "I'll catch up in a little bit."

"Right."

Nathan nudged her and she blinked. "Oh, sorry. I don't suppose anyone saw someone drop this, did they?"

"Not that we can tell right now. We had eyes on everyone in the crowd. We even filmed some of it. We'll watch the footage and see if we can find something on there."

She nodded. She'd done all she could do here. She'd revisit the scene tomorrow. "I'm going home." She had to think. And do a little research. Maybe the fires weren't connected to her after all. Well, they were, but maybe not in the way she was thinking. Maybe they were connected to her father. Which connected them to her, of course. She rubbed her head, thoughts spinning.

"Who's staying with you tonight?" Nathan asked.

"Kenzie. She'll take me home."

"Good." He hesitated. "You know how I said Eli was okay?"

"Yes."

"Well, he is and he isn't. He's going to be staying with me while I'm in town. As long as this case takes. When it's time for me to head back home to Asheville, then we'll figure something else out."

"Okay. Is that a good thing?"

"Guess we're going to find out."

Jesslyn said her goodbyes and finished up at the scene, then headed to Kenzie's car. She hadn't had time to arrange another rental.

"Rough scene?" Kenzie asked.

"Not really. Just more of the same. I don't understand the point of the fires." Then again, if she understood the *why*, she could probably pinpoint the *who*.

She fell silent, thinking, until Kenzie pulled into the garage. After Jesslyn disarmed the alarm, they walked inside, and Kenzie started checking the windows.

"They're locked," Jesslyn said.

"I'm sure they are." She continued her checking and Jesslyn smiled. Kenzie finally returned to the den. "All good."

"Told ya."

Kenzie merely smiled.

"I'm going to take a sponge bath," Jesslyn said. And get some Motrin. Her head had started throbbing, her hands ached, and her leg itched. And while that was a sign of healing, it didn't make it any less annoying.

"Go to bed, Jess," Kenzie said.

"Yeah, think I might do that. After I clean up a little." Her research would have to wait too.

Fatigue hit with the speed of lightning, and she stumbled to the bathroom. It took every last ounce of energy she had to bathe, throw on a T-shirt and sweatpants, and wrap her hair in a towel. She walked to her bed and face-planted.

Then rolled, pulling the comforter over her.

She wasn't sure how long she slept, but the crash woke her. Then Kenzie was in her room, shoving her shoes at her. "Put them on. Someone threw a Molotov cocktail through your window."

Sleep fled as adrenaline took over. She slid into her sneakers and grabbed her coat. "First my car, now he wants to burn my house down?" Fury snaked through her, and she grabbed the fire extinguisher from her closet and handed it to Kenzie. "Can we put it out?"

"We can try."

"I've got another extinguisher in the kitchen!" She raced to grab it from the pantry, smelling the smoke coming from her den area.

Kenzie was already dousing the fire with her canister when Jesslyn got hers going. It didn't take long to get the fire out, but damage had been done. She'd have to assess that later. She grabbed her weapon and raced for the door.

"Jess! Wait!"

"Call 911! He's not getting away this time!" But she stopped at the door. No sense in bolting out without checking the area.

Kenzie was right behind her, hand on her shoulder, letting her know she was there. Her grip was tight, silently but clearly expressing her displeasure at Jesslyn's determination to go after the arsonist. "If you insist on going out," she said, her voice low, phone tucked at her ear, "at least use a different door. This might be what he wants. Set your den on fire and wait for you to come out the front door."

"Good point."

"Yes, someone threw a Molotov cocktail through a window." Kenzie identified herself as law enforcement and gave the address while Jesslyn slipped from her friend's grip and bolted for the garage. She pressed the button and the door rose, then she aimed herself for the sunroom. "Maybe that will throw him off a bit."

"You're not a cop anymore, Jess. The cops are on the way."

"Maybe not on paper, but you know as well as I do, once a cop, always a cop."

"Fine. I've got your back and I'm calling for backup."

"And thanks to that streetlight, I just saw someone head for the trees at the back edge of my property." She took off after them, adrenaline masking the pain in her leg, with Kenzie on the phone behind her.

NATHAN PRESSED THE GAS and the engine purred smoothly to the faster speed. Maybe he'd keep the vehicle after all. If it got him into a position to save Kenzie's and Jesslyn's lives, it would be worth it. The call had come from Kenzie that Jesslyn's home had been attacked and Jesslyn had gone after the attacker. Kenzie was racing after both of them. He was to get there with backup and put his comms in.

When he pulled into the drive, he saw two police cars, two fire engines, an ambulance, and neighbors on the front porches. He also noted the broken window as he shoved the comms into his left ear, praying he was in range. "Kenzie, talk to me."

"We're still chasing him." Her voice came through loud and clear. "He's running in and out between the houses. No clear path or obvious destination. Just running. I think we're off Sycamore coming up on Dumas."

He knew where that was. He passed the information to the nearest officer. "Spread out!" The officers started the foot chase while Nathan spun the wheel and took the next left, then braked to a stop in the middle of the intersection.

A figure came into sight, spotted him, and swerved between two houses. More sirens sounded in the distance and Nathan reported in his position. He shoved out of his vehicle and took off on foot after the disappearing person. The fleeing attacker was fast, and Nathan marveled that the guy's feet barely touched the ground. Even knowing there was no way he was going to catch him thanks to his now throbbing hip, he kept on.

Because at least if the guy was running, he didn't have Jesslyn.

TWENTY-THREE

Jesslyn finally slowed to a stop to catch her breath. Nathan was about ten yards ahead of her. They'd lost the person who'd just tried to burn her house down.

With her and Kenzie in it.

She bent double, coughing. Stressing her lungs and leg so soon after all the trauma they'd endured probably wasn't a good thing.

She coughed again and dragged in another breath. Okay, *definitely* not a good thing. She wasn't running another step. Couldn't if someone held a gun to her head.

The sirens drew closer and she straightened, dragging in a few more deep breaths. Her fingers were clamped around the grip of her Glock. She loosened them slightly, then the sound of footsteps spun her around.

Kenzie. "Are you crazy?" her friend asked. A mixture of anger and concern glittered in her dark eyes, and she'd lowered her own weapon to aim it at the ground.

"No. Not crazy," Jesslyn said. "Desperate. And determined. Mostly desperate." The words came out hoarse and harsh, and she cleared her throat. *Just breathe.*

At her honest response, Kenzie's anger faded to be replaced with compassion. "I know, but you can't take off like that. Jess, this person wants to *kill* you."

"I know that!" She caught another breath. "I know." The second time came out softer, but still held the punch she needed. And she did know, but they both knew she'd do it again if it meant catching the person terrorizing her and burning down her city.

"On that note," Kenzie said, tucking her weapon into her holster, "did you get a look at him?"

Jesslyn frowned. "A glimpse, thanks to the streetlights, but there was something different about him this time."

"Different how?" Nathan asked, joining them but favoring his hip, weapon still drawn, eyes on the shadows.

"He seemed . . . smaller. Lighter." She shrugged. "I don't know. And faster."

"Definitely faster," Nathan said.

She started walking back toward the house. No reason to stand out in the open and invite a bullet. Kenzie walked at her side. Nathan stayed behind her. Covering her back, no doubt.

"Different person?" Kenzie asked.

"If I had to testify, I couldn't say with one hundred percent certainty, but that makes the most sense to me." She raked a hand over her hair. "So, I have two people trying to kill me?"

Nathan and Kenzie exchanged a look. "Cole and Andrew are at your house. Let's go assess the damage."

When they walked up to her home, she had her second wave of relief for the day. The window to her den was broken, but the damage to the outside was minimal.

The inside? Relief fled and she dreaded looking.

But it had to be done. She walked up the porch steps and entered the foyer. The smell hit her first, of course, and then she surveyed the damage. "Okay, floor is burned in areas, but the trucks didn't have to flood it with water. We got the worst of it with the extinguishers. Repairs are needed, but it's not a gut job. Furniture will have to be aired out and so on. Looks like everything can be fixed."

She was talking to herself, not sure who was listening and didn't really care.

"Grant could probably take care of this for you," Kenzie said. Lainie's brother owned one of the best restoration services in the state. "In the meantime, I think you need to come stay with me. Pack a bag. I'd love to have you. Not glad of the reason, but you can help me plan a wedding."

"You have to pick a date first," Jesslyn said absently.

"I've picked it."

Jesslyn raised a brow, her attention now fully on Kenzie. "Do tell. When?"

"Valentine's Day."

A snort slipped out before she could stop it. "You're lying." There's no way Kenzie would pick that day. It was too "mushy" for her. "Stop messing with me. It's not nice."

Kenzie smiled. "Okay. Yeah. We decided on New Year's Eve. New marriage, new beginnings, new start, new life. All that."

"Now *that* sounds lovely."

"So you'll help me plan?"

"Sure. But what if this person decides to toss a cocktail through your window?"

She held up her hands. "I'm moving in with Cole after the wedding so I'm not worried."

"Kenzie! Not only is that a year from now, that's your grandmother's house you just renovated. You *should* be worried." How was it she found herself on the verge of laughter when her house was in a shambles? Tears pinpricked her lids. God might have allowed the evil that had taken her birth family, but he'd given her people to love and who loved her, people who'd become her family by choice if not by name. She was grateful.

Kenzie slid an arm around her shoulders. "To the bedroom. Pack. I'll get Lainie to call her brother to come assess what it'll take to fix the damage. You can call the insurance company later to get that ball rolling. We've got this."

With Kenzie's assurances ringing in her ears, Jesslyn packed a suitcase, grabbed her go bag, then looked around her room and followed her friends outside. She slid into the passenger seat of Kenzie's car and made a mental note to check on her own vehicle. Her insurance companies were going to drop her if she had any more incidents, but that wasn't why she wanted to catch this person. She wanted to look him in the eye and ask him why he'd chosen her. What it was about her that made him turn her into a target.

Yeah.

She wanted those questions answered ASAP.

NATHAN TUGGED THE SLEEVES of his black blazer down to his wrists. Tuesday, Jesslyn had been quiet and moody, but busy on her laptop. Whatever she'd been doing, she hadn't shared. If the person after Jesslyn had hoped for another chance at her, he'd been sorely disappointed. She stayed in with her self-appointed bodyguards, and thankfully, there'd been no more fires.

Wednesday morning, the day of Brad's funeral, was overcast, cold, and gray. Seemed fitting. Carly had come to Nathan's rental to hang out with Eli, and Nathan had picked Jesslyn up from Kenzie's home. Now they stood back from the gravesite with the other detectives assigned to the case, watching those who had shown up.

Detective Gil Saunders was a good man in his early fifties who'd solved a lot of cases during his years on the force. Nathan leaned toward him. "So you guys don't think he jumped?"

"We haven't ruled it out, but no, we don't think he did."

Gil's partner, Miranda Peterson, crossed her arms and shook her head. "The evidence is inconclusive. And he's got a pretty insistent friends and family base who say no way. We'll get to the bottom of it."

The size of the crowd indicated that Brad had been well loved and would be sorely missed. His parents and three siblings, an assortment of cousins, aunts and uncles, and friends from all the places he did life had turned out in droves.

Nathan stood beside Jesslyn, favoring his hip that had decided to throb despite the meds he'd taken. His running after the guy at Jesslyn's home hadn't helped matters, and now he was paying for it. It wouldn't keep him from doing what was needed, but the annoyance put him on edge.

His gaze swept the crowd once more. The family had opted for a graveside service only, and the pastor was mid-sermon with no end in sight. The fat gray clouds threatened to release their bounty while the wind grabbed at hair and clothing with icy fingers. People shifted, pulling their coats tighter around them with gloved hands.

Nathan nudged Jesslyn, and she looked in the direction he indicated. "Has to be students from the math competition team," she murmured for his ears only. "They wore their uniforms in his honor."

"Yeah."

They stood with heads bowed, gazes on the coffin. Morgan and Claymore bookended them. Kenny stood next to Heath and refused to meet Nathan's gaze.

Jesslyn leaned into him slightly to get a better view, and he got a whiff of her shampoo. Something light with a hint of vanilla. He breathed deep, his arms almost twitching in his desire to pull her close. He resisted. She'd made no response to his declaration Monday.

She shook her head and auburn strands teased his nose. He shifted backward and she looked at him.

"Who are you looking for?" he asked.

"No one really, just trying to memorize faces."

"You think the arsonist is here."

"Don't you?"

"If he killed Brad, then yes." He paused. "But that's confusing. What's the point in killing him? Making sure he couldn't talk?"

"If he had something to do with the fires," Jesslyn said, "then grew a conscience and the killer saw that, then . . . yeah. If the arsonist *didn't* kill him, then Brad could have jumped because of a guilty conscience. None of that's out of the realm of possibility."

"True."

"Then that probably means Kenny knows more than he's saying, which I've always believed."

"I agree, but we just don't have the evidence we need to arrest him. Nothing links to him except his presence at the fires."

"And honestly, we only know he was actually at one fire. I can't tell you if that was him at the church or not. Or the hospital. Or at the inspection sites. Or all the places I've been and someone's shown up."

"Well, Kenny doesn't drive that make or model car, but that doesn't mean much. The car's probably stolen."

"I know."

Finally, the minister stepped back and the family filed past the coffin to drop flowers and dirt on it. Sobs echoed and a hard fist squeezed Nathan's heart. He wanted to know who had done this to a kid who'd had a lot of living left to do.

Brad's mother spotted them and broke away from her family to walk over and hold out a hand. "Thank you for coming."

"Of course," Nathan said. "We're so very sorry."

"Just find out the truth, please. I need the truth. One way or another." She rejoined her family, and Nathan watched for a moment before turning his focus back to the math team.

"They all seem pretty broken up," he said.

"They do." When the funeral was over, she walked to the car with him. Once they were buckled in, she turned. "I've thought about what you said."

"About . . ."

"Dating. You want me to go on a date with you."

"Ah, that."

"I . . . want to do that . . ."

"But?"

She swallowed and looked away. Out the window, then down at her hands.

"But?" he asked again.

"But I'm not sure I know *how* to do that."

"Do what? Date?"

"Yes."

He honestly wasn't sure how to respond to that. "Jesslyn—"

"No, let me explain."

He glanced around and noted the people leaving the service. He'd keep an eye on the crowd while she talked. "Okay."

"This is embarrassing to even say, but the truth is, I don't know how to date. I've never had a boyfriend. Not a real one. There was a guy in high school who liked me and we hung out some, but when I got a B on a test, I dumped him because I couldn't afford the distraction. Since then, I've never done more than go out with guys in friend groups. I've never allowed myself to dream about what it might be like to be normal, to have a relationship. To want something other than justice for my family."

Nathan swallowed, trying to figure out how to navigate this situation. "I can't imagine what that was like for you."

"No, you can't, but it's okay. It was my life. It's not like I knew anything different. And I didn't care. Not really. I had my goals and I was achieving them one by one." She shot him a sad smile. "And then you came along."

"And?" Dare he hope?

"And I like you too, Nathan. A lot. But you could be the same kind of distraction that boy was in high school and I can't let that happen."

His hopes plummeted and he cleared his throat. "I see."

Silence fell between them. He started the car, needing a moment to think.

"But," she said as he pulled out of the parking lot, "Lainie asked me a question that I can't stop thinking about."

"What's that?"

"She asked if I thought my family would expect me to sacrifice my life, my happiness for their justice."

"Wow. That's pretty deep."

"Very."

"Did you have an answer?"

"No. I mean I know what the *right* answer is. Or what the answer *should* be. They'd never want me to do that. But then again, I didn't really have the chance to know them long enough and well enough to know if that's true or not."

"What would your aunt Carol say?"

"That they'd want me to live my life, not sacrifice it. She's encouraged me to do that for years. Especially when she saw how driven I was to excel in my career choice."

"Then why do you feel like you have to? Sacrifice your life, I mean."

"I don't feel like I *have* to, I feel like I *want* to know who killed my family. No. I *need* to know. I *need* someone to blame, Nathan. I need to put a face and a name to the arsonist. And now, I need to know why he's suddenly decided to target me."

So she *did* think the guy they were chasing was the one who'd burned her house down and killed her family twenty years ago.

Frankly, he didn't think she was wrong. "Then let's get back to work. We can put our personal . . . whatever it is . . . on the shelf and when it's all over, we'll revisit it if that's what both of us want." She nodded, her eyes cloudy. He frowned. "Was there something else?"

"Well, I've come this far in unzipping my baggage for all to see. Might as well admit that after all this is over and if we finally manage to catch the person who killed my family, I'm worried I won't know who I'll be."

"What do you mean? You're still you."

"No." She shook her head. "I've never been me. I've always been the poor girl who lost her family and then grew up to be a fire marshal with the whole intention of catching her family's killer. Other than that? I don't know who I am or who I'm supposed to be."

Nathan's heart slugged a painful beat. He wanted to fix it for her. To help her understand she was amazing and wonderful and that God had a plan for her life. And while part of that plan might entail finding the arsonist who killed her family, there was so much more than that.

"We all have a purpose for being here, Jess," he said softly. "Some of us just take longer to figure out what that is. I've known ever since Danny was killed that I had to be able to protect the people I loved. That I had to have skills and resources to keep them safe."

"And being an FBI agent is the way that you chose to do that. Makes sense."

"Yeah. Well, a cop first, but I found I was good at it and loved climbing the ladder. I love my job. Most of the time."

"And so do I."

"Then that's a start, right?"

She offered him a small smile. "Yes. It's a start."

TWENTY-FOUR

Jesslyn settled onto the Airbnb's comfortable couch with a printed report of all the people who'd owned homes in the neighborhood she'd lived in the first seven years of her life. The Nelsons were still at the top of her list to talk to since they'd been close friends with her parents—and they still lived there. And ever since Chief Laramie mentioned her father's connection to the general store, she'd meant to check on that.

But with her conversation with Nathan still ringing in the back of her head, she found it hard to focus. She shut her eyes. *Focus. Focus. Focus. This is your purpose for now. You can worry about everything else later.*

She scrolled down the rest of the list. It was a large neighborhood with a hundred and seven homes. She didn't recognize or remember a single name other than the Nelsons. And she only knew that name thanks to Aunt Carol's sharing.

Nathan walked in from the back of the house and stopped. "Can you tuck that away?"

She followed his gaze to her weapon on the end table. "Yeah, sure." She slid it into the shoulder holster. "Eli okay?"

"Yeah. I'm just jumpy about any weapons being in the open or within his reach."

"I got it. You're right. I wasn't thinking. Sorry."

Eli walked into the den. "Aw, Jess, you don't have to apologize. I'm the one who needs to do that."

She smiled. "Hey."

He nodded. "I'm hungry. Thought I'd do some cooking. You got anything to eat around here?"

"A fully stocked freezer and fridge," Nathan said. "Help yourself."

"I'll do that." He looked at Jesslyn. "Anything you don't eat?"

"Fungus and mold."

He raised a brow. "'Scuze me?"

She laughed. "Mushrooms or blue cheese. Can't stand either."

He shot her a smile, then nodded. "Got it. Homemade pizza without fungus or mold. Should be easy enough."

He made his way to the kitchen and Nathan watched him go, his eyes cloudy with emotion she couldn't identify. Guilt, anger, compassion? All of the above?

"I think I need my aunt to look at this list of neighbors," she said. "She might be able to give insight into some of them." She snapped a picture of the list and texted it to Carol with the request for her to look it over and see if anyone stuck out as a possible woman her father may have been involved with.

While she waited for Carol's reply, she texted Kenzie her location and explained that Nathan would bring her to Kenzie's home when they were finished going over the case.

Kenzie sent her a thumbs-up emoji, and Jesslyn started her search of all the fire locations. She also wanted to know every building in Lake City that had Owen McCormick's name associated with it, and she was almost done. She closed her eyes and brought her father's face to the forefront of her memory. The familiar pang of regret was there like it always was whenever she thought about him.

He'd obviously had his mental health issues and dealt with stresses in his marriage in an unhealthy way. Her mother had been stubborn and determined to save her marriage. What would her life have been like if her family hadn't been wiped out?

It wasn't the first time she'd wondered that. Probably wouldn't be the last. The more she searched, the more her breath caught. "I have the connection between all the buildings."

"What's that?" Nathan looked up.

"We thought it was me, but it was actually my father. He was in commercial real estate."

"Right."

"And he either built or sold all the buildings the arsonist is targeting, including the bank."

Nathan's eyes widened. "No kidding."

"Not even a little."

"Coincidence?" She raised a brow at him and he shook his head. "Yeah, probably not. But why target you?"

"Because I'm trying to stop him? Because I'm my father's daughter and the last one alive?" She shrugged. "Take your pick."

He nodded. "That's definitely a connection." His phone buzzed and he glanced at the screen. "Andrew said he could join us for dinner if we wanted. He'll just be late and for us not to wait on him to eat."

"Okay. What's going on with him and his family anyway?"

"I'm not entirely sure. His parents moved here shortly after Andrew was assigned to the Asheville office. They own a bookstore here in Lake City, did you know that?"

"Hm. I think he's mentioned it."

"So one of their employees just up and quit. His mom has some doctor's appointment his dad had to take her to, so he's manning the store. In the meantime"—he sniffed—"I'm getting hungry."

They walked into the kitchen to find Eli pulling a pizza out of the oven. He looked up. "Hope you like a meat lovers pizza."

Jesslyn's stomach growled in anticipation. "Bring it on, my friend."

Eli set it on the wooden block he'd found, and Nathan grabbed a pizza cutter from one of the drawers. Plates and napkins were on the table along with a pitcher of tea.

After they said grace, Eli smiled. "Dig in."

While Jesslyn ate, she studied the brothers. They looked very much alike, but were very different in personality and temperament. From what she could tell.

"You're an excellent cook, Eli," she said. "This is amazing. The spices are just perfect."

"Thanks." He shot her a soft smile. "Cooking helps me think. And it's fun to share with people who like to eat." He seemed to be in a better place than the last time she'd seen him. Maybe Nathan would share with her when he got the chance.

Her phone buzzed and she grabbed it to scan the text. "I have to go back to the scene at the store. The chief said it's ready for my last walk-through and he has something new to show me."

Nathan took his last bite of pizza and rose. "I'll take you." He looked at Eli. "Tell Andrew we had to go, will you?"

"Sure, I'll save him some pie."

"Great. I'm sure he'll appreciate it."

She glanced at Eli, who was snagging another piece of pizza from the tray, then raised a brow at Nathan, silently asking if it was okay to leave his brother alone. He nodded and she smiled, then told Eli goodbye and aimed herself toward the door.

NATHAN HAD CALLED TATE and Stephanie to come over and hang out with Eli. The three got along well and usually wound up playing cards when they found themselves in the same room for any length of time. He'd never betray his brother's confidence about what was going on with him, but he didn't have to. All he had to say was Eli would benefit from their company while he was gone, and they'd dropped everything to come over.

He had no idea what he'd done to earn this kind of friendship, but he'd never take it for granted. Gratitude swamped him and he glanced at Jesslyn beside him, thankful once again that she was a part of that circle. "You okay? You look pensive."

"Pensive?" She raised a brow, an amused look in her eyes. "That's a five-dollar word."

He shot her a narrow-eyed look. "You're laughing at me."

"Never."

"Hm. So what is it?"

She sighed, all signs of humor fading. "Just thinking about everything. Wondering why I haven't heard from Aunt Carol about the names on the list."

"There were a lot of names."

"I know, but still, I think I'm going to send her a text asking her if she saw any name that made her look twice."

"Couldn't hurt."

"Right." She tapped her screen and within seconds, gasped. "Seriously?"

"What?" Nathan asked, spinning the wheel to turn right.

"*Been busy with the fundraiser. Will do that as soon as I get home,*" she read. "I want to shake her."

"I know it's disappointing, but your emergency isn't hers."

"Doesn't she understand what's at stake here?"

"She's focused on the fundraiser. That's what's important to her right now." He cocked an eyebrow at her. "Because she knows it's important to you."

Jesslyn gaped at him. "Well, I appreciate that, but finding out who killed her sister and family isn't important?"

"No, of course that's not what I meant." Was it? "I just . . . well, okay, maybe it is. Sort of. I'm not saying she doesn't want you to find the person, but maybe she believes you're chasing your tail, so why put everything else on hold to work on that? I'm not saying that's her reasoning, but it could be something to think about."

Her lips snapped shut and she rubbed her eyes. "You could be right about that," she finally said. After another short pause, she looked at him. "In hindsight, she's been supportive in this whole endeavor, definitely. But not overly . . . enthusiastic? Is that the word I want?"

"Maybe."

"I mean she never offered information unless I pushed her for it. She's had that jewelry in the safe deposit box for twenty years. She's known about my father's affairs for longer. It's . . . weird to know that. I honestly don't know how I feel about her silence."

"She didn't want to hurt you."

"I get that, but this is the closest we've—*I've*—been to finding the person responsible for my family's deaths. I guess I expected her to be as eager to figure it out. But maybe she just doesn't want to get her hopes up only to have them crushed again." She bit her lip. "I remember as a kid, we'd go to the police station twice a week to ask about updates, what the investigators were doing to find the arsonist. We did that for years until I think she finally just gave up."

"Or maybe it was just keeping the pain alive to go and then leave without any progress made?"

"You have an answer for everything, don't you?"

The words held no heat, but a twinge of guilt twisted inside him. "I'm sorry. It's not my business."

"It's your business. I made it your business and you're making me think, so thank you. I appreciate your input." She reached over and squeezed the hand resting on the gear shift. "Seriously. Thank you."

"Sure."

He pulled into the parking lot of the general store and scoped the area. The fire was out, the store a shell of its former self. Grief hit him. The place was insured and would be restored, but the wanton destruction twisted him in knots.

Chief Laramie spotted them and hurried their way. "Thanks for coming so quickly," he said.

"Sure thing. What was it you wanted to show me?"

He held out a bag. "Another piece of jewelry."

"But you already found one from here."

"Yep. And just found this one shortly before I called you. Didn't know if you wanted to do another walk-through or not, but figured the detectives would want to add this to their stash."

"I'll take it," Nathan said.

"I'll get my gear on and you can show me."

"Actually, I need to take a call. One of my guys can walk you through. He should be inside taking samples for testing."

"Great. Thanks."

She gave him a smart salute, then looked at Nathan. He was scanning the last of the holdouts of the former crowd standing on the other side of the yellow tape and he figured she was looking for the same thing he was. The arsonist.

"Do you see anyone that says arsonist?" he asked.

"No. You?"

"No, but I'll keep watching."

She nodded and bit her lip. "Right. Thanks. Hopefully I won't be too long, then we can go. We're getting close, Nathan. I can feel it. We're going to get him."

"We are."

She hesitated, almost said something, then smiled. "Okay then. Time for me to change and get busy." She left and he watched her go, marveling at her stamina. Her hands weren't yet healed, her leg was bothering her if her slight limp was anything to judge by, but she wasn't letting it stop her. This was what she did and she was in her element.

He had no doubt the arsonist would be caught. He could only pray it would be before the arsonist caught her.

TWENTY-FIVE

Once she was dressed in her PPE gear, Jesslyn made her way to what remained of the general store. When she stepped over the threshold, she gasped at the sight of the soot and char. Not that she hadn't expected it, but she'd shopped here less than a week ago.

Lights had been set up outside and part of one filtered through the broken windows, casting shadows across her path. She swept her high-powered flashlight over the area and stopped. The damage patterns caught her attention, and she noted the deep char along the western wall just above the purple stain on the floor. "Well, guess you started there," she murmured. "And with exactly the same materials." She'd known it, of course. Hadn't doubted it, but having it confirmed just fueled her determination to catch this guy.

Jesslyn moved cautiously, the smell of burned wood mingling with the acrid sting of melted plastics. Debris crunched beneath her feet.

She stopped, listening for any hint that the structure might collapse, but so far there was nothing.

"Excuse me. Jesslyn McCormick?"

She turned to see a man dressed in the same gear she sported. "That's me."

He walked over to her. "I'm Pete Bennett, one of the fire marshals from Boone. Chief Laramie asked me to come down and take a look at this one."

Jesslyn blinked. "He did?"

"Said a new pair of eyes might be a good thing."

"I see. The chief didn't say anything to me."

"Oh, right, well, maybe he just hasn't had a chance to."

"He did say someone would be here to show me where the second piece of jewelry was found."

"Second piece?"

"Yes. That's why they called me."

"Oh. Right. Um, well, we can talk about that in a minute. I wanted to show you this place back near the freezer." He waved a hand for her to follow, and she did so, looking back over her shoulder. She and this guy were the only two people inside the scene. She could see others walking past what used to be walls, but she suddenly felt very isolated.

"I think that's where the fire originally started," he was saying. "I also think that once the people were scared out of the store, the guy set more fires."

"I had the fire starting on the west wall over there." Jesslyn pointed, then followed. "Why do you say it's over here?"

"Well, there may be multiple starting points. Come take a look."

He wasn't wrong. In fact, he was very right. And he was saying all the right things, but there was something about him . . .

The closer she got to the back of the store, the more her nerves itched. She stopped. "Who are you again?"

He turned and grabbed her wrist. "Don't fight me. I don't want to hurt you."

"What?"

She took a step backward and her ankle twisted. She went down with a grunt, leaving him holding her glove. He grabbed for her and she swung. The angle was awkward, but she managed to clip him on his mask. He jerked back and she rolled to her knees in an attempt

248

to scramble to her feet. Before she could rise or call out for help, he pushed her once more and she went flat to the ground, face down. A knee went into her lower back and she gasped.

"Be quiet. I don't want to hurt you."

Her heart hammered in her throat. She tried to buck him off, but he was too strong and the gear was weighing her down. He pulled her arm back.

"What do you want?" she gasped.

Something stung her exposed wrist and she flinched. He stepped back and she rolled over to glare at him. He stood with a syringe in one hand. A strange lethargy started to invade her.

"What did you do?"

"It's okay, it's just scopolamine."

"But . . . why?"

"For your own good," he muttered. "I tried to warn you."

The drug was taking effect. "How much did you give me?" Would this be the way her life ended? An overdose?

"Not too much. Just enough for you to follow my direction."

"No," she said, but found herself doing as he bid. He kept an arm around her shoulders and guided her toward the back exit . . . or what used to be a back exit. It was now a gaping hole. Her body refused to obey her brain's commands to fight back. Resist.

She simply couldn't.

"Why are you doing this?"

"Because it needed to be done."

JESSLYN HAD BEEN INSIDE the scene for a while and Nathan was ready to lay eyes on her again. Just as he was about to, someone dressed in the same gear as Jesslyn came stumbling out and went to his knees.

"Hey!" Nathan raced over to the man and pulled off the helmet. "Who are you? What happened?"

"I was at the back waiting on Jesslyn McCormick when I was attacked." He pressed a hand to the side of his neck and groaned.

"Did you get a look at him?"

"No, he came up from behind me."

Nathan motioned to a nearby officer and the woman hurried over. "Call an ambulance."

"On it."

He turned back to the firefighter. "What's your name?"

"Carson Tillman." He slipped out of his coat and lay back. "Sorry, feeling sick. They jabbed me with something."

"It's all right. Just lay there until the paramedics get here." He paused. "Your PASS alarm didn't go off?"

The guy checked his gear. "I didn't have my air tank on. Didn't need it."

"Where's Jesslyn?"

"I don't know. I never saw her."

That familiar bad feeling crept into his gut and settled there. He raced toward the burned shell that still had a few charred walls and places where someone could hide.

Or come in from the back.

He stopped at the threshold, knowing he shouldn't go in without the protective gear, but Jesslyn—

"Nathan?"

He turned. "Andrew. What are you doing here? I thought you were helping your parents."

"I was. I did. Then decided to swing by here to check on the scene, talk to the chief. What's going on?"

"We're looking for Jesslyn. She was supposed to meet with one of the firefighters and went in to find him." He glanced into what had once been the interior of the general store. "Someone knocked the guy out and I haven't seen Jess in a while."

Nathan waved over a firefighter who still had his gear on. "Can you see if anyone is in there?"

"Sure thing." He stepped into the mess and Nathan paced while the minutes ticked past.

Finally, the guy returned and pulled off his helmet. "No one's in there."

Nathan stilled. "That's not possible."

"I assure you, it is. There's no one in there."

He headed inside and scanned the area. Still and dark. And maybe still smoldering in some places. Dank in others.

But definitely empty.

He yanked his phone from his pocket and dialed her number.

It went straight to voicemail. He spun and stepped back out into the fresh air. "Andrew!"

Andrew looked up from talking with one of the firefighters. "What is it?"

"She's gone. He's got her." He thought fast, searching his mind for the next best step, trying to keep the panic at bay. He pressed a hand to his mouth and turned his gaze on his partner. "We've got to find her fast." What if it was too late? Why take her when the guy had been trying to kill her? Why not just shoot her and run?

Morbid speculation that made his heart ache, but valid questions nevertheless.

He sent a group text.

Jesslyn's been taken. Need your help.

Within seconds, his phone started blowing up. He tapped another message.

That's just a heads-up. Stay tuned for the plan.

Andrew scrubbed a hand over his chin. "Okay, Jess thought there was someone in her old neighborhood that would give her a clue about who her father was spending time with. Maybe we should chase that lead hard and fast."

"That's going to take time," Nathan said. "Time Jess may not have."

251

"I'll get everyone on it. We've got the best resources in the world at our fingertips. We'll use all of them."

Nathan nodded. "And I'm going to have to call her aunt Carol. She's not going to take this well."

"Who would?"

"Yeah." He found her number and dialed.

TWENTY-SIX

A groan woke Jesslyn. She tried to raise a hand to her throbbing head only to discover both hands were cuffed in front of her. She also realized the sound had come from her. What—

She sat up with effort, her gaze scanning the area, swallowing hard against the bile working its way up the back of her throat. She was in . . . an office? There was a desk with a chair in front of the far wall. Two wingback chairs faced the desk. She rolled her head the other way and spotted a door. With a floor-to-ceiling rectangular window next to it. The blinds were closed. And she was *hot*. Was she sick again?

She shook herself and took inventory.

No. She had her fire gear on except for her helmet and gloves.

Memories came flickering back.

The fire scene, the guy dressed in matching gear. The struggle. The pinch in her wrist. Then . . . what?

She had nothing.

It was a complete blank.

Panic wanted to scramble her thoughts and she fought to keep the fear under control. "Oh Lord, help," she whispered. She was going to be sick.

She rolled to her feet in desperate search of a bathroom and spotted it right next to her. She raced to the toilet and lost what was in her stomach.

Then sank onto the blue-and-white tile floor.

The *clean* tile floor. In fact, the bathroom fairly sparkled.

Okay then.

She waited a few more minutes to make sure her stomach was going to behave, then awkwardly rinsed her mouth, wishing she could take her gear off. The water in the sink ran clean, so she drank deeply, getting her fill, then turned to walk to the door, thankful he hadn't bound her feet.

She eased the blinds aside and glanced out, surprised to see a large warehouse-type area filled to the brim with—she squinted—pool supplies and other assorted chemicals. Was this the arsonist's stash? Had to be, but where *was* she?

She tried the knob. Locked. Of course.

Jesslyn pulled in calming breaths. Screaming and pounding on the door would get her nowhere. And might bring her abductor.

So no screaming and pounding. She could do that later when she was safe.

If she ever got safe.

She looked at her wrists. The cuffs needed to come off.

She shot a glance at the desk, then at the window one more time. She could break the glass easy enough, but there was no way she'd be able to slide through the narrow opening. Not in her gear. Sweat dripped down her temples and neck.

Maybe. She might have to try.

A watercooler in the corner gurgled. In the opposite corner, there was a coffee station with a Keurig. She pulled open the double doors of the cabinet. A small bag of sugar, enough K-cups to last her forever, and packets of fake cream. There were also to-go cups and a box of stir sticks along with birthday plates and napkins.

She shut the doors, then hurried to the desk and pulled a drawer open. Empty. She tried them all and heard something rattle in the

LYNETTE EASON

last one. She reached into the very back and scooped out birthday candles and a book of matches. Well, three matches.

Wow. Helpful. She tossed them back in. She would have preferred a stapler or a safety pin or a paper clip. She shut the drawer and pressed her palms to her forehead. *Think, Jess.*

Nathan would have noticed her absence by now and started looking for her. He'd probably alerted everyone else and they'd be searching too. But where would they even start? *She* didn't even know.

Footsteps sounded outside the door. She darted around to the other side of the desk to keep it between her and whoever entered the room.

Of course if they had a gun, the desk wasn't going to be much protection, but maybe she could toss it over on him if she had to. She tested how heavy it was and couldn't budge it. Okay, no tossing.

More sweat beaded on her brow even as she shivered and her palms slicked with a combination of nerves and fear. *God, help me, please.*

The door opened and a man stepped into the room. Her eyes widened. "You?"

Professor Derek Morgan nodded. "Hi, Jesslyn."

"What in the world? Why would you want to kill me?"

"I don't."

Okay. Right. She leaned forward and placed her cuffed hands on the desk, a plan forming. "Who are you?"

"You know who I am."

"No, not really. I know you're a professor at the local university and you used your students to set fires."

He blinked. "They didn't set the fires. Kenny was just there to watch and leave the jewelry. He didn't know why, of course. Just that I needed him to do that and keep his mouth shut about it."

Could he be any more cryptic? "So you set them? And why leave the jewelry?" She hesitated. The Morgans were on the list. "You lived in my neighborhood, didn't you? Your mom was the woman he was seeing, wasn't she?"

"So many questions. It doesn't matter who set them. And yes, she was. I was thirteen when I knew something was wrong with my family—between my parents. And when I found out your father drove my father deeper into the bottom of a bottle and turned his fists even harder . . . well, that wasn't a good feeling."

Her heart ached for the confused child he'd been, but fear of the man he'd become pounded through her. "Why take me?"

"Because I need you."

Her brain hurt. "For what?"

"A couple of things." He glanced at his phone. "But we'll get to that in a bit. I have to take care of something first."

He wanted to play games and she wanted answers. She drew in a ragged breath and tried to think through the fear. First things first. "Are you going to kill me?"

"If I was going to do that, I would have just given you enough of the drug to ensure you didn't wake up."

Okay, valid point, but he seemed evasive as well. "But . . . but you've been trying very hard to do so, and now that you have me, you're not going to—" What was she doing? Trying to talk him into killing her? She snapped her lips shut.

"No," he said. "Not at the moment."

"Why not?" She couldn't help it.

He laughed. "Again, it doesn't matter. What matters is you're here." He offered her a small smile. An empty one that sent a shiver up her spine. "Enjoy your little . . . vacation. I'm not sure how long it'll last, but I'll get you some supplies so you'll be more comfortable until . . ."

Until? She held up her hands. "I'm a prisoner. I don't think comfort is going to factor in."

"But you won't be dead. Yet."

He was infuriating.

Swallowing a scream, Jesslyn studied him, her heart thudding but her fear under control. Her confusion was another story. "What do you need from me?"

"You're going to pay a debt for me." He smiled again, but it didn't reach the flat dark eyes that stared at her. "And I'm not a killer."

A debt? Somehow she had a feeling he wasn't talking about money. She also had a feeling he wasn't ready to reveal exactly what the debt was and how she was going to help him pay it.

"Were you the one who tried to grab me at the restaurant?" He was certainly the right height and everything else.

"Yes." He scowled this time, that weird smile fading away. "If you had just come peacefully, this would all be over by now."

Over how? She wasn't sure she wanted to know. "So you just plan to keep me here indefinitely?"

"No." His frown deepened. "I just need you to cooperate with me for a while, then you'll know everything. But if you give me any problems, then you'll have to die—and then I guess I'll be a killer too."

"Too?"

He sighed. "I don't have time for nonsense and drama. I have enough to deal with. Understand?"

"No. I actually don't. Can you be a little more clear? Who's trying to kill me?"

"That's not for me to say." He studied her. "You don't remember me, do you?"

"Should I?"

He leaned forward. "I'll be watching you, Jesslyn," he whispered.

Jesslyn gasped and recoiled against the wall behind her, her childhood nightmare coming to life and facing her in the flesh. "You were real. You were there. In my room."

"I was."

"Why?"

"I'm not sure, to be honest. I was . . . jealous of you. You got to start over with life. I wished I could do the same."

She ignored that last part and stared at him while she let his identity sink in. "You killed them."

"Me?" He laughed, then scowled. "No, of course not. I told you, I'm not a killer."

She didn't believe him. "You were in my bedroom at my aunt's house. I remember you. I remember your words."

"Yes. I was compelled to see you, to see what a survivor looked like in some ways, but I also thought about killing you that night."

Jesslyn shuddered. "Why didn't you?"

"I told you I wasn't a killer."

She was so confused.

"My sister thought you had all died in the fire. That's what she hoped, but you beat her. You survived all of it—losing your whole family, starting a new life. I admired that. Relished it, even. I overheard her ranting one night when she didn't think I was there. At the park where she used to watch our mother meet your dad. She saw me there and started screaming at me, like it was my fault you weren't in the fire too. I asked her what she was going to do and she said nothing. Our mother was dead because of your father."

Jesslyn flinched. His mother had made choices too, but she didn't think now would be a good time to point that out.

"But that's neither here nor there," he said. "That's all in the past. Or at least it was until you went on television and told the world about your wonderful father and how you were going to honor him by building a youth center. What this boils down to is that your father was not a good man. There can be no building with his name on it. That's just laughable. Why would you want to honor a dishonorable man?"

"He'd changed," was all she could offer.

He snorted. "Right. You don't understand. My family was all I had. Do you know what it's like to grow up as the odd one? The quiet one? I was smart so I was expected to achieve great things, right? I loved chemistry so that was great. I could become a famous chemist. But one summer I worked at the country club and discovered I also loved pools." He gave a humorless laugh. "Have you ever heard of anything so dumb? Maybe it was all the chemistry involved in keeping them clean and balanced. Whatever. But that's what I loved. I can't explain it so anyone really understands. But when I'm out there with just the pool, I can just be me. I don't have to worry about what anyone thinks of me and I don't have to worry about measuring up. Basically, I just wanted to own my own company and serve customers. Help them keep their pools in great working order. Clean and fun. But that wasn't good enough for my dad. He hounded me about making something of my life, so I decided I would do both. Teach and work with the pools. But because I have to give all my money away, I'll never be able to see that dream come true. Until now. It's just about to be within my grasp and I can stop this stupid teaching thing and start my own business." He shrugged.

"And I'm somehow going to help you do that."

He glanced at his phone again. "Yes."

"What about the other fires?"

"Again, not my work."

He seemed in a hurry to leave and yet at the same time wanted to stay. Like telling her everything was a relief of some sort.

"But you used your students to watch them? What were they watching for?"

"It was just Kenny. No one else was involved. I promised Kenny I'd make sure he got his degree with honors if he helped me and kept his mouth shut. He was desperate and wasn't about to say no. Kenny dropped the jewelry at each fire for me. I told him if he got caught, I'd make sure he lost everything. But good old Kenny. When he got caught, he kept his mouth shut."

"Why drop the jewelry?"

He straightened. "I have my reasons. Don't worry. They'll put it together soon."

"Who'll put what together?"

"Where to come. They'll find the check."

Her brain hurt. "What check? Who'll find it?"

"My neighbor called and said officers were looking for residents of our old neighborhood. It's only a matter of time before they connect me to the neighborhood and the school, right? And then come here?"

"Right, but you want them to come here?"

"Yes. I'm sure they missed you almost immediately at the fire scene and started looking, right?"

She frowned. "Yes."

"Then they'll be here soon. I just have to pick the right time to call her. They'll stop her."

"Her? Who?"

He shook himself and backed toward the door. "I've got to go."

"And Brad?" she asked, ignoring his insistence that he had to leave. "Someone pushed him off the dorm roof. Was that you?"

He whirled back to face her. "No! I told you I wasn't a killer." He glanced at his watch. "I'll be back in a bit."

"Wait! Why the jewelry? Tell me! Why leave it at the scene?"

"It was my mother's. I'm the only one who knows about it. I walked in on her trying it on and wondered where she got it. There was no way she could afford those pieces. But she wouldn't tell me, and she swore me to secrecy. I figured it out, though. I thought about selling them, but the very idea of using that money . . . money that came from the man responsible for her death?" He shook his head. "I couldn't do it. I didn't want anything from him. It would have felt like a betrayal of my mother. I've always wanted to get rid of them, so when the fires started, it seemed a good time to do that. You were supposed to use them to figure out who was burning the buildings, but apparently y'all aren't that smart."

"My father bought those pieces. Is that what you wanted me to know?"

It was his turn to stop and stare at her for a moment. "Well, well," he finally said, "what do ya know? Maybe you're smarter than I gave you credit for."

"Why drop them at the fires? If you wanted us to figure out who bought the jewelry, why not just tell us? And how does the jewelry connect to the fires and who started them?"

"Because I can't have any of this coming back to bite me."

He didn't think kidnapping her would come back—

A door slammed overhead and he glanced up. "Like I said, I have to go." His phone rang. "That's my cue. I have a client coming to pick up supplies, but I'll be back with some food. There's water in the cooler. It's fresh."

His reference to a customer sparked an idea. "Is George Harlow a customer of yours?"

He froze again, then tilted his head. "Yes. Why?"

"You managed to get your hands on his key fob somehow, didn't you?"

"Wow." He looked impressed. "You figured that out?"

It had been a shot in the dark but explained the gun theft. "Now that I know it was you looking for me, I figured you had to know Harlow."

"I delivered some supplies to his business. I knew he kept the weapon in his car, and when I saw the keys on his desk, I waited for him to turn his back and pressed the button. Then grabbed it out of his car. Easy enough. And now I really must leave. For real this time. I'll be back soon."

"Wait! Please! I need to take this gear off. It's too hot."

He hesitated, then shook his head. "No, if I take the cuffs off, you'll just attack me. I can't deal with that right now. I have a customer. I'll turn the air on. Now I've got to go."

"I have more questions."

But he backed out of the room and the key twisted in the lock and she slammed her hands against the door. "Who needs pool supplies this time of year!"

NATHAN SWIGGED ANOTHER MOUTHFUL of coffee, then set the cup on the hood of the sedan. He, James, Andrew, and Kenzie were at the entrance to Jesslyn's old neighborhood. They'd requested the help of Lake City's finest and had about thirty cops canvassing the area, going door-to-door to speak to those who'd lived in the neighborhood when Jesslyn's family had been there.

Those who weren't home were being located.

It was taking too much time.

But what other choice did they have?

On the iPad, he scanned the list once again, noting the names that had been checked off the shared sheet.

One name snagged his attention. "Wait a minute."

Andrew looked up. "What?"

"I think I've got it," Nathan said. "Morgan. It's common enough not to jump out at me, but put the word 'professor' in front of it and now I'm curious."

Andrew leaned in. "You think it's the same family?"

"I'm thinking the connection is there. Look at all the kids from the school who are overly interested in the fires. Kids with a professor named Morgan."

"Yeah, it's definitely worth looking into."

"The homeowners were Todd and Patty Morgan." He leaned over to work on his keyboard for a few seconds, then looked up. "Two kids. A son and a daughter. Daughter's name is Samantha Morgan Ashcroft and the son is Derek Morgan." He raised a brow. "Derek Morgan could be a coincidence, but I don't think so. Patty Morgan is deceased. She shot herself the night of the fire. Todd is in an assisted living home. Derek still lives in the house and Samantha lives about twenty minutes away with her husband and three children."

"Derek's a professor, Samantha is . . ."

". . . his sister. Yeah. We had the pleasure of meeting her at the school." He tapped the keyboard. "She was in the Army. Enlisted after high school and was a . . . firefighter."

"Okay, that's interesting," Kenzie said.

Andrew nodded. "No kidding. Think her little brother picked up some tricks on how arson works?"

James nodded. "Let's find both of them and their spouses too. But mostly, I want eyes on Derek Morgan ASAP. If Jesslyn's father was involved with their mother, then that would explain the nighttime walks."

"Maybe. But with his students' interest in the fires and Kenny's running from the scene . . . it's all connected somehow. What's Samantha doing now?"

"I don't see a job status. Looks like she's staying home with her kids. They're two, four, and six."

"Littles," Nathan said.

"Let's go."

TWENTY-SEVEN

Jesslyn stomped a foot, her anger bubbling, but was grateful the room had cooled down significantly. He'd actually turned the air on for her. She was so confused. Was she in danger or not? She was going to go with yes but was still turning over their very weird conversation. He never directly answered a question but insisted he wasn't a killer. And yet he'd threatened her all those years ago. He'd kidnapped her. He'd played mind and word games with her.

But she was still alive.

And standing there thinking wasn't going to get her out of the situation. She went to the bathroom and pulled the ceramic lid from the back of the toilet. She then dismantled the piece of wire from the chain that hooked to the handle used to flush. Working quickly, she managed to get the cuffs off, then slipped them in her pocket and shrugged out of the fire coat.

She'd leave the boots and pants on. The heavy sweatshirt over the T-shirt would keep her warm enough. She hurried to the door and examined the lock. The deadbolt required a key, presumably from both sides. Lock picking was not her strong suit. Anyone could open cuffs with a paper clip—or toilet part—but picking a lock was another matter altogether.

So, she was in a room and the only window in the office was the skinny rectangular one. If she broke it, she could try to slip out, but it would be tight . . .

Slowly, a plan formed. She hurried back to the bathroom and grabbed the tank lid from the toilet and rushed back into the office. Using the lid, she rammed it into the window. The glass shattered and spilled out onto the concrete floor. She ran the ceramic piece around the edges, getting rid of as many of the broken shards as possible, then stopped to listen.

No one seemed to be reacting to all the noise.

Derek Morgan. Professor Derek Morgan. She shook her head, still confused, thinking about everything even as she tried to slip through the opening. A sound from above startled her and she shoved harder, trying to force her body through. It wasn't working. More footsteps from beyond. She pulled back and studied the window. She just needed a couple more inches. So if she removed the molding, that would give her the extra space she needed. The question was, could she do it before Derek returned?

She felt quite confident in her ability to overpower the man as long as she could take him by surprise. If it came to that, she'd do it, but for now, she looked for something to pull the molding off. She'd get the answers eventually if she could just get out alive.

Because she needed to know who set the fires. And how did Brad's death fit into the grand scheme of things? Heath had seemed as confused as everyone else and simply wanted his own answers.

Yes, answers please. And as soon as she had Derek locked in his own cuffs, she'd get those answers.

AFTER LEARNING THAT DEREK wasn't at the school, officers went to his home with the SWAT team and, after no response, forced entry to do their search. In the meantime, Nathan and Andrew had made several attempts to reach Samantha Ashcroft by phone with no success. They arrived at her home and pulled to the curb. It was a lovely home painted a light baby blue, situated on about an acre in a middle-class neighborhood with well-manicured lawns.

Nathan hurried up the porch steps and knocked on the front door while Andrew walked the perimeter toward the back. No sounds came from within, and he highly doubted anyone was home, but he peered through a parted curtain into the den anyway, looking for signs of life.

Still nothing.

Andrew came around from the back. "No one's here, I don't think."

"Yeah." He looked around. "Let's see if we can scrounge up a neighbor. Maybe one will have an idea where she is." They lucked out on the second knock.

"Oh sure," the seventy-something woman said. "Sam's probably out looking for a job. She was a firefighter in the Army but said she wanted something different. She finally finished her degree in business a couple of months ago. Got those kids in full-time day care while she looks, so I reckon she's going to need to find something pretty quick."

"What day care, do you know?"

"Um, the fancy one on Long Shoals Drive."

"Right. Thanks."

"Of course. You know where to find me if you need anything else."

"Yes, actually. One more question, please. What about her brother, Derek Morgan? What do you know about him?"

"Just that he's a professor at Lake City University. Oh, and he works at a pool supply company. Guess teaching at the university doesn't cover all the bills. I will say we have quite a few people in the neighborhood who use the company he works for and seem to be happy with the service. That's really all I know. Samantha doesn't talk about him much, and the most interaction I've had with him is to wave if I pass him coming or going."

"Pool supply company, huh?" Nathan said. He glanced at Andrew. "Interesting."

"Very," Andrew said. "Can you tell us where that company is located?"

"I don't have a clue. You can check with Carl Baxter on the corner. I think he uses him."

"Do you know if Mr. Baxter's home or does he work?"

"He works for the post office."

"Right. We'll track him down. Thanks again."

They tried the Baxter home just on the off chance the man was home, but he wasn't, so fifteen minutes later, they pulled into the parking lot of the Adventure Sanctuary Childcare. Interesting name, but he supposed it was intended to convey something . . . expensive. He could only hope the care lived up to the ideal.

Once out of the car, he checked in with Lindsay. "Any luck tracking Derek Morgan down?"

"Not yet. He's off the radar at the moment, but he was at Brad's funeral. The person I spoke to said his chemistry class this afternoon was canceled."

"Chemistry class? I thought he taught math."

"Yeah, he does. Two math classes and two chemistry classes."

"Okay, that's interesting. Thanks. Let me know when you track him down."

"You know I will."

He hung up and looked at his partner. "You hear that? Morgan teaches chemistry."

"Well, he'd certainly know how to mix together those two simple chemicals to ignite a few fires then, wouldn't he?"

"So he didn't need the sister."

"Maybe not, but *we* might if we're going to find him."

He buzzed the door and the speaker on the wall crackled. "Yes?" the voice on the other side asked. "May I help you?"

"Special Agents Carlisle and Ross. Could we possibly come in and speak to you?" He and Andrew held their badges where she could see them.

"Um. Yes, all right. I just need to get the director. Can you wait just a moment, please?"

"Sure thing." *Hurry up, hurry up. God, please be with Jesslyn. Protect her. Keep her safe. Let her know help is coming. Please let it be coming.*

A few moments later, a voice said, "Hello, gentlemen. I'm Cecelia Brown, the director. Badges again, please?"

They complied. The door buzzed, then opened. A woman in her late fifties who had a style that reminded Nathan of Jesslyn's aunt Carol peered at them. Her short salt-and-pepper hair was styled in a classy bob, and she wore comfortable jeans and a long-sleeved denim shirt with the cuffs rolled at the wrists. Stylish and functional enough to get on the floor with children if necessary.

After handshakes, she motioned them to follow her into a conference room just off the side of the main entrance. "Sorry for all of the hoops, but I can't be too careful with the children here."

"We completely understand and are glad to see it," Andrew said.

She motioned to the chairs. "Have a seat."

"That's not really necessary," Nathan said. "We're in a bit of a hurry." Time kept slipping past. Time Jesslyn might not have. "Could you just confirm that Samantha Ashcroft's children are in care here?"

She frowned. "I can."

"And they're here today?"

"They are. What's this all about?"

"We're having trouble getting in touch with Samantha or her husband. Could you give us the emergency contact information you have on file?"

She hesitated for a moment, then nodded. "Sure. Wait here."

While they waited, Nathan paced from one end of the room to the other. He checked on Eli and got a thumbs-up from Carly, who'd taken over "babysitting" duty from Tate and Steph.

"All right, gentlemen." Cecelia glided back into the room. "Here we are. I've written down everything I have under emergency contacts."

Nathan took the piece of paper. "Thank you."

"Anything else?"

"Actually, yes," Andrew said. "Could you call her phone and see if she answers? And could you just put it on speaker? It could be that she's just not picking up a call from an unfamiliar number."

"Oh." The woman blinked her heavily mascaraed lashes, but nodded. "All right."

Nathan held out the paper so she could see the number, and she dialed it on the landline conference room phone.

She looked up. "It's ringing."

Another few seconds passed and then, "Hello?"

"Yes, hello, Mrs. Ashcroft," Cecelia said, "I have some men here who've been trying to reach you—"

"Are the children all right?"

"Oh yes, they're fine, but these agents have been trying to get in touch with you—"

"Agents?"

"With the FBI."

"FBI! What in the world do they want?"

Andrew leaned toward the speaker. "Ma'am, this is Agent Andrew Ross. I'm here with Agent Nathan Carlisle. You're on speakerphone. We'd like to speak to you about your brother, Derek. Do you have any idea where he might be?"

"Um, at the school?"

"We've checked there and he's not."

"Then I . . . I don't know. Why are you looking for him?"

"We just have some questions for him about a woman who's disappeared. You may know her. She used to live in your neighborhood before her house burned down. Jesslyn McCormick?"

A gasp echoed through the line. "You say she's disappeared and you think Derek had something to do with it?" She laughed. "Is this a joke?"

Andrew frowned. "I assure you it's not."

"No, you don't understand. Derek doesn't know how to separate colors from whites, and you think he has the ability to pull off a kidnapping?"

"That's what it looks like from our perspective."

"I say you need another perspective. Regardless, what do you want from me?"

"We were hoping you could tell us where we might find him," Nathan said. "We understand he works for a pool supply business in addition to his job at the school?"

"Yes."

"Does he have a physical address for this business?"

"Yes, of course, but I'm not sure . . . hold on." There was a pause, then, "I think it's this one." She gave them the address.

"All right, thanks," Andrew said. "Does he have another phone number? Any other way to reach him?"

"No, just the one cell phone. And I mean, his office phone, but if he's not there . . ." She huffed. "This is so stupid. I'll try to get ahold of him. What's your number if I find him? I'm going to wring his neck . . . uh . . . not literally. I just don't have time for his drama."

"Ma'am, do you know if he's setting these fires?"

"The fires in the news?"

"Yes, the church, the gym, the general store, the bank."

"I'm confused. Is he a kidnapper or an arsonist?"

This wasn't going well. "Would you mind meeting us to continue this? I think it would be better if we did this face-to-face."

"Um . . . sure. When?"

"The sooner the better. We're trying to find a missing woman."

"Of course. Of course. I uh, can meet you in an hour? I'm sorry it can't be faster. I have to go to this interview. I can't miss it. I need this job. My kids are in full-time day care, my husband left me two months ago, my friends are tired of babysitting, and—"

"Mrs. Ashcroft, I'm sorry to hear of your marital troubles and understand the need for a job. I'm sure we could let the company you're interviewing with know we had to talk to you right away. We need to do this now."

"I've got to go." She hung up.

Nathan blinked, then shook his head. "Seriously?"

Andrew grunted. "I'll get Lindsay to ping her phone."

The only prayer Nathan could think to offer was, "Please, God."

TWENTY-EIGHT

Jesslyn had been working for what seemed like an eternity, but the clock on the wall said it had been an hour and twelve minutes. The molding was off, her fingers sore and bleeding in some places, but she'd found a ballpoint pen to help pry some of the wood loose. She listened. Faint sounds from above reached her, but Derek didn't appear to be coming back anytime soon. Maybe he had more customers. If she made a lot of noise, would someone hear her? Yeah, Derek. And then he might come back down and . . .

She set the tank lid aside and considered putting her jacket back on. Derek had promised to keep it cool inside and had definitely followed through. And if she hadn't been able to get out of the coat, she'd be glad of it.

She took off her boots, then kicked off the heavy pants. Her station gear underneath wasn't exactly the height of fashion, but the polyester and nylon material might offer her some protection against any glass shards.

Guess she was going to find out.

She slipped her boots back on, then tossed the pants and jacket through the window's opening and well away from the broken glass.

"Well, here goes nothing," she muttered. She checked once more for any glass sticking out, then turned sideways and stuck one foot

272

through, sucked in her gut, and pushed her upper body through. Her full hips might be her downfall. She pressed hard against the opening.

Please, God, get me out of here. Don't let me get stuck.

But it was going to be tight. She wiggled and rocked and broke out in a sweat, but with one final twist that must have pleased whatever physics rules were necessary to torque her way out, she was through the opening and standing next to a stack of boxes as tall as she was. Pool chemicals.

She glanced around, ears tuned for Derek's return. To her left was a worktable loaded with more boxes of chemicals. Chemicals, chemicals everywhere. And he kept matches in the desk drawer.

Idiot.

Jesslyn walked through the stacks of supplies and chemicals, realizing there was order in the chaos. She found a door in the far wall of the windowless room but, after close inspection, realized it was reinforced steel. Not going out that way. She wove through the chemical maze, noting the pool nets, PVC piping, pool floats and toys, and more until she finally found the bottom of the stairs. The door was shut at the top. Okay, that was her way out, but first a weapon. She searched for a moment, every ticking second a scrape along her nerves. Nothing was going to work. Everything was unwieldy and awkward.

She paused.

Except maybe the PVC pipe. A piece the size of a baseball bat would do the trick. Jesslyn managed to find one that was a tad shorter than she had in mind, but it would work.

With the piece of pipe gripped in her right hand, she took a steadying breath, realized her nerves were just about shot, and started up the steps. *Lord, please, I need your help, your wisdom how to get out of this situation, your—*

The deadbolt unlocked.

"Yes, we have everything you need in stock," a voice said from the other side of the door. "I'll have it ready when you get here."

She spun and hurried back down the steps as fast as possible with as little noise as possible. At the bottom, she swung behind the nearest stack of boxes and willed her heart to slow down.

Stay cool, Jess, stay cool. Keep it together.

The door opened and heavy footsteps started down. Okay, he'd check on her while he was down here, see she was gone, and . . . what?

He didn't seem like he'd thought this whole kidnapping thing out very well. The room he'd kept her in had been fairly easy to escape. Anyone wanting to keep someone should have thought about the window. Or maybe he just didn't think she could squeeze through it. And if she hadn't lost the few pounds from being sick, she might not have.

Thanks, God, for knowing what I need when I don't have a clue.

A door slammed overhead and the footsteps paused, then continued on. Derek muttered to himself, walked right past her, and grabbed something off the top shelf of the stack. When he turned, she whacked him in the head. He went down with a thud.

"Derek!"

The shout came from the top of the stairs, and for a moment Jesslyn thought she'd been seen but realized the person was looking for him upstairs.

"Derek! Where are you? I need to talk to you now!" The woman's voice came closer. "Derek!"

Did she dare hope that this was someone who could help? Or should she stay hidden and wait for the person to leave?

Possibly locking her in once more.

Jesslyn stepped into view as footsteps started down the stairs. "He's a little incapacitated right now."

The woman let out a low cry and planted her hand over her heart. "What are you doing down there?"

"Derek Morgan kidnapped me. Who's he to you?"

"He's my brother." She narrowed her eyes. "Why would he kidnap you?"

Derek's sister? The one who wanted her dead? Uh-oh.

"What are you doing here so soon?" Derek rasped behind Jesslyn.

Jesslyn whirled to see Derek awake and holding a hand to his head, his eyes dark and furious.

"Soon?" the woman asked.

"I-I haven't called you yet. I was just getting ready to, but . . . how did you know to come here?"

"Because this is where you work when you're not at the school?" Her tone implied he was an idiot.

"B-but you never come here."

"Derek! Pay attention! Why is she here?"

"Because I want to be free of you, Sam!" He waved a hand at Jesslyn. "You want her dead, so here she is. My gift to you. But not here. You can't do it here. It's too dangerous. Too many chemicals."

"Are you out of your mind?" the woman yelled.

"I'm trying to help you!" Derek's shout echoed.

"You've never wanted to help me in your life. Why start now?" Before the man had a chance to answer, she said, "You're the dumbest—" She growled. "I had everything under control and you had to go and interfere! I told you to stay out of it and now I have to fix it!" She pulled a weapon from her pocket and turned it on Jesslyn.

Jesslyn moved even as the woman's finger was tightening on the trigger. "Don't shoot! You could send this whole place up!" The words flew from her lips as she ducked behind the nearest stack of boxes.

Boxes that wouldn't stop bullets. "Stay at the steps, you idiot," Sam said to her brother. "Don't let her up. She can only hide for so long. I'll find her and be done with it."

"You could at least be grateful," Derek said. "You kept trying to kill her, and with each failure, you became nastier and nastier. Here she is. You can stop blackmailing me now. I can't live like this anymore!"

As far as she could figure, the siblings had both been after her, with Samantha starting the fires, tossing the bombs, and trying to kill her and Derek trying to *take* her. So his sister could kill her? Jesslyn wanted to ask so many questions, but keeping quiet was the

only way she was going to get out of this alive. Who was going to
be on the way? What did a check have to do with anything? She was
confused but couldn't worry about that now.

She had to figure out a way to get the path to the door free because
she was pretty sure it was still open.

NATHAN'S PHONE RANG while they pulled out of the day care parking lot, desperately trying to figure out their next move. "Carlisle."

"Detective Lee here," the voice said. "I took another look inside
Derek Morgan's home and came across something interesting."

"What's that?" Nathan had a tight grip on his emotions and managed not to yell at the man to just spit it out.

"A paycheck from a pool supply company, but it's not the one the
Ashcroft woman sent you to."

"Okay. So, you're saying she lied about Derek working there?"
Nathan asked.

"Looks like it."

He caught Andrew's gaze. "Samantha Ashcroft played us." Back
into the phone, he said, "What's the name of the company on the
check?"

"Bowman's Pool Supplies."

"Definitely not the pool company Samantha sent us to," Nathan
said.

"Because she wanted to get to Bowman's first?" Andrew asked.

Nathan nodded. "Yeah. Let's go." He said goodbye and hung up.

Please, God, keep her safe. Nathan spun the car around and breathed
the prayer with every ounce of faith he had. *Please let us be in time.*

TWENTY-NINE

Jesslyn stepped to the side, doing her best to hear over her thundering heart. She'd trained at the academy and learned coping mechanisms, but they were failing her at the moment. She pulled in a slow breath and closed her eyes for a second.

Think.

She needed a distraction.

"I'll just burn the place down with you in it," Sam said, her voice low and harsh. And straight ahead on the other side of the boxes. "I'm sure you have questions. Want to ask? I'm happy to answer them."

Jesslyn stilled. She so wanted to ask questions but bit her tongue and moved as silently as possible, needing distance. But at least if the woman was talking, Jesslyn could keep track of her.

"I've never understood why your mom and sisters went to your aunt's house while you were with a friend, but then went home. How could your mother want to stay with a man who didn't want her?"

But he did. Jesslyn stayed quiet. Arguing with the woman in her head had to satisfy the desire to verbally fight back. The clunky boots were a nuisance, so Jesslyn stepped out of them and the cool of the concrete leeched through her socks.

A distraction. She needed one desperately.

She had a chemistry degree. And chemicals at her disposal. She even had matches. She should be able to come up with something. *Think.*

"I was twelve years old when the affair started," Sam continued, "and had started following my mother when she left the house at night. She never went far. Just to the park down the street. To meet him. Off and on for *two years.*"

Jesslyn listened while she planned, her heart aching for that twelve-year-old girl who knew her mother was doing something she shouldn't. Jesslyn didn't want to set anything on fire. That was too big a risk. She had no idea where she was or what kind of houses and businesses were nearby. But she could possibly make Samantha and Derek *think* the place was on fire. And send them running for the exit. Even if they locked her in, thinking she'd burn to death—that would work. But she would have to do something that wouldn't sear her lungs.

Just a simple high school chemical reaction. She ran through a list of everything she knew she had to work with, then unscrewed the cap from the PVC pipe and hefted it. Four inches in diameter. It would work. Next, she moved to the aisle that held the potassium chlorate.

"Come on, Jesslyn, stop this stupid cat-and-mouse game. You're just delaying the inevitable. If you come out, I'll answer all your questions. Every last question you have."

A pause while Jesslyn continued to stay away from the voice.

"Or maybe you think I don't have the answers. Like did you know they were going to leave together? I was so excited. I hated my father. He was a drunk and an addict and liked to use his fists when he was mad. I thought I was finally going to get the father I'd always wanted. Your father always smiled at me when he saw me out in public. And he never hit my mother."

A thud much too close sent Jesslyn scurrying to the next aisle with the box under her arm. She set it on the nearby shelf and pried it open, then used the cap to scoop out some of the powder. Now she had to make her way back to the room where she'd been held for the other items she'd need.

278

Could she get in?

"So, they were planning to go away together," Sam said. "I over-heard them. Every time she made some excuse to leave the house or even when she just left without saying anything, I followed her. And listened. One can learn a lot that way."

Yes, one could.

She worked her way to the door, wishing she could see Derek. Or at least have him say something. She wanted to ask about Brad. She couldn't imagine his role in everything. She bit her lip and kept moving.

Finally, she made it to the office area in the back of the room. Thankfully, she was able to weave and dodge, keeping track of the woman who'd fallen silent.

From her position behind the row of supplies closest to the door, she eyed the deadbolt. The key was still in it.

Oh, thank you, Lord.

She wanted to dart to it but stayed still. Silent. Listening some more.

"What else do you want to know, Jesslyn? Do you want to know how I followed my mother to your house that night? How your father came outside and told my mother that he couldn't meet her anymore? That it was over. My mother yelled at him, told him he was breaking his promises. That they were supposed to go away and make a new life together. He told her that he couldn't leave his family and that he was sorry. He cried while he told her all of this. I was furious and crushed. I didn't want to go back to the house and back to my father and his vicious rages."

Tears fogged Jesslyn's vision and she brushed them away, staying as silent as possible. *Focus. Get it done.*

"So, Mom went home and I followed her, wishing I could take away her pain and hating your father for causing it. But she didn't go inside. She got gasoline from the garage and went back to your house. I was super curious, you know? She took that gas can and walked around your house, splashing the walls and making sure it was good and covered. I knew what she was going to do, and I have to say, it was the moment that she struck the match and walked away that I loved her most. And then she shot herself in the head. At least after that, my father stayed drunk and passed out most of the time. But I never forgot your father could have taken us away. Given us a new life. In fact, promised it. And then he just . . . didn't. He backed out." The woman's voice was growing hoarse from her rant. "He stole that life from me! He deserved to die! And so do you. You dare to want to honor him? There's no way I'll allow that to happen."

More tears crowded her eyes and Jesslyn ground her molars. She couldn't react, couldn't process that the woman's mother had killed her family. Samantha had to be just three rows over and wasn't going to stop looking for her.

Jesslyn stepped forward, spied her fire coat, and set her concoction on the shelf while she pulled the jacket on. Then the pants. Then she twisted the key in the deadbolt, opened the door, withdrew the key, and stepped back inside the office. She left the door cracked, then hurried to the desk drawer and grabbed the matches. She turned to the coffee station, found the bag of sugar, and carefully poured it into the pipe with the potassium chlorate. She needed a 60 to 40 percent ratio. Eyeballing it would have to do.

She carried it back to the door. Glanced out the broken window to make sure Sam wasn't in view, then stepped back into the warehouse area.

"I'm done with this, Jesslyn," Samantha screamed. "I'm done!"

A loud crack echoed, and Jesslyn gasped when the bullet whipped past her left ear. She ducked, careful not to spill her mixture, and hurried through the maze of supplies. She just had to get to the front of the building near the stairs and light the match.

She made it back to the front where the stairs were and saw Derek still guarding them, rubbing his head. She set her science experiment on the floor next to a wall of boxes and lit the match.

At the scrape, Derek grunted. "Sam? My head is killing me. I'm leaving!"

His sister stepped around the edge of the aisle. "You're not going anywhere. You've brought all this on us and now I'm going to end it."

"I took her to help you! And to find out what she knows. I needed to know what the police knew and—"

"They didn't know anything!"

"You killed Brad, didn't you? I know you did."

The smoke started to build. Soon, they'd notice it and hopefully rush out. Then she would too.

"Stupid boy. He saw me at one of the fires and had to ask why I was there."

"You didn't have to kill him."

"He tried to blackmail me! So, yes, you idiot, I did have to kill— What's that?"

"What?"

"The smoke! What did you do?"

"Nothing!"

"Find the source before we go up with this place. This is taking too long. I've already set up the chemicals upstairs and time is ticking down. Soon they'll combine and ignite."

"You what? Upstairs?"

"Yes!"

"But why this place?"

"Because *her* father built it. Everything he touched has to go."

"He was in real estate! Are you going to burn down every building he had a hand in building?"

"Every single one. Now find her!"

The smoke was thick and provided ample covering.

Jesslyn darted for the stairs.

"THERE!" NATHAN SHOUTED, and Andrew spun the wheel into the parking lot of the small warehouse tucked behind a row of shops and up against the side of a mountain. Just as he put the vehicle in park, an explosion rocked the front of the building.

Nathan threw himself out of the vehicle and watched a ball of yellow and orange fire roll heavenward. "Jesslyn!" His heart pounded and a sick feeling churned within him. "No, please," he whispered.

Fire trucks and other officers were minutes out. Minutes Jess might not have. But to find her, he had to go inside that raging inferno.

And everything in him was screeching to get away from it, flashes from the past nearly paralyzing him. He raced around the side, looking for an entrance.

The ground sloped down to a basement.

He bolted to the door.

Locked. Reinforced steel. No windows on the wall but steps led up. He took them and came to a door with a window at the top. Cupping his hands, he placed them against the glass to get a look inside, and his heart stuttered at the flames licking along the wall next to him.

"Carlisle, where are you?" Andrew's voice came over the comms he'd shoved in his ear without even thinking about it.

"Around the side," Nathan said. "I think I found a way in."

The flames licked closer, and he gasped and stepped back. No, he couldn't go in there, but he tried the door anyway.

"Nathan!"

He spun. "Eli?" His brother stood at the base of the steps, eyes wide, hand outstretched. "Get out of here!"

"You can't go in there!"

"Eli, I can't deal with you and this at the same time. Get away!"

"I talked Carly into bringing me. I told her I was coming and she could help me or not. So she did. I was going to just stay in the car, but when I saw what you were doing—"

"Get out of here! I got this!" The door swung open and he pushed through, pulling his weapon and scanning the area. The smoke wasn't thick yet, but it was billowing from below. "Someone get Eli away from here. He's around the side, near the entrance to the basement. I'm inside and looking for Jess."

"Nathan, the firefighters are here," Cole said. "Get out of the building."

He hesitated. Heard a cough. He recognized that cough. "Jesslyn!" She was on the floor, scrambling to her feet.

The door behind her burst open and Samantha and Derek Morgan appeared. Samantha aimed her weapon at Jesslyn and Nathan lifted his. "FBI! Drop it!"

She paused, and for one heartbeat of a moment, he thought she would. Then she let out a scream of pure rage and Nathan fired. Three pops center mass. She dropped. Derek cried out and went to the floor with her. Then raised his head, eyes wild. Accusing. Determined. "No!" He launched himself at Jesslyn and latched on to her arm. "This isn't how it was supposed to go down! I wasn't supposed to be here! No one was supposed to know I was involved. They were just supposed to kill her! You ruined it all. It's all your fault!"

"Stop!"

But he started dragging her back into the fire. She kicked hard and threw out a hand, catching Derek on his cheek. His head snapped back and he let go. Jesslyn went to the floor once more.

The smoke was so thick now, Nathan was having trouble keeping her in sight. "I need help in here!" The comms buzzed with promises that backup was on the way, but if he went much farther in, he was going to lose all sense of direction.

"Here!"

He spun. "Eli? You followed me?"

"I need to help. I *have* to help if I can."

"And I have to get Jesslyn out. Please, Eli, help by staying safe. I can't help her and you too."

"Stop, Nathan. You can't. You're terrified of fire."

"I'm more terrified of losing Jesslyn!"

Eli moved toward him and handed him a hose. "I tied it to the porch. Tie the other end around your waist so you don't get lost."

Nathan took it. "Okay! Now, get out!" He didn't have time to see if Eli obeyed, he had to get to Jess. He tied the end of the hose around himself and dropped to the floor. He was able to drag in some fresh air and army crawl. "Jesslyn!"

And then he was practically on top of her. She had Derek face down, hands cuffed behind his back.

"Nathan!" James's voice was in his ear.

"Yeah! I'm okay."

"Firefighters are coming in to get you. The whole place is about to go! Call out so they can track you."

"Over here!" he yelled and choked. Then grabbed Jesslyn. "Are you okay?"

"Yeah. Peachy." Her raspy voice, hoarse from the smoke, was the sweetest sound he'd heard all day. "Grab this guy," she said. "I may have knocked him out."

"I can get him if you can follow this to the exit." The smoke was so thick and swirling, making visibility nil. "Hold on to the hose." He coughed and forced himself not to drag in a deep breath. "It'll take you right out."

"I got it."

"Then I've got Morgan. Go!"

She disappeared into the smoky haze, and for a moment he panicked, but could feel her tugs on the hose so he knew she was okay. He gripped Morgan by the collar, turned him on his hip so his hands wouldn't drag on the cement floor, and pulled the man behind him toward the exit.

Finally, lights from flashlights greeted him along with firefighters and paramedics as they took Derek Morgan from him and helped him out the exit and down the stairs. He coughed and gagged until someone slapped an oxygen mask over his face. He looked around. Eli ran toward him.

"Jesslyn," he croaked.

Eli reached him. "She's okay. Smoke inhalation and a few bumps and bruises, but she's all right."

"Where?"

"Ambulance next to you."

James, Andrew, Cole, Kenzie, and others on the SWAT team closed in. He was going to be in so much trouble for running into that building. And he'd probably killed Samantha Ashcroft. Grief gripped him by the throat, but he also knew if he hadn't dared, Jesslyn would be dead.

Movement from the building caught his attention and he turned to see firefighters bringing out Samantha. An EMT rushed to her side and checked her pulse. Then shook his head and covered her with a blanket. Face and all. She was dead. His heart constricted, a heavy weight in his chest. He hadn't wanted to pull the trigger, but she'd given him no choice. His gaze slid from where he sat at the back of his ambulance, searching for Jesslyn. His eyes locked on hers and she held out a hand to him. He pulled off his SCBA mask, went to her, and took her hand to pull her, mask and all, into a hug. "I'm so glad you're okay."

"How did you find me?" she said, her voice muffled by the mask.

"Samantha sent us on a wild-goose chase. But one of the detectives found a pay stub from the pool company he actually worked for. We came straight here."

She closed her eyes and leaned against him. "Thank God."

"Definitely."

THIRTY

The night of the benefit had swooped down upon her, arriving so fast her head was still spinning. The high school gymnasium might seem like an odd place to hold a classy fundraiser, but in Jesslyn's mind, it was perfect. It embodied the spirit of the reason for the whole thing. Giving kids a safe place to hang out—and get help. The gym atmosphere would be a reminder throughout for why they were there.

Once everyone had a chance to finish their dinner, her aunt, dressed in black jeans, a white turtleneck, and a black jewel-studded blazer, took to the stage while dessert was served.

Jesslyn caught Nathan studying her. "What?" she asked.

"You ready?"

"I think so. I better be." She shot him a smile, then turned to Eli, who was looking happy and healthy. It was amazing what hope could do in such a short time. "I can't thank you enough for your part in this."

"I'm excited, and it's you I should be thanking."

"Without further ado," Carol said, "I'd like to welcome my lovely niece to the stage. She has a few words she'd like to say."

Nathan squeezed her hand under the table, and she rose to walk to the stage. Carol hugged her and passed her the microphone.

"Thank you all for coming," Jesslyn said. "I know you're familiar with my story. My family's story. What you may not know is that I've recently learned that my father suffered from mental illness." She caught a few raised brows, but she had the attention of everyone. Including a few of the servers. She pulled in a steadying breath. "I also learned that he grew up in and out of the foster care system due to neglect. With no family and slipping through the cracks of an overwhelmed system, my dad was basically on his own throughout his entire childhood and into his adulthood. By some miracle—proof that the Lord is always working—he finished high school and got a full scholarship to college where he studied real estate and business. While he was still in school, he went to work with a company who took a chance on him and from there, built his career. Dad met and married my mother and had us kids. For the casual observer looking at my family, one would never know anything was wrong. For those on the inside, such as my aunt, there were so many problems. As a result of his formative years, my father suffered PTSD, fear of abandonment, and so on. I've talked to a psychiatrist who pinpointed multiple things, and out of respect for my father, I won't go into detail, but I want you to know that since discovering who my father was and how my mother supported him, I still want to build this youth center, but I want it to be so much more than that. I want it to be a place where kids can come from all walks of life. A place where they will find someone in their corner. People who genuinely care about them and are willing to mentor them through this thing we call life. The Bible calls us to do so. In Matthew, Jesus says, 'When the Son of Man comes in his glory, and all the angels with him, then he will sit on his glorious throne. . . . The King will say to those on his right, . . . "For I was hungry and you gave me food, I was thirsty and you gave me drink, I was a stranger and you welcomed me, I was naked and you clothed me, I was sick and you visited me, I was in prison and you came to me."'

"Folks, we want to reach these kids before they have to go hungry or thirsty. We want to welcome them and clothe them, get them medical help if they need it. And make sure they never see the inside of a prison." With each word, her voice rose, her passion ringing in the silent gymnasium. All eyes were on her, dessert left untouched in front of the attendees. "And most of all, we want to make sure they get the mental health help they may need. Tonight, I'm asking you to join us on this journey to influence the future. *Our* future. These kids are our future too, right? We must invest in the next generation and the generations after that. Some of us can do that by volunteering our time. Others can dig into their pockets to get this place built and keep it running for many years to come. And I'm thrilled to say, Dr. Eli Carlisle will be joining our team. He's a psychiatrist with many years of experience and a story of redemption that will change the lives of those he counsels." She motioned for Eli to stand, and he gave a small wave to thunderous applause before taking his seat again.

Jesslyn gripped the mic and took a breath. "You know why you're here. And I don't have the words to express my gratitude that you showed up. If this is a project you can get behind, there are envelopes on the table. Our goal is to raise enough to build this place and fund it, including Dr. Eli's salary, for the next five years. Thank you again. And don't forget to eat your dessert. It's really good."

Laughter broke out and then murmured conversations floated around her as she made her way back to the table.

Before she could sit, Nathan stood, the look on his face making her stomach do that flippy thing. He snagged her hand. "Could I borrow you a moment?"

"Sure."

He led her out to the empty lobby and over to the painted sunset scene on the wall.

"That's Lake City's sunset over the lake near James's house," she said.

"I recognize the spot."

"I never get tired of seeing the gold and oranges and reds all coming together to create a scene that's never the same, but always painfully beautiful."

He reached out and stroked a finger down her cheek. "That's a good way of saying how I feel when I look at you."

Her breath caught and she bit her lip.

"Too bold?" he asked.

"Um. Maybe a bit."

"You have to know how I feel. It's not like I've tried to hide it."

"I know. I think that's why I'm so comfortable with you. I never have to wonder about you."

He shrugged. "I don't like games. Never have."

"Then I won't play them with you." She sucked in a steadying breath. "You've given me a lot of space up to tonight. There, but not pushy. Allowing me to think and process. I appreciate that."

"Of course."

"So, here goes. I like you, too, Nathan. The same way you like me. I think you're amazing and wonderful. You have a compassionate and giving heart and I . . ."

"You what?"

"I don't deserve that," she whispered. "I don't deserve you. I don't know what to do with you. I don't know how to *have* a relationship."

"Does anyone really know how?"

"I mean, aren't there rules?"

"The only ones I'm aware of are the ones laid out in the Bible. You know, leave and cleave and be faithful, trust in the Lord and let him direct our paths."

"You make it sound easy."

"I think the concept is easy. Following it might not be. A relationship is work, just like anything else. But you make a commitment and stick to it. And let's face it. Following through on your commitments is one thing you do well."

She laughed. "Oh, Nathan, I do appreciate your humor, that's for sure."

He pulled her close. "I told you before, the ball is in your court. I want to date you, but I will walk away if that's not what you want. So, are you ready to tell me what you want?"

And all of a sudden it was very clear to her what she wanted. "I want to kiss you."

He blinked. Then laughed and obliged. The feel of his lips on hers, his strong arms wrapped around her, and the thud of his heart under her palm were nothing like she'd ever experienced before. It was right. It was what she wanted. It was home.

When he lifted his head, he smiled. "I like that."

"So do I."

"So does this mean we're dating?"

She giggled. "I guess. I have no clue. You tell me."

"Perfect. That's exactly what it means." He pulled her into a tight yet gentle hug. "I'd walk through fire for you, Jesslyn."

"You already have."

"I'd do it again."

"Please don't. That was terrifying. I could have lost you."

"But you didn't. We're here and the future looks good." He paused for a moment and she relished the silence. "You were amazing in there," he finally said.

She smiled against his chest, happy to stay there for eternity, but she pulled back slightly and looked up at him. "Thank you. I'm thankful to know the truth now. My father was trying hard to make things work with my mother. He sent Derek and Samantha's mother away that night. Told her it was over."

"He was definitely trying hard. He'd overcome a lot in his past. I feel sure he and your mother would have worked it out."

"It hurts that they never got the chance. But it's over now. It's really over. I haven't had time to get the details. All I know is that Derek confessed to everything, that he was terrified of his sister and didn't dare turn her in. Instead, he schemed to have her killed by the police while they rescued me."

"Yep. It was such a long shot, someone finding that check, but I guess even criminals get lucky."

"I don't believe it was luck. God knew I needed you to find that."

"Very true." He shook his head. "That Samantha was a piece

of work. She'd picked up their father's abusive habits and went from hitting Derek to blackmailing him. He said he saw the fires as his chance to get rid of her once and for all. She'd snooped on his phone one day and read a text message thread between him and a student and knew he was taking bribes to change grades. From then on, she extorted money from him in exchange for her silence. Samantha didn't know about the jewelry, so Derek figured he could use that to lead us to her. He convinced Kenny to drop the jewelry for him and keep his mouth shut. Derek knew we'd put it all together eventually, but apparently, we weren't working fast enough for him. He planned for Samantha to die in a shoot-out with the police. When he kidnapped you, he knew she would come after him. But before he could tell her what he'd done, we alerted her to the fact we were closing in on Derek and she panicked. He *says* he didn't want you to die, but that he couldn't see any way around it. We were too slow to figure it out and he got desperate. He decided the only way to stop Sam was to bring you to her and convince her that his debt was paid and she was to stop blackmailing him."

"He's an idiot. He was going to call her and tell her I was there at the store and for her to come get me. She was supposed to arrive about the time you guys showed up. Although I'm not sure how he planned to make that happen time-wise. But apparently he thought he could."

"Weirdly enough, his plan did kind of work. She went to find him and set the chemicals up to ignite to destroy the building she'd been stealing her supplies from. She's on camera. Anyway, she'd given herself thirty minutes to get in and get out."

"She planned to kill Derek too?"

"I'm not sure about that. He was her money source. If he died, that would have dried up."

"Not technically, if her kids were his beneficiaries."

"True. If he died, her kids may have inherited. He seems to really care about them."

"Wait a minute. That jewelry was worth a lot of money. Why not just sell it and run?"

"I asked him that. He said she would have found him wherever he went. He needed her dead." He pursed his lips. "I'm not sure if that's true or not, but he sure believed it. He knew that jewelry would eventually lead us to his family—and then his sister. He also said he knew that she'd fight to the death. And if he could instigate that, then great." He pulled in a breath. "But we're done with that until Derek's trial. Now we can focus on us."

Us. Right. She swallowed hard and looked away, trying to figure out how to tell him everything.

He tilted her chin to look at him. "What is it?"

"How are you so in tune to my feelings?"

"Because I care about you."

She smiled, then sobered. "Oh, Nathan, I'm still trying to figure out who I am if I'm not looking for the arsonist. My whole identity was wrapped up in that. And now he's—or rather, she's—caught and I feel at loose ends. Like I'm no one now. I don't know what to do with that." Tears slipped down her cheeks. "Sorry, I didn't mean to do this here. Now."

"It's fine. No one's missed us yet. Keep going. Get it all out."

"It's like I need to let them go now. Let my family just fade into the past. Justice is served so we can all just move on."

"No, Jess, no." Nathan pulled her down onto the couch and took her hands in his. "You don't have to let them go. You'll never have to let them go. They're a part of you. A part of your past, your present, and even your future. You're a fire marshal because of them. Every family you help in the future will have your family's stamp on that. They'll be a part of each person you help. That's who you are. And besides, you know your identity is in Christ, not what you do."

She sniffed. "I know that. In my head. I'm having trouble convincing my heart of that, though."

"Maybe it'll just take a little time to figure out where to go from here, but you will. We'll pray about it together."

Jesslyn scrubbed her tears away and looked at him. "Thanks."

"And you have the center. It's going to be something that will keep you busy. I don't think you have to feel lost or without purpose, I think you need to lean into a new purpose. A new chapter in your life."

"A whole new book, you mean?" But his words struck a chord and she let them settle in her heart. He was right. Her shoulders relaxed, and for the first time in as long as she could remember, she looked forward to the future. "I've been living day to day for so long, not daring to dream about . . . anything. My focus was solely on catching my family's killer. And now . . ."

"What about now? Tell me what you've been thinking."

"What do you mean?"

"You're a thinker, Jess. A planner. If you could do anything in the world with your job, what would it be?"

"Cold cases."

He blinked. "That was fast."

She stared at him, her jaw swinging. "I have no idea where that came from."

"I think you do."

"Maybe. I guess I have been thinking about it. A little."

"A lot? But let me guess. Solving cold cases would allow you to bring closure to other people. Like yourself."

"Yes. Closure is a good thing."

He pulled her tight. "I like to be *closure* to you."

She laughed, then groaned. "That was terrible." But she kissed him again anyway. "I like you being close to me too."

"Now for the big question."

"Sure."

"Where do you want to go on our first date?"

She laughed again. "I'll think about it, but it needs to be somewhere where we can do lots of kissing."

He kissed her again. "I'm okay with that."

When she could breathe again, she said, "We should get back in

293

there, but will you be my date to James and Lainie's wedding? They've changed the date to sometime in the next couple of months. 'More details to come.'" She put air quotes around the last four words.

"What?" He laughed. "She's scared she's going to forget her wedding date, isn't she?"

"I think she might be. So, will you come with me?"

"I'd love to."

"Good. I was nervous about asking."

"Then I'll just have to kiss those nerves away."

"What a brilliant idea."

He lowered his head once more, and Jesslyn thought she heard clapping and cheering over the pounding of her heart. She shot a sideways glance at the entrance to the gym and spotted James, Lainie, Kenzie, Cole, Andrew, and Kristine. After more cheers, they stepped back into the gym and shut the doors, buying her and Nathan a few more minutes of privacy. Then all of that faded away and she knew with Nathan at her side and God at the center, they'd figure out life together.

Turn the page for
a sneak peek at the next book
in the Lake City Heroes series,

FINAL APPROACH

COMING SOON

ONE

Air Marshal Kristine Duncan leaned back in her seat, her eyes skimming over the sunrise outside the Airbus 319's window. Minutes ago, they left the Lake City, North Carolina, airport and had just leveled out at cruising altitude after a smooth climb. When the Lake City field office had opened a little over two years ago, she'd been offered a position and taken it without hesitation. Moving away from Asheville had been a good thing. In many ways.

The hum of the aircraft was a familiar comfort, but it was a smaller craft than she usually flew, with only one aisle and three seats on either side. She and the others were about halfway back in the body of the plane. Not her favorite seat, but she wasn't complaining.

Despite being off duty, she couldn't help going through her usual flight check, scanning the passengers and the luggage being brought on board. Thanks to her job, when she was on a plane, she was never truly off duty. Even though she was trying very hard at the moment to simply enjoy the flight.

Lainie Cross had already fallen asleep in the middle seat, her head tilted slightly to the left. How the woman could sleep like that was beyond her. In the window seat, Jesslyn fiddled with her new camera, the excitement on her normally reserved features making Kristine smile. She'd just gotten into photography and her fiancé, Nathan, had purchased the Canon R5 for her birthday along with two very nice lenses. Kristine couldn't help wondering how much that had set him back. Detective Tate Cooper and his fiancée, Stephanie Cross, had settled in and had their heads together, talking quietly.

"I can't believe we're actually doing this," Jesslyn said, leaning forward, her voice low. "How long have we been planning this? Six months? It felt like six years to get to this point." She had her red hair pulled into a casual ponytail with a few stray tendrils curling around her temples. A smattering of freckles crossed her nose and fanned out over her cheeks. "Ten days at an all-inclusive resort in Key West, snorkeling, scuba diving, parasailing—"

"I'm not parasailing," Kristine said. "No way."

Jesslyn raised a brow at her. "But you love to fly."

"In a plane. With a skilled pilot—or two. Or frankly, myself flying. With safety protocols in place. Not at the end of a rope attached to a boat with a driver who may or may not know what he's doing."

"Could be a she."

"Exactly. And neither of them may know what they're doing."

Jesslyn laughed and tilted her head. "You're still taking flying lessons?"

"I am. It makes me feel like I have more control."

"You've been doing that forever. Don't you have your license yet?"

"Just got to take the test."

"And when are you doing that?"

"I don't know." The truth was, she'd been putting it off. Something about the test and flying solo terrified her and she wasn't sure why.

Her tone must have conveyed her desire to terminate the subject, because Jesslyn went back to her camera with only a raised brow.

Kristine glanced around at her friends sitting nearby. Kenzie King and Cole Garrison were engrossed in a travel guide, plotting their adventures—and probably their wedding—while James, Lainie's husband, was lost in the latest bestselling thriller by Kate Angelo. Kristine drew in a deep breath, taking in the atmosphere of anticipation and relaxation. It was a hard-earned break from their often-hectic lives. With the exception of Lainie who was a physician's assistant, they were all in some form of law enforcement and the last couple of years had been chaotic. Thankfully, the last nine months had been "quiet." Or at least "normal" for them and their occupations.

Her gaze drifted across the aisle and back one row, where a man sat immersed in his notes. FBI Special Agent Andrew Ross. Smart, dedicated, and definitely too handsome for anyone's good. His blond hair was slightly long and his five-o'clock shadow was making an attractive appearance on his usually clean-shaven features. She and Andrew had known each other for a while now, but it was only lately that they'd acknowledged they wanted to get to know each other even more. She had to admit spending time with Andrew on a sandy Key West beach sounded like an amazing adventure. If she could just get past her fear. She cleared her throat and pushed that aside, wishing she could dump her baggage once and for all.

Maybe one day.

Andrew looked up and caught her gaze. His soft smile stole the breath from her lungs, but she forced herself to smile back before returning her gaze to the passengers once more. She studied the ones she could see. All seemed well, as, thankfully, it usually was. So why were her nerves itching?

"Come on, Kristine." Jesslyn nudged her. "Surely, you can switch off for this trip."

"You know as well as I do that as a federal agent, I'm always on duty on any flight I take."

"Well, yeah, but still . . . relax."

"I'm trying," she said. "Seriously. It's hard, though." She forced her features into a serious expression. "But keep your camera ready. Nathan may decide to cut loose and dance down the aisle or something."

Jesslyn smirked and Kristine laughed. That was about as likely as below-zero temps in the Keys.

The laugh felt good. It was a bubble of normalcy in the midst of a tension Kristine couldn't shake off. She glanced around the cabin, her trained eyes scanning the other passengers once more. Most were absorbed in their own worlds. Sleeping, chatting with seat mates, reading, snacking, and trying hard to keep restless children occupied.

But one man, five rows ahead, sitting in the aisle seat to her right, caught her attention. He seemed on edge, his movements rigid, jerky. She'd noticed him as they boarded, but he'd settled down so she just decided to keep an eye on him. It appeared his restlessness had returned, though, and Kristine narrowed her eyes. Nervous flier? Personal problems? Or something more?

Or nothing?

The aircraft jolted, a brief but rocky turbulence that silenced the occupants of the plane. Kristine gripped the armrest, her body tensing.

The captain's voice came over the speaker. "Sorry about that, folks. Hit a little pocket there. We're back to cruising smoothly, so go back to your book or your movie and we'll be on the ground in about an hour and a half."

Kristine relaxed. She wasn't usually jumpy. She flew all the time, but today there was just . . . something.

Lainie quirked a brow at her. "You okay?"

"Yeah. Yes, of course." Again, the turbulence was nothing major. It happened.

The uneasy passenger stood up. Looked around. Then headed to the back restroom. Kristine shifted so she could watch down the aisle. At the ten-minute mark, she was about to ask Amanda or Jeffrey, the two flight attendants working the flight, to go check on him. Just as she started to rise, the man exited the lavatory and passed Kristine to take his seat again. Andrew rose and walked to the front of the plane and slipped into the lavatory before Kristine could snag his attention. Instead, she caught Amanda's eye. Jeffrey was at the tail of the plane. Amanda raised a brow and nodded in the direction of the man who'd captured Kristine's attention.

Kristine gave a subtle nod back.

Amanda moved toward him, her smile friendly and professional. The passenger jumped to his feet again, his hand diving into his jacket as he stepped into the aisle.

Kristine reached under her jacket to release the snap that held the SIG in the holster. She'd only intervene if the cockpit was threatened. But Andrew and Nathan were FBI. They had their weapons and would handle it for the moment.

Amanda stopped next to him. "Sir, please sit back down," she said, her voice calm but firm. "Everything is fine. If you'll just put your seat belt on—"

"Stay back!" He pulled out a makeshift knife and held it to the neck of the person in the aisle seat next to him, then pulled the woman to her feet. Amanda let out a startled yelp and stumbled back. The passenger's shocked whimpers reached Kristine's ears even over the eruption of the panicked, screaming passengers.

Nathan rose. "FBI," he said. "Put your weapon down, sir."

"I'm getting in the cockpit," he shouted. "Open the cockpit!" His words were directed at Amanda.

A threat to the cockpit. That was Kristine's cue. She stood. "Everyone, stay calm!" The command in her voice stilled most of the people. "I'm an air marshal," she said. "Sir, please drop the knife." The cockpit had a keyless entry. A code that only certain people knew. Amanda was one of those people.

"I got your back," Jesslyn murmured. "We all do." Jesslyn was a fire marshal, but she was also trained law enforcement.

Kenzie was also on her feet. A SWAT medic with the Lake City Police Department, Kenzie was a member of the SWAT team, along with Cole and James, who also stood ready to assist. They wouldn't have their weapons on them, but they were still powerful backup.

The man's gaze flicked around the cabin, his desperation clear. "This plane is not going to Key West! Let me in the cockpit. Now!"

Kristine kept her focus on him and moved into the aisle toward him. "We can talk about this," she said. "No one needs to get hurt."

Andrew had stepped out of the lavatory, his eyes bouncing between Kristine and the hijacker who had his back to Andrew. It took him a nanosecond to read the situation. She shot him a quick glance and he gave a subtle nod indicating his readiness to help. His hand went to his weapon.

Passengers whispered prayers, some crying, as the hijacker's hand trembled.

In a flash of movement, the passenger across the aisle lunged at the man. The cabin erupted into chaos as the hijacker, caught off guard, plunged the homemade weapon into his hostage's shoulder.

The wounded woman's scream echoed through the cabin and she went to the floor—and left the knife still in the attacker's hand. He swung the blade and caught the passenger who'd tried to take him down across the raised forearm. Blood spurted and the man screamed and fell back.

Quick as a blink, the hijacker shoved the weapon against another woman's throat. "He shouldn't have done that! He shouldn't have . . . I didn't . . . She's . . ." He turned his attention to his new captive. "Get your seat belt off or I'll cut you too!"

Lainie rushed to help the fallen woman while James looked like he wanted to protest but clamped his mouth shut.

"Now!" The assailant's scream jolted the woman. She squeezed her eyes shut but made no sound while she unbuckled her seat belt. He grabbed her and propelled her to her feet, pressing the knife against her neck, nicking the skin. A trickle of blood slid down and disappeared into the collar of her T-shirt. The passenger who initiated the attack on the hijacker slid back on the floor of the plane, his eyes wide.

Kristine stepped toward the assailant but motioned to Andrew to go to the left. He nodded and moved in accordance.

The attacker swung the knife in front of him, keeping everyone at bay. Then pressed the weapon once more against the neck of his hostage. "Stay away. I need in the cockpit. Someone open the cockpit door now or I'll—I'll slice her open! I will."

The woman bit her lip. Kristine caught her gaze and tried to convey she needed to remain calm. The woman stayed quiet, but her fear was a tangible thing.

Kristine didn't blame her.

Andrew moved in sync with Kristine, edging closer to the hijacker. Slow, calculated steps. Each second stretched into an eternity while her mind raced, planning her next move. She had to end this before anyone else got hurt. Her mother's death flashed in her mind. Had her mom been as afraid as Amanda? Kristine could see the flight attendant's tremors from her position in the aisle, but she was trying to be brave, to be strong and pull on all her training for a scene like this.

"Sir," Kristine said, "no one can open the cockpit. You know that."

His eyes swept the sea of passengers. Some who were on their feet. He was looking for someone. His gaze locked on one of the passengers, and tears trickled down his ashen cheeks.

"Th-then she dies!"

"No!" Kristine held out a hand. "Wait. Tell me. Once you get the cockpit door open, what do you plan to do?"

"Take control and fly where I want to go."

"You can fly a plane?"

He snorted. "Of course not. The pilot will."

Andrew had settled into an empty seat so when the man swiveled his head to look behind him, Andrew looked like any other passenger. When the guy turned his attention back to Kristine, she caught Andrew's movement from the corner of her eye. He stood and moved closer.

The attacker held the knife out in front of him once more, briefly removing it from the woman's throat. "Stop moving!"

Kristine froze and he swept the knife back beneath the woman's chin. "I'm sorry. I have to do this. It's time."

"TIME FOR WHAT?" Kristine asked, as Andrew moved into a position right behind him and his captive. He had a good line of sight with

Kristine. He met her gaze, and she blinked to acknowledge him while keeping her attention on the hijacker.

"Time to do what I ask," the guy said. "I'm not afraid to use this to do what I have to do."

Kristine took another step forward. "Where do you want to go? What's your plan?"

He shoved the knife at her. "Stop!" Then back to his victim's throat. "I don't know. I don't know."

"What's your name?"

"It doesn't matter. Stop moving!" The knife swept out and back one more time.

Kristine stopped. "What are you going to do?" She took one more small step toward him.

Come on, do it. Andrew silently willed the man to move.

As though he read his mind, the hijacker swung the weapon out toward Kristine, his right hand tight around the hilt. "Stop moving! I'm not playing with you!"

Before he could pull the knife back toward his hostage, Andrew moved fast, coming up from behind on the attacker's right side. He jammed his left arm over the attacker's right forearm, and in one fluid motion, shoved the woman away and grabbed the guy's wrist with his right hand. Andrew then twisted the captured right arm down and back. The man screamed and struggled, but his one-armed fight was no match for Andrew's vicelike grip.

Kristine had lunged in and snapped a cuff around the man's left wrist while Andrew finally put enough pressure on the hijacker's other wrist that he released the weapon. It clunked to the floor. Nathan swooped in to snag it with a gloved hand, Andrew cuffed the defeated man's other wrist, and it was over.

Then the clapping started. Passenger by passenger until the plane was filled with thunderous applause by those who weren't capturing the moment on their phones.

Ugh.

"I'll stay with him," Kristine said. "You call it in."

Andrew nodded and got on his phone.

Lainie had the plane's first aid kit and had put it to good use to help the woman who'd been stabbed.

"How is she?" Kristine asked.

"Fortunate. Her name is Bri. I've cleaned and bandaged it as best I could, but she needs stitches and pain meds. Thankfully, the blade went in just above her collarbone, and while painful, I don't think it went deep enough to cut anything major. Jugular is intact and she's breathing great." Lainie smiled at the woman who blinked up at them from her position on the floor and patted her shoulder. "You're going to be fine, Bri."

"Thank you," Bri whispered, then closed her eyes.

Thirty minutes later, they touched back down on the Lake City tarmac and rolled to a stop at the gate. The prisoner sat still and silent, chin touching his chest, refusing to talk or look at anyone.

As soon as the door was opened, Andrew hauled the sullen man to his feet, and he and the others escorted him into the hands of waiting FBI agents. He'd be taken to the Buncombe County Detention Center, where Andrew and Nathan would head to question him. Andrew could only hope the guy was in a more talkative mood than he had been, once detained.

Andrew stood on the tarmac and gripped the bag holding the weapon. He marveled at the creative piece of "art." Sturdy wire cut into pieces, fashioned into a blade and held together with superglue. Then superglued to the end of a toothbrush. Everything that fashioned the "knife" was allowed in a carry-on or could be purchased in the airport after going through security. Except for the wire and possibly the glue. That was kind of weird that the glue had made it through security.

"Unbelievable," he muttered. He couldn't wait to search the guy's bag.

"That's the weapon?"

He turned at Kristine's voice. As always, her beauty threatened to unnerve him. He cleared his throat and ordered himself to focus. "Yes. It's clever, I'll give him that."

Nathan and the others joined them. "Who is he?" Nathan asked.

Andrew held up a black leather wallet. "ID says Marcus Brown. Fifty-seven years old. Lives in Boone, North Carolina." They walked into the airport. "You ready to go talk to him? I had a friend drop off a car for me."

"Great minds think alike. I'll see you there."

Lainie oversaw the transport of her patient to the waiting ambulance and said goodbye to the others.

Andrew glanced at his phone. His mother had texted him.

I saw the news. Are you all right?

He tapped,

> I'm fine, Mom. Back in Lake City at the airport, but fine. I'll fill you in soon.

She sent him a thumbs-up and a heart, and he tucked his phone back into his pocket. His brothers would be messaging any moment now. Instead of waiting for them to do so, he sent them a text on the family loop.

> I'm fine. Busy wrapping things up. Will text or call later. Love you all.

His brother Carson was thirty-three years old and an architect in Atlanta, Georgia. He was older than Andrew by twenty-three months. Felix, their younger brother at twenty-nine years old, was a professional photographer, high in demand in the wedding and family portrait industry. He worked out of Greenville, South Carolina, and was married with two girls. Andrew found it rather odd his parents tended to land where he was and not with their grandchildren, but he was glad whatever their reasons were. He climbed into the Bucar and headed for the detention center.

ACKNOWLEDGMENTS

Writing acknowledgments is always terrifying for me. I'm so afraid I'm going to forget someone. So just know that if you helped me in ANY WAY on this story, you get a big thank-you from the bottom of my heart. I'm so very grateful.

This book—and every other book that has been written by me—would not have been possible without the unwavering support of my family. To my husband, Jack, thank you for your endless patience, encouragement, and love. Even when I know you're tired of me having my laptop in my lap! LOL.

Thank you to Dru Wells, FBI Supervisory Special Agent (retired), Behavioral Analysis Unit/CIRG agent, who deserves so much more than this measly little shout-out. Thank you, Dru, for EVERYTHING!

A heartfelt thank-you to my literary agent, Tamela Hancock Murray, and to my editors, Andrea Doering and Barb Barnes, for your brilliant guidance and dedication to making this book the best it could be. Thank you for always making sure my books are worthy to be published even when I strain your brains to exploding! Tamela, you're an amazing agent and friend and I love you dearly. Thank you for your unwavering support and belief in me. You're awesome.

Thank you to all of my Revell people, from editors to cover designer to marketing pros. You all are amazing, and I thank you so much for making it possible for me to do what I love.

Thank you to my brainstorming friends! You know who you are!

And last but never least, always first, thank you to Jesus. Thank you for letting me do what I do. I pray these words bring you honor and glory and hopefully even a bit of entertainment.

Lynette Eason is the *USA Today* bestselling author of *Double Take* and *Target Acquired*, as well as the Extreme Measures, Danger Never Sleeps, Blue Justice, Women of Justice, Deadly Reunions, Hidden Identity, and Elite Guardians series. She is the winner of three ACFW Carol Awards, the Selah Award, and the Inspirational Reader's Choice Award, among others. She is a graduate of the University of South Carolina and has a master's degree in education from Converse College. Eason lives in South Carolina with her husband. They have two adult children. Learn more at LynetteEason.com.